FORT OF SILENCE

FORT OF SILENCE

by

HELEN FOLEY

*But do recollect—that all is at stake—the present—
the future—and even the colouring of the past.*

Lord Byron to his wife.

HODDER AND STOUGHTON

First printed 1963

Printed in Great Britain for Hodder and Stoughton Ltd., St. Paul's House, Warwick Lane, London, E.C.4 by T. and A. Constable Ltd., Hopetoun Street, Edinburgh.

TO R.H.L.F.

CONTENTS

CONTENTS

I

LAURA

SCALES SWAM through her dreams like a cascade of fish in a glass tank; she watched them bubbling, rising and falling and then suddenly, in transition, could only hear them, a ladder of notes which played over her body, over the bed and the walls. Under exploring hands the sheet was coarse and satisfying. She could not open her eyes yet. But the sounds were now more localised, they had ceased to be part of her and became, instead, a noise outside, drifting in through the open shutters. She could feel the air, cold with autumn. Mingled with the piano scales now were other sounds from the courtyard: dustbin lids, saucepans rattling, a distant harangue, someone whistling.

But David had not woken yet. His breathing, even, secure, controlled, she could also hear in the room. Reluctantly she opened her eyes. The wallpaper had not been so pink last night but daylight had diminished the toppling effect of the armoires and overmantel. In her hurry to go to bed and to sleep, she had looked only glancingly at their room as they came in late from the last London plane. She had an experienced eye for seeing there was all they wanted. What David wanted she could not pretend to see. She had developed a knack of stepping nimbly aside: direct recognition of anything David wanted would by now have seemed embarrassingly real.

It was a Monday in October in Paris and whoever was

playing scales redoubled the pace of his arpeggios, which seemed to glance through the air like arrows too swift to see. Her hands stretched themselves to octaves on the sheet. She would be clumsy now. The days of the Good Friday eisteddfod were over; Schubert or Brahms or Bach on a black piano which reflected one's hands so surprisingly that one almost lost one's head, like seeing the car one was driving in a shop window and veering towards it fascinated. The audience, alert but mellow in their best clothes, applauded critically: the adjudicator, in a thick black suit, had eyebrows that crowned the crags of his sunken eyes like a copse on a precipice. But they were not as alarming as her grandfather's in his presidential chair; his witty words belied their alarming growth, only her Welsh was inadequate to follow him. The audience laughed constantly at his introductions, interpolations and set speeches with that ready, tumultuous Welsh laughter like shallow thunder. So long as he was chairman she had to compete; her piano playing was competent if unexceptional. She had no dreams about it and priggishly resented the emotional antics of those who bowed and swayed at the keyboard, crooked their fingers and elbowed their way flamboyantly through the set pieces. "Elbows well into the side, always," her piano mistress said, or was that an echo of a riding lesson? One girl won constantly; she was pale and long and by now probably a grandmother.

That was the next stage.

"David, do you think you will know how to be a grandfather?"

"Give them time. They were only married on Saturday. That confounded fellow's been playing scales for hours."

"You were asleep till I spoke to you."

"I've been listening to him carousing through the dawn. Must be some damn student."

"It's almost half-past eight and breakfast will be coming. I've been remembering playing the piano. Perhaps I ought to take it up again now."

"Why now? What's different? We still have no piano. It's not a standard issue for a general so far as I know."

"I see one with pink shaded lamps. The one at home had nasturtiums inlaid into the wood."

"I don't know what you are talking about."

"It was sold because we had nowhere to put it and the carriage would have been so costly. I cried myself to sleep."

"At thirty women don't do that."

"Was I thirty? Have I not seen Plas Newydd since then? How terrible. And you never knew I cried. A pillow is muffling and you drop to sleep like a tree falling anyway."

"I present that illusion of sleep, as this morning. Do you think there will be croissants and enough coffee? There never is enough coffee abroad."

"It's expensive. Are you thirsty?"

"I'm still tasting my thirst from the wedding. Why was I so thirsty? I drank five glasses of water before dinner, I could feel it gurgling down dry pipes."

"Nerves."

"Ridiculous."

"You shook all through the ceremony. I expected to hear your money and your studs rattle and the pew behind to start putting out restraining hands. You shook when we were married too. Your sword vibrated; I could feel it in my teeth like a pain. Was it the same sword that Antonia cut the cake with on Saturday?"

"No. I borrowed one for our wedding."

"Even if you hadn't, you would tell me that."

A waiter brought their breakfast with a French flourish and closed the window on the pianist, tidied the curtains and withdrew.

"Apricot jam, David, and quite a large pot of coffee."

"Thick china is very deceptive. They used to have bowls, do you remember? Perhaps somewhere they do still."

Laura warmed her hands on one in recollection. That would have been in the first family she stayed with, before she left school: a summer of tennis and the smell of lime flowers and provincial snobbery. When Antonia was sixteen, Laura was reluctant to believe she also could perceive the same languors of an alien country life. Laura had been married at Antonia's age, nineteen, and was still disturbed and shocked that her daughter had followed her example so exactly. Would they be happy? The absurdity of the idea choked her and she spluttered over her coffee.

"I was remembering some of the speeches and the hats. One always hopes that it's only at other people's weddings that these things happen."

"A wedding is a wedding is a wedding."

"Yes, David."

It was not the idea of happiness that amused her, but people's care for the future. "I do hope you will be very happy." "With best wishes for your future happiness," was written on cards with presents. Presumably people married because they were happy; to marry in the hopes that they would be, seemed calculating. She had never speculated

12

about happiness with David. Life with him, yes, but happiness was the present bubble.

The pianist had broken off his scales and was playing Schumann's *Carnaval*; Laura crumbled her croissant with pain and thought of John. This was something she must cure, like smoking. But scales were one thing at breakfast and *Carnaval* another: haunting, bitter sweet, snatchy little tunes nudging memory, prompting desire.

"More coffee, David?"

"Please."

"I wonder whether that cottage will be comfortable. Probably we should have insisted on a hotel. The fire will smoke, the Calor gas cylinder expire and they will quarrel."

"One, Jack's hard up, two, we couldn't have persuaded them as it's nothing to do with us, three, if they can't surmount trivial discomforts now, how will they ever survive . . .?"

"I wish you wouldn't muster your facts; it's pedantic."

"Shows an orderly mind."

"We quarrelled all through our honeymoon; the car kept breaking down and we blamed each other."

"And we've never quarrelled since."

"No."

For their honeymoon they had that golden splendour of September, 1938; in the Welsh border country the hedges were full of honeysuckle, flower and berry together, ripe blackberries and bloomy sloes. They ambled down the lanes and scrambled up the hills; she was never a good climber. "Make you a lance-corporal if you get to the next bush." "Take away your stripes if you malinger like that." She laughed when she had enough breath. David had been good about Wales. If she had encouraged him, Plas Newydd would never have been sold and the furniture and the piano with the inlaid nasturtiums. But she had not wanted to keep these roots. It would have seemed unfair to have sold Aldengrove and kept Plas Newydd. Aldengrove was too large, too demanding; Plas Newydd remote, uncomfortable. From the beginning she had shied away from roots with David, the house they would come back to when he retired. Both houses were now scarcely remembered by the children. Their grandfather had died when they were very small, David's mother at the end of the war.

The pianist came back into her consciousness; the notes made little leaps in the air like a hurdy-gurdy waltz. There would be no barrel organs for her grandchildren, only other people's wirelesses heard in the street with exasperation. Antonia and Mark had never had their day changed because of a tune ground out with a handle, two streets away, making people step more confidently on the pavements. Sometimes in London, perhaps there were still some in the sequestered, modish streets of Kensington and Chelsea. The first time she had gone to John's studio, she had heard one like an omen and bought roses at the street corner, those thin, frail roses only sold by flower-men in London, never seen elsewhere, which seem grown only to look splendid for an hour or so and then to droop and fade as if some vital wire had been withdrawn. The roses were red and yellow, and, for the moment, sweet-smelling. She was carrying too much when she arrived on his doorstep and dropped the roses when he opened the door. She walked over rose petals into his house and never forgot it, ridiculously. The hurdy-gurdy waltz was still audible, now a scratchy little tune, which did not explain the secret of roses and love.

14

John had short legs like pillars of iron and she could not admire him as she walked behind him, then. It was a tiny house, with a large studio and a couple of other rooms. It looked on to a blur of London trees rain-bowed in retrospect with sun or rain or lamplight. He had thin, fair hair, grey now, like David's; it was absurd that John had precise hair and hands and David an opulent thatch and long graceful fingers, now curled round his coffee-cup.

"Did you bring enough cigarettes to last you, Laura?"

"Did you?"

He made an accustomed ironic movement of his mouth at her.

"What time is our train?"

"Not till noon. Do you want to do anything special before that?"

"I might take a walk, but it's raining."

"Raining?"

"Haven't you looked? It rained all night."

"You were sound asleep."

"I kept waking to hear it."

It was an old argument, meaning nothing, carrying time between them a little further on. She walked to the window now and undid the shutters behind the velvet and the muslin. On the courtyard below the rain splashed down, on to the dustbins and an old handcart, some abandoned potted plants and a wicker chair with its broken fronds appealingly in the air.

"It isn't too good for our holiday, David. Why does the weather always change and the currency alter for us? We've never been lucky at holidays."

She watched him review twenty years of holidays regretfully.

"Surely not as bad as that, Laura. There was Brittany and Killarney and Dublin."

"I was sick in a tram, a terrible tram, bending and swaying fast round corners and they lit a peat fire in my room and we had huge pale eggs, like china ones, for breakfast. Why did we go to Dublin? You made me watch a Rugger match in December, wrapped inadequately, because the team played with clockwork cars over the hotel lounge floor. There hadn't been any clockwork toys in England during the war. They were sweet, so we watched them play Trinity College. Were they Oxford or Cambridge?"

"I don't remember them at all."

"But you must. Don't you remember our hotel bedroom, with the trams outside till the small hours like Trieste and the newspaper boys selling clothing coupons and the barefoot children and the steaks?"

"Vaguely. Do you think we could get an English paper?"

"Will the announcement be in? The hotel might know where you could get a *Times* or a *Telegraph*. Ring down to the porter."

"I can't bear talking French on the telephone. My French needs gestures. Have a cigarette? Do you think that chap plays the piano all day? I wonder the hotel doesn't complain."

"Perhaps he's part of the amenities."

"If we were staying longer, I'd ask for a room on the other side. What's he playing anyway? Sounds a muddle to me."

"*Carnaval*. Schumann."

She found it almost unbearable. But that was absurd.

Everything was bearable. One lived to forty-two to realise that. Is that what one should tell one's children when they ask mutely for a message? All is bearable. Nothing lasts, only pride and habit. If a jingle of music in a Paris hotel bedroom exaggerates a mood, stirs recollections, one should enjoy it, not suffer it like a boring dinner party.

"Who's having first bath?"

"You do, if you want to go out. I shall write letters, then I won't have to at Rocamadour."

"Letters. Put it on a postcard like me."

"And where has that got you?"

"To be a general unencumbered with personal correspondence."

"You're not a general yet."

He had turned the taps on and would not have heard. She put the breakfast tray outside the door and rummaged for her writing-case. Did she write to the children? To Mark at Sandhurst, to Antonia on her honeymoon?

"My dears, I have waited twelve years for this moment; twelve years, not daring to hurry time into its grave but noticing the months and the years as they passed, imperceptibly faster, regretting that they were taking your childhood and my youth away, but hopeful for the future, for the house in France with John. And now the twelve years is up, you are safely stowed away from your childhood and my care and where am I? In a hotel bedroom with your father, en route for another of our dim, comfortable, habitual holidays. To Rocamadour, why? Some guide book reference, some impulse. Some fate. And everything is just the same as it ever was, except that twelve years have gone and I've spent it idly in a dream."

But she never wrote letters like that, not to the children

anyway, relying on brisk inquiry and humorous anecdotage to fill out the pages. David, whatever he might boast about postcards, relaxed his rules for Antonia and Mark and wrote long discursive letters to them, which they adored. He had always been better with them than she was; she saw them always as entirely vulnerable, whether for disease or bombs. When they flew out in school holidays to David and her stationed abroad, she suffered agonies which David scorned. They stepped off the plane gay, confident, hardly crumpled, into his holiday plans and mood. When they went ski-ing together, she sat in the hotel knitting and writing letters to John which he could not reciprocate, seeing the children brought back on stretchers still and dangling. David took them to his cottage in Scotland, to walk and to fish and to live rough, while she snatched greedily at the opportunity to be with John and he tried to explain her guilty anxieties to her. It was assumed that Achranish was not for her and she did not resent this. She disliked rain and the smell of paraffin and tinned food cooked over a primus, and endless patient conversations with people whose dialect she imperfectly understood. Perhaps it was too reminiscent of Wales; she had escaped from uncomfortable living and sad weather and Celtic obsessions. John was laborious about her childhood; he had tried to cure her of everything and, finally, perhaps of love. He had a diffident voice and hesitated over the interpretations he would put inevitably into her mind. "Father dead, mother a G.P., holidays with grandfather. What do you remember about your grandmother?" "Her death more than anything, the long, slow drama, with the village knocking gently, perpetually, at the back door, the jolly doctor who should have had a pony and trap, my mother with her professional façade woefully dropped, weeping in the pretty Victorian chaos of the drawing-room. I was sent away for the funeral and the village was shocked. Perhaps they were afraid that I should not know what to do. I stayed with a school friend and pretended a grief in a bid for her sympathy. It was cosy when it was all over and I came back next holidays to a promoted cook-housekeeper and Grandfather singing 'Hob y derry dando' as he polished his shoes or the car.''

"And how often did you see your mother?"

"At Christmas, when she came for a few days because her partner never wanted to go away then; in the Easter holidays I went for a week and we bought clothes and went to the cinema and had snacks on trays; in the summer when she came home for a fortnight and people were asked to supper and we went for picnics. But she was alarming – a good doctor, cool and scrutinising, quick-moving. I liked people telling me how good she was and told boring stories about her at school, the lightning diagnosis, the quick whip of the knife; G.P.s then had more scope than now in a factory town with a fear of the hospital.''

"Yes, yes." John pushed away her irrelevancies. "But what did you *feel* about her?"

"I don't know. That was the life I had. One takes too much notice now of children and their feelings." And he smiled teasingly at her while she blushed for her anxiety for her own. He had never persuaded her to leave them, he had only wanted her not to grieve over them. She had found this touching.

Now, faced with a blank page of writing-paper and twelve years behind, she was not sure at all.

She thought of Antonia and Mark in a long series of snapshots; the starfish stance of their infant years, the

legginess of their growing, the sudden shaping to precocious
maturity with the look and the voice and phrase not quite
in the true till she came face to face with them on Antonia's
wedding day, handsome, self-contained strangers of her
creation.

David came out of the bathroom.

"You don't seem to have written much. What have you
been doing? Brooding about Antonia or the rain?"

"Is it still raining?"

"Indeed. Let's hope it's just local rain."

"I'm glad it didn't rain for the wedding. Being married in Aldershot in the rain would be a terrible recollection."

"Worse than Goofy Marksby's speech?"

"No. I saw an aunt or two wince. We shouldn't have
suggested it."

"I didn't. Goofy rises too frequently to occasions."

"It's only the civilians who'd mind. He's like a surviving mammoth in a cave, drooling tusks, not fierce only
funny."

David was looking out of the window.

"He's all right in his way."

"In his cave. Do you think Jack will turn into Goofy
when he's stopped looking like an advertisement for making
the Army your career? I only really see him from the waist
up peering masterfully from that turret."

"Any other interest in your son-in-law would be improper. The Army's different now anyway. The ad man has
to combine the glamour of the old with the material comforts of the new. How my father would have grieved."

"One can't judge what the dead would think. They are
frozen into attitudes like children playing statues; your

20

father leaning on his stick shouting to Aeneas, mine impaled on some No-man's land wire fence or did he slip on the duckboards and drown in mud? My mother never knew; better to gloss heroically. But I always see him with a hand outstretched, you know. He had beautiful hands, my grandfather said. He used to talk about them to me. He thought they were wasted."

"So you've said before."

"I'm a repetitive woman. What can you expect after twenty-odd years? I wish you'd stop looking out of the window. Rain is the same, is the same, or is there some drama?"

"I like to study windows."

"If you dressed you could go out and look."

"The pianist has stopped. He has remembered an appointment. Good. Yes, I will dress. Are you sure you don't want to come? I probably shall only go and sit downstairs."

"There's no point in sitting in a train all day in wet clothes."

Two hours before the train goes; seven hours in a train, second class. David was thrifty and it was not worth bringing the car for only ten days' holiday.

She watched him dress, in and out of the bedroom and the bathroom, packing his suitcase as he went along, everything meticulously folded and stowed, some mental list ticked off. He moved about as if she were not there, wrapped in some concentration of thought and effort. She put out a bare foot to trip him as he passed but he saw it in time.

"You shouldn't take your slippers off in a hotel bedroom, Laura. Surely by now at your age . . ."

"I shall do as I please at my age."

21

He was folding his silk dressing-gown, taking a lumpy handkerchief out of the pocket. She had bought a dressing-gown like it for John, because his camel one took up so much room, and then hated it because it reminded her of David when she packed it or hung it up. John was untidy and dependent: clothes slid off him on to the floor and were left there; his suitcases would never shut. "You do it for me, Laura, you're so competent."

She had never been allowed to pack for David; in their first years he had always packed for her. He mistrusted her arrangements for the children, and it was with difficulty that she kept school clothes lists from him. He pounced on half-heard remarks about the number of handkerchiefs and unmarked pyjama trousers. Laura had learned to be vague, soothing and evasive.

When the school trains had gone and she went to see John, he scarcely listened to her recital of difficulties, until she learned not to take her catalogue of minor woes to him as to some neighbouring Army wife.

"For God's sake, Laura, it doesn't matter. You're here and they've gone for the moment."

Here was the secure world where John and Mrs. Malcolm reigned, untidy in a clean and dashing way which is Bohemian without being sluttish. There was dust on the china and the painted Italian furniture, but it was beautiful. But in Aldershot or Catterick or Mönchen-Gladbach or Singapore, there was no dust on the Army furniture and the scrolls of improbable colours sang loud and clear from innumerable ugly brushed carpets. Bright mirrors in bevelled frames reflected rooms of nonentity and in them her face steadied to the sensible managing look of a good Army wife, humorous, patient and ready to dress up with a smile and a hat to draw the raffle at a Wives' Club or present the cup to the Relay Team. In John's house, the mirrors were blackened and patchy in their ormolu frames; slightly distorting, it was necessary to find the one place where they would faithfully reflect instead of inserting a bulge or a wavering line and even then Laura's face, shadowy, seemingly beautiful, seemed only uncertainly hers.

Mrs. Malcolm waved a cheery goodbye at noon with her plastic shopping-bag.

"Ta ta, be good and remember you're only young once." She never varied her farewell as she went home to an invalid husband and querulous clutching children. They never tried to explain themselves to Mrs. Malcolm. She adored John and only mildly resented his paintings of her.

"To think of that in an exhibition. I could have put a better overall on and my hair in curlers for a night or two. But you know best, sir, it's your living, as you might say. You find things out, like the Bible says and that's what matters."

The reference escaped them for some time and then they were greatly touched. Laura was John's friend and that was good enough for Mrs. Malcolm. She talked about John's wife sometimes:

"She was nice enough in her way, but it wasn't her country or her life. She was homesick, you know. I'd come in in the mornings and she'd be sitting in her dressing-gown, only she called it a wrapper, drinking coffee at the kitchen table with tears running down her face and not reading her letters or the paper. The little girl was sweet enough but she spoilt her, Mrs. Ledcome did, and her grandmother sent all her clothes from America and she didn't look like an

English child at all. She used to hand them on to me, quite new, mostly, when the next parcel came, but my kids— well, I suppose they were all right for them sometimes and it's no use looking a gift horse in the mouth. Mr. Ledcome —I think he was glad in a way when they went, though it was only supposed to be a holiday, but we all knew—I never like to ask whether she's coming back or whether there's been a divorce. It would be easy for her, but mind you, she loved him. She'd fling her arms round him, right in front of me, Ma'am, and give him a great kiss like a close up. I was sorry for them all. Gail, she called the little girl, but Mr. Ledcome called her Elizabeth. Well, here I go running on and what does the enemy say—twelve o'clock as near as makes no difference. See you tomorrow, be good and remember you're only young once.''

The house folded them up when she went, as if some great bird of silence dropped from the London sky and touched it with its wings. That noonday quiet seemed precious each time Laura was there for it; the stream of chatter, then the smart bang of the front door, the trotting footsteps receding down the little street, then not a sound for a time, only the sensation of being alone with John, gathered into peace. He was always working in the mornings and did not stop for her. She would sit and watch him and catch his eye occasionally and smile, wrapped in a knowledge of love. An hour later they drank a glass of sherry and made lunch from what she had brought or Mrs. Malcolm had left: if she were feeling extravagant, she brought the first asparagus or the first strawberries or some exoticism from Harrods or Fortnum's en route, but often they had scrambled eggs and coffee and listened to a record or two or gossiped or held hands and kissed between mouthfuls and when lunch was over they went to bed. Depending on where David was stationed at the time, she went away to catch her train from, invariably, Waterloo, covering her tracks sometimes with a visit to a gallery, tea with an old friend, a series of telephone calls, two hours at a cinema. Waterloo was fraught with the sensations of triumph and partings. The monotonous voice giving unintelligible information, the brisk and hollow music, the soldiers and sailors with their loaded kit-bags and young faces, the late commuters, formed the background for Laura's transition from one world to the next. Sometimes she sat, too early for her train, on one of those long, ranked benches; the footways between were silted with the detritus of endless vigils, the litter of the impatient consuming time away with blank eyes and moving mouths. Conversations washed over her. She remembered to make them funny for David at dinner. Sitting there, she felt lost between one identity and the next. In London, bar the chance meeting or the planned appointment, she was unknown, a face under her latest hat. In Aldershot or Camberley or Tidworth or Wilton she would be labelled and put in her temporary compartment, to be forgotten in a few years, except, possibly by some grocer who liked her jokes or a daily who recalled a kindness. On some document, she supposed she was a dependent charge to the Army, a card in a file perhaps and that was all. As David Kingsley's wife she had a shape and a purpose, to herself she seemed to have no identity except when she was with John. Waterloo was a No-man's-land of noises and terrors.

She had always collected herself by the time she reached the other end; emotion drained away, she read the evening paper and a magazine, looked at her diary, saw that they had a young Captain and his new wife to dinner tomorrow, that she had a S.A.A.F.A. meeting the day after and a fork luncheon to plan a 'teenage dance' for the next holidays. David would ask about her day at dinner; he could not bear London and could not understand her pleasure at going, but was thankful she did not require him to drive her up or take her to shows, or, Heaven forfend, sit conspicuous in a gilt armchair until madam emerged from a fitting-room to ask with mingled diffidence and excitement if he liked the dress. He separated their lives as if with a sword and it was this sense of severance which kept her calmly chatting in the evenings about the traffic congestion in Regent Street or the new tulips she had seen in St. James's Park, without any stab of guilt, only of pity for them all.

And now David had shut his suitcase and gone down-stairs. He intended cashing some cheques and paying their bill and making various small arrangements: it was too wet to go out for long: he might send a boy for an English paper. Laura wrote a note to Antonia and a note to Mark: Antonia had looked beautiful and must be happy: Mark had behaved commendably and been solicitous about her in the evening. She thanked them both and was proud of them, but did not say so, since this smacked of age and they would tease her. It seemed impossible to her that they had turned out so well and so conventionally. Almost she had egged Mark on to buy the wrong clothes, sneer at the Army, take various in-substantial jobs and the wrong girls out. Antonia had been a year too early always with her high heels, shade of lipstick or nail varnish, but this was the limit of her rebellion. Laura had hoped for a career, a flat shared gaily between three or four girls, a flourish of difference, but no, she had fallen in love with Jack Truscott, able, eligible, sensible Jack and would make a trim, competent young wife. When she had first told Laura of her hopes of marrying Jack and Laura had been first astringent and then a little maudlin, she had said in her rather high young voice,

"But I don't *want* to be any different from you, Mummy. I just don't understand what you mean. I never wanted to go to a university and my shorthand's rotten, and being bossed about by some smooth young executive is not *my* idea of independence. I know Grannie was a doctor and all that, but she was a widow and it was more of a thing in those days anyway."

John had laughed at her too, in his teasing, warm way, taking her hands in his.

"Darling girl, it's what you've always wanted, *their* independence, *their* growing up."

She had cried ridiculously:

"It's because of that, don't you see? I've been wishing their childhood and their lives away and now I feel guilty. If Antonia were really my daughter I would have been firmer about it, but I can't be. That's what always happened."

Even John's cleanest handkerchiefs had a residual smell of paint and turpentine about them; she had mopped her eyes with the current proffered one, seen the tree tops outside for an instant pointed and starred with green and they had all wavered and blurred as her eyes filled with tears again.

"All my relationships are sterile," she had said in a broken, choking voice, like a ham actress in an over-emotional play.

She knew she was going too far and did not care. For years she had maintained her serenity with John; no outbursts, no scenes, no surrender to self-pity; time with John was too precious to squander on moods. Even on their rare holidays their happiness had to be cherished like a candle-flame in the wind. Perhaps that was what had been the weakness of their relationship. They had both known of the range of their griefs and vulnerability. John's wife's desertion and the loss of pride this entailed for him, the removal of his daughter whom he had painted with a transcendent tenderness which revealed all that needed to be known about his feelings, Laura's frustration over her childless marriage and her consequent, or imagined consequent constrained relationship with David, her intermittent jealousy of Christina, Aeneas, his mother: all that appertained to his childhood and background; of all these they were fully aware. But their concern for each other had a fastidiousness about it which prevented a continually prying finger on to the sore place to see if it were better; they were wary of relying on each other's sympathy as a stimulant for love. They had been clever, Laura had always thought until recently.

The pause in the piano playing ended; perhaps he had been out for coffee or to telephone or there had been an importunate caller. Laura imagined a lean young man with impatient fingers, blank to everything but a perfection of phrase or technique, living on black coffee and *soupe à l'oignon*. He warmed up with a scale or two and then was launched on *Carnaval* again; the pygmy battle of David against the Philistines.

Laura went to have her bath. If she were not dressed when David came back, he would be cross and she could not bear an ill-humoured day. The only chance they had was in keeping their tempers. He had been impossible on Antonia's wedding morning about the time: awake at six he had been at the windows to look at the weather like a small boy about to be denied a picnic. It was too dark to be sure of anything but an absence of rain. She had woken to remonstrate with him.

"There's only eight hours before she's due at the altar – think of what there is to do by then. Of course it's not too early. I'll make you some tea."

"Don't disturb Antonia."

"I won't."

But he had and she had come into their room to sit huddled in Laura's eiderdown and drink tea with them, laughing at remonstrance. There was a curious Christmas gaiety about it all that had reminded her of those early morning sessions with stockings and pillowcases, sleepiness, winter darkness, childish sharp excitement, infectious to Laura, and a curious sense of apprehension, as of a mystery. Mark's arrival, roused by their giggles, completed this illusion. They had cheerfully wasted away an hour of David's eight in fantasy and reminiscence and comfort; even David had not looked at his watch more than twice. It was for this hour and for others like it that she had stayed with David so long. Had they been her children, it would have been easier to hurt them and abandon them, she thought. But one cannot abandon a contract or a trust.

She had insisted, conventionally, on Antonia's return to bed for breakfast, where, in contrast to her dawn sprightliness, a skimmed-milk pallor and languor enveloped her. Whatever David might say, it was a long morning which unnerved Laura. She didn't want to be alone with anyone in the family in case they made some startling disclosure or asked some telling question. The air was taut with emotion and excitement; Laura was afraid of it and kept seeking safety in the kitchen with Brownlow the batman and Mrs. Curtis, the daily. The reception was to be in the Mess, and Brownlow should have been over there polishing glasses, but he kept remembering chores for the Brigadier and over cleaned shoes in his anxiety not to miss a moment of the house's preparations. It was warm in the kitchen with that sense of endless security that goes with familiar sounds and smells, a casserole bubbling, eggs being beaten, a sauce stirred. Mrs. Curtis took Laura's edginess for granted as her privilege that day, gave her cups of coffee and a morbid sympathy. She was a bulky woman with dyed hair, a flat voice and an unrivalled knowledge of Army families, her shoes turned over ludicrously at the sides as she waddled about, expostulating with Brownlow half-heartedly for cluttering up her kitchen.

More than anything Laura dreaded that Antonia would think of her real mother, even talk about her with that tactless candour she affected when worried. In her cooler moments, Laura could grant that speculation about her mother was natural. Antonia had a quality of innocent affection; she would wish to impart something of her happiness to her proper mother. No one could ever bring themselves to think that they were just a temporary physical mishap to their parents. Mark took a different line from Antonia; he minded much more that she was not really his sister than that he was only an adopted son. Laura had told them they were not her children from the earliest age, before they could understand what she meant, indeed, so that they would grow with the implicit knowledge and have no shock or doubts. She had an intuitive feeling that she could not have been wiser in what she had done. When they were older, the most natural of references were made to their situation. Mark astonished her, a placid, absorbed boy, by raging fiercely against his unknown mother once and never mentioning her again.

"You are my parents; there's no one else I want to care about."

Antonia probed sometimes, but Laura had been careful not to find out anything about their background. She thought it would be fatal to know about their mothers, to agonise or tyrannise over them in her thoughts. She was afraid of having to dispute her possession even mentally. That they had emerged with unplebeian faces and with some intelligence was a happy accident. Remembering an arrogant old uncle who always had the best of everything, she echoed his declaration which had been a family joke through her childhood, 'Ah, but I picked a good one'. In fact it was David who had made the final choice in each case, although it was a limited choice. There was too long a waiting list for children and even to be accepted on to the list was a difficult and lengthy process.

"You must not think, Mrs. Kingsley," her doctor had said, "that the adoption of a child is a recipe for restoring an impaired marriage. That would be grossly unfair to the child; selfish, improper. You must want to give someone else's child the love and concern you would have given your own. That love must be singular and positive." She had been frequently hysterical in his consulting-room and resented his calm sympathy over problems of sterility.

"Have you thought of adopting children?" he had asked. Laura had, but David was against the idea. It was her doctor who had finally persuaded him. She wondered what he had said. It was unlikely, holding the views which he did, that he would have implored David to help stabilise his wife or his marriage; the appeal must have been on wider grounds. David had always retreated into a black silence when she at first diffidently had raised the subject. She had grown vehement and emotional afterwards, hating her easy tears. Laura had never been able to argue coolly, it had been the handicap of her childhood and adolescence. However perfect a case to present to her school or grandfather, some favour to request, some injustice to right, the minute any argument developed Laura felt the tears welling up and choking her carefully thought out logic. "Highly strung", they said dismissively in those days. It was for this reason perhaps that she chose the calmest and easiest of paths now with John or with David. She could not afford to lose her serenity. In those early years of marriage, with the imminence of war and then war itself, the necessity of children had seemed piercingly urgent. She had gone to consult doctors after the first year and taken their treatment and advice through the second year. They had been lucky in some ways in being able to live together, with few interruptions, for nearly three years. It was after that that Antonia and a year later, Mark, had been adopted. She was very young and bitterly in love. David was ten years older.

It had been a rapturous marriage; she could still recapture the dizzy exultant time of courtship. Stepping out of her bath and into her clothes, Laura gave herself the luxury of its recall. Schumann mingled with the bathwater whirling and gurling in a foreign way down the waste pipe and with the rain splashing in great rivers down the window. There was only an hour before their train. She looked at herself by habit in the mirror, wiping away the steam with her hand, seeing herself emerge from a blur to a travesty of beauty. *But I was pretty once, attractive, on tiptoe, like Antonia, for love and admiration and for something, someone to love.*

Cole Porter, not Schumann, had spilled into her ears. It was a wicked world, of unemployment and hunger marches, of bread and butter and tea as a staple diet in Wales, of Hitler's threats and the mounting thunder of the jackboot, but Cole Porter's melodies sang sweetly to hopeful youth through it all. She and David had met dancing to *A fine romance with no kisses*, in the spring of 1938; she was staying with cousins in Chester; David was stationed there and they met at some regimental dance on the fringes of two parties who knew each other. It had been a love that ignited like a rocket, whizzing with growing speed into an unregarding sky. He came to stay at Plas Newydd, where her grandfather twinkled at him under his impressive eyebrows.

"You must make him laugh, David," she had said before. "Tell him a funny story; amuse him. Welsh men like laughing. You'll never gain his sympathy by being serious. Tease him a bit."

Reluctantly her grandfather was wooed; David made him laugh a great deal. They went for walks over the moors and fished together in silent amity. Her visit to Aldengrove and his mother was more difficult. David had been posted to Colchester; she had taken a job in London as a doctor's receptionist, living with the family (her grandfather's condition for accepting the situation) and had a long, free weekend. David was prevented at the last moment from driving her down; she had to catch a Saturday train in June. It had not occurred to her that the Isle of Wight was a popular place until she had to fight her way on to the train amongst an ebullient crowd of Cockney holiday-makers. It was a hot day and the air was loud with the crying of over-excited children and the anticipatory glee of their fathers in braces and the exhausted shrill remonstrance of their mothers. Laura felt like a hard pebble in a warm sea; her tidy presence an irritant in the spilling, crowded carriage amongst the sweet wrappings, the orange peel and the empty fizz bottles, her unheard voice an affront to the rich torrent of joyous abuse and gibe.

She had, then, a native contempt for other people's scenery and did not care for the comfortable Southern Railway landscapes. In Portsmouth there was an endless queue for the boat and in her anxiety to do the right thing she had brought too many clothes in too heavy a case. There were no porters. One shuffled slowly on, picking up, putting down one's case, enveloped still by one's neighbours, seeing no end to the journey. There was the long platform to crawl along, then a shuffle down the stairs, then the length of the quay; it was all intersected by barriers; officialdom was harassed and merely sheep-dogged round the good-humoured queue. Laura began to blame David for letting her face the journey alone and not telling her about summer Saturdays. A sour displeasure with him mounted in her so that by the time she had manœuvred her suitcase awkwardly in front of her up the narrow, steep gangway, she could feel the taste of it in her dry mouth and prickles of heat stung her like nettles. She almost fell into another girl, jerked forward by an eager woman with full, bulging shopping bags. Laura apologised and took in with envy her appearance — long hair surrounding an unexpectedly strong and capable face; she felt dwarfed and awkward under her height and amused gaze.

34

"I'm most terribly sorry."

"This is something of a summer scrum, I'm afraid. There's more room, a little more, over there." She led the way to a small space by a funnel.

"You'll jump when she hoots, I'm afraid. At least I always do."

She was wearing, Laura always remembered, slacks and a shirt with a cardigan loosely knotted on her shoulders and stood amidst the jolly press of people with a slightly arrogant air.

"I've never done this before or I wouldn't have been so silly as to travel on a Saturday afternoon."

"Coming to stay with friends?"

"Yes, in Hatherstone."

"Goodness, my village." She put a peremptory hand on Laura's arm and scrutinised her.

"*I* know, you're David's girl."

Laura had blushed under her stare and guess. At that moment the hoot of departure sounded and deafened her. She felt that was the last discomfiture of the day.

"And you are?" She put a certain amount of hauteur into the question to regain her self-respect.

"Christina Field."

"Oh, you're Christina. David didn't tell me you were so beautiful." The words slipped out and Christina was laughing at her.

"Ho, ho. There's been a lot of chat about you. David has been our prize bachelor for a long time."

Laura was rapidly working out Christina's age; she was only a year or so younger than David. At first glance, she had looked very young, now Laura surveyed the signs of age keenly and was disappointed that they did not matter, nor, she told herself coldly, ever would with a face and a disregard for it like Christina's. But she was drawn to her, there was a strength and warmth about her. She talked amusingly about Hatherstone, about David's mother and the old gardener Aeneas; she refrained from quizzing Laura.

"You're going to be asked heaps of questions all weekend, so I won't now. And we're all coming for drinks tomorrow night to meet you, so I can get you in a corner then, ginned-up and one of the family. At the moment you look as if you're dying of heat and people. It's no good my suggesting a lemonade below. That will be worse. Twenty minutes and you'll be there. Is Mrs. Kingsley meeting you?"

"I have to telephone, because the arrangements were altered. I expect David knew we should be late."

"Now, now. We're all at the mercy of the mainlanders in this season. I'm being met by a brother. We could give you a lift in our anything but limousine."

"I'd better telephone first."

"Yes, yes, of course."

Christina and Ian had whisked away in a sputter of gravel and dust as Mrs. Kingsley came down the steps to meet her.

"So like Christina to have rescued you and given you an unconventional welcome. I hope you don't mind."

Laura was conscious that a crouched journey in the battered car had laddered her stockings, further creased her skirt, jolted her hat, that her face shone and her lipstick had been eaten away in anxiety. Mrs. Kingsley was a tiny commanding woman, like a fierce, small bird, with elaborately dressed hair, flashing diamonds and no resemblance to

David. She drew Laura to her and put a silken cheek against hers.

"Such a journey naughty David put you through. Betty will take you to your room and then come down to tea."

In the drawing-room there were blinds over the balcony to keep out the glare. It was an oval room full at first glance of china and pictures and the striped reflections of sea and grass. Far below the lawn and the pines and tamarisk was the sea wall. The tide must have been in for the marshes and millpond David had talked about were under a blue wash of sea, distantly decorated by red-sailed little boats. It was calm, improbable and beautiful. Her hand trembled absurdly from fatigue and excitement so that her cup when she put it down rattled in the saucer and she splashed tea over herself when she drank. Mrs. Kingsley, handing her cucumber sandwiches and chocolate cake, seemed unaware of this. Her detachment from malaise and its symptoms was a quality Laura grew to appreciate more than anything else in her mother-in-law. She had a clever way of not noticing anything from tears to egg stains to too much gin to unhappiness. It was soothing to be with her and have one's distress ignored. She had no warmth, no cosiness, but a cool and critical mind and a touch of ice. With her stature one expected something else before being confronted with the elegant beak nose and the fine thin bones of her face. She read a great deal and despaired of David and yet had channelled him relentlessly into the Army. A portrait of his father, dead of influenza in the post-war epidemic, dominated the library; in dazzling and outmoded military rig, bland and commanding, Laura could trace David's lineaments to his. But the photographs in their silver and tooled leather frames around the room had less of the timeless quality of the painting. Colonel Kingsley looked old-fashioned, whether in uniform or mufti; even his stance and what he did with his hands dated him. He had looked more shyly and diffidently at the camera than at the artist or the latter had been anxious to reflect the military glow not only of the scarlet jacket but of the traditionally blue and piercing eyes.

She had tried so hard then to be clear-sighted about David, to view him out of uniform and circumstances, to view his detachment from her as an unexpected inheritance from his mother. It was not the last fearful journey she would be left to do by herself. She told herself later she had seen then prophetically the houses she would have to pack up alone or find alone, the sea voyages and endless train journeys with small children she would be left to endure, while David was comfortably looking to his men's welfare, the solitude that would press in on her while he went off to courses or Mess nights. Women can only fight back by falling into that most ridiculous attitude of "our regiment, our men, our mess". Viewing the colonel's portrait gave her a flicker of doubt but probably no more at the time, and as her hand stopped trembling in his mother's drawing-room, she viewed the day with the amusement that would subsequently go into her relation of it.

When David came, within half an hour, he had her out cockling, postponing dinner, lending her old plimsolls, waving aside his mother's protests. They went first to visit Aeneas, who greeted her with the civil dourness David had warned her of. He had a long, bony, contemptuous nose like a sheep's.

"Ye'll not be getting married yet awhile," was the first remark she remembered him making.

"Oh yes, in the autumn," Laura had said with a staunch smile.

"Gey soon, gey soon," he had shaken his head. "And you're away cockling: nasty, filthy things they are too. I mind gathering them for Miss Christina's grandfather and taking them crabs and lobsters too when the men were lucky. Some people would eat anything."

She remembered then the connection between Christina and Aeneas. Brought up on her mother's family estate in Scotland, the Fields and the Kingsleys were old friends.

"Were you always expected to marry Christina?" she said when they were on their way to the beach.

"Our mothers no doubt planned it. We spent our childhood together, dodging Aeneas, eating his peaches and strawberries, but that's different."

She pulled a face which she hoped he did not see. The tide was receding and the sky rich with fading sunset light. Cockling is a concentrated affair; head bent till the neck aches, a survey of the pool at one's feet in silence till the sand and ripples of one's approach die away and all is clear again; the hard crusted wave marks, the pebbles, the vivid green strands of silky seaweed and then the tiny white-rimmed 'eyes' of the cockle; scoop, snap, bubbling shut and there is another one for the bucket. One becomes impervious to one's surroundings; conscious only of what one sees in a narrow range. Then straightening to ease one's aching back, there was sudden immensity around, the sea and the sky paling into a bleached slate blue with the sting and strength of the day's colour abated. The sand in great curves and spits engulfed one's landward horizon. Voices from the harbour were clear as bells but wordless, figures on the sea wall were silhouettes only. The tide was going out fast now; great lagoons of stranded water drained away leaving only an occasional shine on the sand. They walked further and further into the bay; sounds from the shore receded, only the gulls wheeled round them and the harbour swans drifted in the remaining channel of sea, one after another in a long flotilla. Laura and David stood up to watch them pass. It seemed to Laura in restrospect, as if caught in some last cloudy beam of sunset, a recollection of perfect happiness. They had set down their pails of cockles and David had put his arms round her and kissed her, gently first and then hungrily. All round them was light and silence.

On their way back across the sands, they met Christina, also in rolled-up trousers, hair knotted in a cotton scarf, her face streaked with sand and salt where she had wiped a careless hand over it.

"I didn't know you still went cockling, David."

"Always given the tide and the opportunity and the right girl."

He had squeezed Laura's hand and she watched Christina's amused glance as it rested on them. Almost she waited for "Bless you, my children," but no, Christina was talking about a fish soup with cockles in it. They walked slowly back to their cars together and stayed, shuffling their feet about in the sharp marram grass of the stony paths, prolonging their goodbyes.

She was still glowing from her bath and recollection of youth and happiness, humming an echo or two of the pianist's music, folding a nightgown, combing her damp hair, dark still, when David came back, pulling a resigned face at the confusion of the bedroom. He finished her packing, handed her her coat and hat and scarf and inspected briskly bathroom, cupboards and bedside tables for stray possessions and then stood hunched moodily before the streaming windows.

"If we have to wait long for a taxi we'll miss the train. I've been looking on a map. It's much further than we thought, the Austerlitz. We should have started earlier. It's ridiculous since we hadn't anything to do except catch the damned train."

"I've been luxuriating in thought."

"Yes, Laura, and a long bath. You always have the water too hot. You still look slightly boiled."

"Darling David, so safe to know what you will say. Couldn't you say it in French for the next fortnight to break the monotony?"

"What's belt-up in French?"

They both laughed and leaned shaking on the bedposts. Laura checked her laughter on the dangerous verge of tears and took out a handkerchief to mop her eyes.

"The Brigadier's a proper caution," she said imitating Brownlow.

"Poor Brownlow, how will he ever face civilian life? He needs a family after that orphanage. He's going to miss us terribly."

"By the time he's helped pack the house up and march us out, I doubt that. Poor Brownlow. How one's life disintegrates; so many neat glossy packets disintegrating in a puddle of rain, that's what I think sometimes, looking back."

David was abrupt.

"For God's sake, come on, Laura. There's the porter for our bags. I hope the taxi's there."

But there was no taxi yet and they stood in the smart

lounge, amidst the rubber plants and the glass screens and the shiny black chairs, David rattled and mottled, Laura tense with calm. One train missed, what did it matter? She could spend the rest of her life missing trains, loitering at stations and in hotel lounges. There was no purpose in catching trains now. The Waterloo period was over. John was gone. She caught her breath with pain; it was like the shock of being soothingly told that some probe would not hurt, a shock not only of sudden agony but of the treachery. No one said it would hurt like that, like this.

She turned to David.

"Talking of Brownlow, I keep wondering why we never heard from Aeneas. Pious Aeneas, practically his grand-daughter's wedding and no wire. Those hideous horn mugs came weeks ago."

She watched David's face twitch into impassivity.

"There was a wire. It got mixed up with the others till old Harry ran through the messages just before we left for the church."

"What do you mean, mixed up?"

"It was to say Aeneas died on Friday, a stroke."

"Oh, darling, why didn't you tell me? For you to have heard then . . ."

"I didn't think you'd be very interested and it would have upset Antonia."

"David, I . . ."

"Not here." He put a cold finger on her wrist. "The taxi is coming."

"Darling . . ."

The tears that stung, the bitter choking in her throat was not for Aeneas; David would know that. Outside she saw through the rain which fell like hurled spears on

42

the pavement, the taxi waiting, the porter putting in their bags.

"Oughtn't you to have gone to the funeral?"

"Yes. It was today. I couldn't disappoint you. Aeneas' last gesture to you."

"David," she clutched his arm, "I'm sorry."

"I wasn't going to tell you for a few days. Come on, *run*. You'll be soaked."

II

DAVID

LAURA IS a fool and I have been unkind to her as always. The game of misinterpretation I started years ago, perhaps from the first time when a look, a gesture, or half-heard phrase telephoning a friend told me she thought I was stupid and simple. Years ago my mother took me to Italy. Squiring her was amusing — I was only sixteen — but she assumed I would be bored by picture galleries because I liked watching the crowds in the streets or the shapes of cypresses on hillsides. Sometimes she would enjoy gossiping maliciously with me over a glass of vermouth about some middle-aged hotel acquaintances, in her conspiratorial way: other times she sent me to bed early, like a schoolboy, and talked me over with them, same conspiratorial smile. Returning for a forgotten key, I heard her voice in the distance.

"Oh, of course David's a complete philistine. He'll make a good simple honest soldier like his father."

At that time the thought of Sandhurst produced a taste of khaki grit in my mouth. I wanted to go to a university; other boys, less clever, were destined for Oxford or Cambridge, to acquire a little learning, make friends, join societies. The trouble was that a heaviness lay upon my mind and reasoning like some impediment in a dream. As in a dream the sense of solitude oppressed me. No one ever dreams that they are part of a loving family or a jolly troupe.

In dreams one is alone and space and time press transparently and heavily upon one like water against the body of a swimmer.

The heaviness and the languor persisted: I have always been a slow soldier but a good one, cramming myself into the subaltern's mould as I crammed myself into the school-boy's mould at my father's old school. I became a simple soldier to spite my mother, who would have liked me to paint, conduct an orchestra or an industry. That is what I tell myself now, interpreting laziness with sophistication. There I lay, summer day after summer day, in the orchard amongst the haycocks, with the smell of cut nettles in my nose, and the bay hedges, like a gently cooking casserole. I read and dreamed and slept, lunched sulkily with my mother or joined her friends for tea, posed in an old-fashioned group under the cedar tree. My mother had easily despairing eyebrows; she would dodge behind the tea cosy and the silver cake stands and raise them at her friends. "I told you so," "I told you so."

When I came back from my first posting abroad, I heard Mother and Aeneas in the garden.

"He's different now, isn't he? More like his father."

"Ay, verra like the Colonel now indeed, ma'am."

Aneas always managed to roll an 'r' into the midst of his pronunciation of colonel which made it sound more splendid. I have been a colonel for a long time now, and now a brigadier; today or next Monday in *The Times* I shall be gazetted a Major-General and in a fortnight I shall take over the Allied Services ceremonially and Laura will give a series of dinner parties and be admired. As an Army wife I can never fault her; as my wife only, I am aware of her imperfections. Laura has always enjoyed playing a part. On

Saturday, as the mother of the bride, she was splendid, half-deprecating her success in the rôle. She does not always look beautiful now, as she did once with her light brown hair and grey-blue eyes, but at the wedding some glow returned, some old fire. For the past week she had looked defeated, worn out, ridiculing wedding bustle, but on Saturday she looked triumphant again. I could not bear to tell her about Aeneas then. She would have said, "How like him to die just at this moment. He never had any sense of timing." For she sees others as actors beside herself, merely players and can only take their rôles seriously. She was so angry when he was ill and there was a long delay about his convalescence, with Jeannie dead. It only meant that the children and I could not go there as we had planned; for her it was some tragedy. Laura likes her plans unalterable, she cannot bend to the wind. She planned to have a large family, seeing herself as a teeming mother with a pewful in the Garrison Church. Look what happened to that. Aeneas was cruel about her then; he must have been visiting that church on the Island with the epitaph on two wives: he saw her only as the unfruitful vine.

"You should have tried her before, laddie, as they did in the old times and waited to see if she bore."

The discussion was too deep for me to be amusedly frivolous about his suggestions; his only child had died at three; they had had none since. When we adopted Antonia and Mark he was even more critical than my mother was.

"Ye don't know what liars and thieves you're breeding up for yourselves or what like their parents were."

It remained for them to captivate him; like a grandfather he was more indulgent to them than he ever was to me or to Christina.

47

Aeneas, pious Aeneas: the adjective fitted with its Latin implications. His name coloured my approach to the classics for years. His nose, bony, long, contemptuous, peered through the lines of Virgil like a horse through a five-barred gate. Once I attempted to explain this to my prep. school headmaster, poised with a slipper at the ready.

"But think of the dogs called Caesar. And I knew a mastiff called Tarquin."

"It isn't the same at all, sir. Aeneas is important to me."

"So is Virgil. Learn to concentrate."

At that time I had my mother's version of life which included Aeneas and my dead father, 'The Colonel'.

When war swept my father from retirement to active service and Aeneas was prevented by some disability from following him, my mother thought she saw her chance to banish her husband's dour gardener to munitions or market gardening.

"If I can't be with the Colonel, my place is with you, ma'am," was all he would ever say to her suggestions.

My father came home old and tired in 1918 and succumbed to influenza, dying almost at once. My mother took me abroad and proposed thereafter living in a London flat. Aeneas had said to her (they both repeated historic conversations to me all their lives), "London's no place for a child, I'm thinking, Mistress Kingsley. The Colonel's boy will not like it at all. And you'll be as lonely there, ma'am, as here."

My mother bought Aldengrove, deciding on a warmer, smaller house and the Fields, old friends of my father's and hers, lived near by. She made a good story of her first visit. My mother had a knack of laughing at herself with the rueful irony of one who had enjoyed being teased. I suppose my father teased her; an easy relationship for an older man to fall into with a younger wife.

"My marriage was a sort of bonus," she would say, "an unexpected treat, a gorgeous picnic, so it didn't matter that it was short and sweet, like the best kind of surprises. After all, I wasn't a young girl and I had a husband out of the blue. *And* a son to be going on with. Wasn't I lucky?" She had a gurgling laugh which dispelled any embarrassed sympathy.

Aeneas had insisted on chaperoning her visit to Aldengrove, since he doubled as chauffeur. He found fault with everything in the house and garden, as the agent showed them round and my mother, anxious to sever herself from Aeneas, to have her own garden and her own way in future, delighted in his gloom. Now she need have no qualms over parting from him, for she loved everything she saw in Aldengrove; she listened happily to his strictures on the dark and poky lodge and the orchard which he judged needed restocking; even the warm, walled vegetable garden with its peach houses and espaliered fruit trees and figs proliferating over the arched entrance, failed to soften him.

"It's verra near the sea," my mother imitated him to perfection. "Sea mist and damp and noise. Verra nice on a day like this but it cannot always be spring and the sun shining. That's a bonny tree — maaagnolia, I doubt. I'm surprised it does so well in the salt air."

"And then," my mother would say as she finished the story, "when we were waiting for the ferry and I was struggling idiotically with my hat and the seagulls were making distracting noises and the gangways were creaking and the wind blowing, at the height of all that, Aeneas turned to me and said, 'Well, Mistress Kingsley, I reckon that house will do us nicely.' I waited till we were on the boat and then I asked him why he'd been so gloomy. He tossed his head, 'Well, ma'am, it wouldn't have done at all to give that creature of an agent an idea of what we were thinking. That's the way of it, whether it's a cow or a house you're buying.' And all I could think of saying then was, 'You want to come then? I thought you would rather find a post with a man and a large family.' 'And leave you, ma'am! Whatever would the Colonel have said?' ''

If I were there on the fringes of the audience, she would wink at me. She was very good at giving me the feeling of being party to some conspiracy. She was too proud and too cool for a sentimental relationship with me, but she made the best of sharing her life with a small boy as she had of being left a widow and heir to an unpredictable, opinionated, crusty retainer.

At worst, when I was a small boy, Aeneas seemed a disagreeable man who counted his bunches of grapes and locked the peach houses and even seemed to know when Christina and I raided the strawberry beds. No strawberries have ever tasted as they did, eaten on our haunches, amidst the tickling straw, warm from the sun and their confinement. I remember looking at Christina's skimmed-milk skin — that's what my mother called it — all dribbled with crimson juice and then nervously over my shoulder to make sure that Aeneas had not suddenly emerged from raking the gravel on the drive or scything the orchard. There was some absolute, if muddled, connection in my mind then between Aeneas, fruit and sin. No wonder that when I was much smaller I confused him with Mr. McGregor and could not quite believe that I had never been caught in a gooseberry net by the brass buttons of my jacket. In the fringes of sleep I sometimes saw my father's ears, sleek as a rabbit's, emerging from a pie. If I outgrew the Peter Rabbit phase, I never outgrew the pleasure of seeing Aeneas in his Sunday best setting out with Jeannie on some rare excursion. Christina and I would watch from one of the peepholes in the wall and then decide which was best: gooseberries, yellow as honey, veined and hairy, strawberries, the first velvety peaches and nectarines (this meant stealing the keys), bunches of red-currants more for the pleasure of the eye than the palate, though one could pop them against one's tongue as one did globules of caviare later in life. It never occurred either to Christina or to me that it was my mother we were robbing. For one thing, she would not have minded, apart from having to placate Aeneas on our behalf, so that would never have done and would have spoilt our delicious sense of guilt, cooled our hot cheeks, slowed down the tearing of our teeth bursting skins and pulping flesh and spoiled the illicit joys of Christina's accompliceship. At best Aeneas was the husband of Jeannie, whose snug kitchen produced shortbread and hot scones and stories of Achranish, the seals and the deer and Christina's grandfather's and great-uncles' exploits. When Aeneas was there, relaxed with his pipe, watching me stuff myself under Jeannie's loving eyes, the stories flowed, vivid and good-humoured. I longed to see Achranish.

"Christina will take you there, all in good time, never fear."

And they would look at each other for a second over my head. Going back to school after the holidays was never agreeable; Aeneas helped. My prep. school always started on Mondays. There was a little mission church in the village, because the church proper was some distance away and it had a tolling, tinny bell. When it rang for Evensong those last holiday Sundays, I was always flooded with a sense of desolation. It was a cracked, implacable, unlovely bell and it symbolised for me the return to a loveless, fruitless climate and Latin. I suppose really it just sounded very like a school bell. Aeneas found me crying once in a greenhouse amidst the geraniums.

"And what's the matter with you, David, I'd like to know?

"I've got something in my eye."

"Aye, so you have. Shall I try to get it out?"

I rubbed my eyes desperately.

"Now, Christina wouldna greet, now, would she?"

"Neither would I. Something went into my eye"; and I tried to turn a sob into a hiccough.

"Christina's a brave lassie. You recall when she fell from that oak when she was hiding from you, she didn't shed a tear."

"She's a girl and they're different."

"Well, well, they're different. Well, that's news to me."

I stopped crying to explain.

"You had Flora MacDonald and that woman who pushed her arm across the door instead of a bolt and Mary Queen of. You wouldn't have expected them to cry, would you? But I bet Charlie cried like anything."

"Now that's a verra interesting view of history, David. Did you learn that at school now?"

"No, I didn't. It's all Latin and Maths. and stories from Greece and Rome."

"Very vaaluable, I'm sure. The Corrnel would have liked you to be a good scholar now and school doesn't last for ever. Just take it as it comes, David now. Your mother misses you sure, but she's a brave woman. Don't be grieving her now."

At Portsmouth station, Aeneas's comfortable voice rang in my ears as I watched my mother's breeziness. If she pulled out a handkerchief it was to wave vigorously. Other mothers raised tentative hands to their eyes. I despised them.

Christina certainly never wept; it would have been out of keeping with her. I have always despised Laura's tears, brimming so easily because I have flicked out crossly at the children or her. Christina was different. Then she was leggy, pale and fanatical. When we were not raiding Aeneas's fruit, we played romantic games with ardour under her instruction in the orchard, on the seaward slopes of the lawn or under the sea wall. In a discarded black velvet dinner-gown of her mother's, Christina laid her thin little neck on a tree stump, previously plentifully stained with mulberries, while I stood perilously above her with a rusty axe. In bunches of brackish reeds, I hid, waiting for her, with her skirts lifted up, to succour me with food or row me to some other insalubrious clump in the mill pond. Once when I dared to whistle, *Over the sea to Skye* on one of these occasions, her eyes blazed. "Victoriana," she said. "Shut up."

Considering our loyal adherence via Christina to Scottish history in our games, it was a pity Aeneas was not more helpful. He disliked Christina's habit of hiding in his neat haycocks when he had scythed the orchard, with me slashing them all to pieces with an old fencing foil to discover which concealed her. He objected to our hiding in his apple loft because it entailed our rolling about on his apples. The smell of apples, sharp and sweet still brings back to me the marbled discomfort of them against my thighs and stomach as I lay with Christina, not daring to move, while Aeneas and the current gardener's boy moved sacks and tins of weedkiller down below, with their jackets turned to scarlet as we peered through cracks, in the intensity of our fear.

My relationship with Christina changed when I went to my public school. I suppose this was due partly to a fashionable anti-girls attitude and partly because we had only played certain kinds of games together, the games which children outgrow. Hiding the young Pretender should have been succeeded by a mutual interest in tennis or sailing. I hated tennis and my sailing was confined to crewing sometimes for my friends. She sailed with her brothers and was rather good, I remember hearing. So we drifted apart and our mothers no doubt shook their heads wisely and thought that when we were through having spots and crazes and falling over things, once the heady and tormented period of our adolescence was over, we would come together again – and marry. I was always a little surprised by my mother's friendship for Christina's mother: they were so different. But my father had been very fond of her and all the Buchanan family and my parents first met at some houseparty at Achranish. I have seen a photograph of that party: foreground guns and dogs, background, Gothic steps and doorway, in the middle, in the soft, slurred browns of old photographs, stand the young men with their tweed knickerbockers and retriever-like eyes and the young women with shirt blouses and steep belted skirts and a gentle melting look. No trace there of the coming bloody slaughter of pheasants or deer or of displays of temper, malice and swung mallets on the croquet lawn. My father was in a prominent place in the group, with his host, the two older men, moustachioed, fierce and bewildered.

Laura has a shrewd phrase for people, sometimes: she described Goofy Marksby as looking like a surviving mammoth in a cave, with drooling tusks, not fierce at all, only funny. I see my father's generation like that. Perhaps Laura sees me like that; she has had a way for a long time of separating our ages. I am ten years older than she but it has now become decades. Perhaps she is right and I have caught the complaint from my old-fashioned profession, though this is odd because I have sometimes noticed that certain professions, like school teaching for men and women, the services for men, nursing for women, keep people curiously young, pickled as it were in some antiseptic preservative. They have grizzled heads, fresh lively complexions and the outlook of innocent and former days. Perhaps it is the habit of command, common to all these professions. The enforcement of discipline keeps one single-minded and away from the dilution and wear of outside influences. One has rarely challenged, one has never been challenged. Acceptance is all. Perhaps religious and enclosed orders also have this gift, if one can call it that, of youth. One rarely sees any nun's face that is neither unconscionably young nor plunged wholly into quintessential and wrinkled age.

This business of growing old is complicated. Some pompous subalterns of my generation have merely now grown into their mannerisms. Others one has seen change, perhaps from gaiety to pedantry, perhaps from diffidence to serenity. It seemed a long way once from a Sandhurst cadet to a major-general: looking back the cadet seems very near to me. This astonishing gift we all have of seeing ourselves and others in the round always disconcerts us: one's children are there all of a piece in one's thoughts from the baby gurgling on the rug to the bride at the altar. I see Antonia all-in-one, inseparable, and Mark too, elegant à la Moss Bros. and yet wearing rompers and a sunhat. I see James also, telescoped from that first sight of him poking in rock pools with determined clumsy gestures, fat legs creased with effort, to my last view, drinking sherry with me in the cottage at Achranish, sweeping his hair back with Christina's gesture: James, my son, my only child, inheriting the world I have learned to want more than any other, that world of solitude and water and hill. If it were not for Laura, it could have been nine years ago, not as James has it, by right, but at least borrowed for my lifetime. Aeneas and I would have been happy there together. But one has one's obligations. I was in love with Laura once, and now I suppose I count her amongst my obligations.

Years ago I took Christina to the fair at Queenbridge, across the harbour. We were, I suppose, about sixteen or seventeen and had not been seeing much of each other. The Fields were always away in Scotland in August and September and let their house to summer visitors, but this August something had gone wrong with their plans and I met Christina suddenly in the village and asked her to come to the fair. It seemed a romantic thing to do as it happened in films. In happy and returned innocence, the hero and heroine capture dolls and teddy bears, ride ecstatically on roundabouts and every ball is a coconut. I saw our faces radiant in naphtha flares; all round us would be the warm crowds I envied in their endless perambulations round the

56

village shops. Collarless men in braces, flushed with sun and freedom, women in flowery dresses and beach pyjamas, with bulging carrier bags and shrieking children, filled me with tenderness. It was not quite as I had imagined it at the fair.

Perhaps the stallholders, with only a glint of rapacity to enliven the indifference of their mean and vulgar faces, would have looked well in a painting or a film; in the flesh they filled me with disgust because they took my money without a smile and watched our efforts with rifles, hoops and rubber balls without interest.

"How can they, Christina?" I bawled above the wheezy music.

"How can they what?" She was wearing a dirndl skirt and white blouse and her hair was tied up with ribbon. This was the only point of my daydream that was better than I had imagined.

"Be so beastly indifferent and sullen. They ought to be jolly."

"It's a dreary life; they're never going to see us again."

"But I *mind*."

"Yes, David. You're such a romantic."

We won plaster lambs afterwards at some stall and clutched them to ourselves in the crowd as though they were Meissen. Then we saw a particular crush of people and went to see what was happening. The crowd had formed a circle and inside were an old man and woman who looked like the ageless pairs of tramps one sees pushing old prams of belongings. They were small but with the toughness of stunted trees outlasting the gales. Her grey hair was in a rough, unkempt bob, her clothes had so grown together in

57

colour and texture that they now looked like a skin from which she could not be separated. She stood motionless while the old man addressed the crowd: she had heard it all before and seen the people. I wondered whether she knew where she was or even who she was. The old man presumably outlined, with showman's exaggeration, what they were about to do. He spoke in a slurred and difficult dialect and was incomprehensible. He had said it all so many times that his expression seemed to bear no relation to what he was saying, but remained impassive and disinterested; not like a machine or a robot talking exactly, but as if some mound of earth or dump of stones had found a voice.

There were some sacks and coiled chain and rope by the old man's feet and gradually his intentions became clear. The old woman stepped into one sack and pulled it up, then he put another one over her head. She lay down and he began to tie her up like a corpse to be consigned to the sea. The shroud was parcelled up with ropes and chains, without a movement from the woman as he heaved her about, grunting and swearing a little. The crowd watched silently; there was a pause in the music from the roundabouts; I could hear the gulls screaming and could see, behind the wasteland at the sand's edge where the fair was pitched, the dark shore stretching to the almost luminous line on the horizon where the sea still glimmered. The old man moved away from the body for what seemed a long time. The old woman had seemed barely human or alive before; her sort of life seemed to have no connection with my apprehension of people, my own sort or those I envied carefree in deck-chairs with newspapers over their faces. But now that she lay motionless in dirty sacking, it seemed that there was a sense of loss.

The bundle began to stir, to writhe, to struggle and gradually, with a great convulsion was erect again, grim, swaying, Lazarus-wrapped. There were more heavings from within, more wrigglings, more sidlings and shrugs. It was an apparition of horror, as of some inert mass fumbling into life; one chain dropped to the ground and then another, the binding ropes were loosened and by frantic rolling by the woman, were worked down to her feet. Her hands emerged, she took off one sack and stepped out of the other. There was a desultory round of clapping, she did not smile. Before the crowd could leave the two of them moved round with greasy caps. Occasionally they said 'thank you' but more as a reminder than in gratitude. The woman was panting slightly, the veins on her arms and neck stood out like cords but her face had the same blankness. I gave her more money than I had intended, but her eyes did not change as they momentarily looked into mine. Some of the crowd walked away and the performance started all over again, but this time it was the old man who was trussed up. She tied him up with a sort of slow competence all the time with a sleep-walker's face in which sometimes I discerned, or thought I did, a faint expression of contempt.

I have never forgotten these two though it is now over thirty years ago and they must long since have become a part of the earth they so adequately represented. It was a curious episode, a disquieting event whose meaning has eluded me like the meaning of some dream on waking but which has left behind a motiveless anxiety. I thought about them afterwards, moving from fairground to fairground. I never thought of them as living in a caravan or eating fish and chips on its steps after a performance. I saw them housed in some hollow of the downs or dunes, some dry ditch, part of the earth, deriving from it, bound to it, moving at a loping, tired trot like animals, knowing only how to curse or demand, beyond comprehension but not beyond pity. Anxiety and pity rose in me that evening, making me careless and slightly deaf to what Christina said, as if I were pre-occupied with some beating I was to get at school for some unknown offence at some unstated time. Since then I see them sometimes with Laura's face and mine, shuffling through an act of possession, loading each other with chains, discarding them to faint applause, bound to each other.

Christina described them as pure Hardy, which meant nothing to me then. She could always indemnify herself from an experience by finding some literary association. For a girl as practical as she was, at home with a car engine or a distemper brush or a sick parrot, she was strangely given to a world of books and poetry. All the Fields had this strange combination of practical ability and dreaminess. Their household had always a temporary look as if they were merely passing the time there en route for some more permanent dwelling. Trunks had remained for twenty years or so in the boxroom, unstrapped but bulging. There were pictures waiting to be hung propped up in the attic. I once ran an old sword through Christina's great-grandmother and lived in dread for years of any one finding the tear in the canvas. I need not have worried. I always wondered what they were waiting for; Mrs. Field stood no chance of inheriting the Buchanan house for she had two brothers. There was always vague talk of some new business venture of Mr. Field's which would entail their moving but nothing came of it. They belonged to that vanished class who possessed small but sufficient private means and who engaged only desultorily in work of any kind. They let their house in the summer and sometimes, when school bills were particularly harassing, took paying guests. Mrs. Field had reddish hair and a pale skin. She had never got used to living in England and I suppose the makeshift air of the house was a symptom of her disbelief that she was not, at any moment, returning to Scotland. Mr. Field was a mild man, given to drinking beer in the summer; he both cultivated and assuaged a thirst; bottles were placed strategically around the house so that the whole place smelt slightly like a pub. Drinking beer usually accompanied some creative phase in his life, some cranky inventiveness, some plotting of a new venture. In the winter he sang Gilbert and Sullivan and smoked cheroots.

Their household, shabby, slightly dishevelled, was a relief from the precision of my mother's. It was a house where one could go and help oneself in the larder when hungry: my mother's cook would have given notice.

After that episode at the Fair, when thinking again, I reckon I must have been seventeen and Christina a year younger because it was the year before I went to Sandhurst, we talked vaguely sometimes of being engaged and getting married. It was a subject which came up when walking in the twilight in the marshes, with the oyster-catchers and curlews making the night air lonely with their cries or watching the blazon of fireworks in the sky in Regatta weeks drooping finally into darkness, or walking on the high downs, where below the immediate sweep of grass or chalk-land, the whole map of the island was visible with a blue paring of sea on the nearer coasts. Given this sort of encouragement, we both felt disposed to talk, incoherently or wildly according to mood, about our futures. We never, either of us, referred to what we both knew about each other; that Christina would never be happy without Scotland to live in and that I, destined for the Army, could not marry for years.

Sometimes I asked her to marry me, when overwhelmed by affection and the scent of her hair in the sun. I always meant it at the time but retrospectively her refusals did not sadden me. I suppose I asked her at the balls at Sandhurst to which she always came. She and my mother came to my passing-out parade, the Sovereign's Parade. I was in a state of icy tremble all day and said things back to front, though why I thought I would be conspicuous to the monarch, I can't imagine. Visiting Mark the other day, watching the ducks sliding between the first fallen leaves in the lake ("These fish will not be fed") I was reminded of Christina's visits (she always fed the fish) on Sundays when she was working in London. She was always taking odd jobs in an impetuous and amateurish way: selling toys in Harrods for Christmas, being a temporary secretary to an actress with the fanmail of a long run. Unfortunately, or fortunately, she never had the sort of education and training which would have developed her talents; I thought her splendidly wasted even then.

Now when every child's gifts and talents are weighed and cherished and encouraged, there isn't this sort of wasting: a pity, I rather like to see unused richness spilling out of a woman's personality instead of being harnessed into teaching and typing and welfare. It makes them unhappy, of course, burning with frustrations, unfulfilled, but I like to see a fine woman smouldering at a dinner party or interfering subtly with her husband's province or prowling round her house with a sense of power exuding from her finger tips. I prefer that to hearing smart prattle about her day in the office (some Ministry, interior decoration, personnel management, what have you?) or how her lectures or tutorials went. Laura was so frightened of being wasted that she had to adopt children.

She was very young then, of course, bursting with warmth and affection, certain that I should be killed, anxious to be a proper Roman matron breeding for the country's future. I minded that she couldn't have children for her sake, but by then I was wrapped in so many anxieties that the situation was unreal. She had an obsession about it: she was frightened that I would stop loving her or that uncemented by the fruits of procreation, our marriage would crumble and fall apart. I wonder sometimes what difference it would have made, not that I haven't most intensely enjoyed Antonia and Mark who have been rewarding in every way: affectionate, interesting, agreeable. But they have been hostages. Without them, I could have retired years ago and lived in Achranish with Aeneas and written my play and dined once a week with Christina. I will enlarge on that dream later. Laura might have come to live with me; she is always on the defensive about Scotland or my play-writing. Women become so maternal about men's hobbies and dreams, diminishing them with their whimsical indulgence. Perhaps basically women think that all time is wasted by men not spent in making love or money.

Regrettably for Laura, neither of these pursuits has played a large part in my life. I am not such a cold or unambitious fish, but circumstances have defeated me. I have cared for the Army and my regiment and I loved Christina and our son and none of these concerns has been so very rewarding. It took me as long to fall in love with the Army as it did to fall in love with Christina.

Perhaps she teased me about the beginnings of both infatuations the day she showed me her discovery. I had just come back from Aden and was in a state of trance at the lush greenery of the Island in June: pale blown wild roses in the hedges, cows deep in varnished buttercup meadows, slow streams winding through creamy mealy meadow-sweet and milfoil, stone cottages crammed in tight posy gardens. She drove, not talking, humming a little in snatches under her breath; I remember watching the curve of her cheek and hair and the competent hands at the wheel, slightly freckled and I had a faintly convalescent feeling. The world had such a beautiful new strangeness to it, tangible, almost edible, that my eyes flinched a little from it; I felt lazy, torpid, as if I were stretching myself continually, stretching and then relaxing. It was a relief to be out of the heat and on leave. There had been so many long hot afternoons on my bed, when I read or lay on my back, turning the pillow this way or that for a momentary illusion of coolness, hearing the shutters creak in the fiery wind and the gritty dust blow up in spirals on the barrack square outside; just at the moment when reality merged into sleep and Aldengrove and the sea wind were near, my batman would always appear, bringing sweet tea slopped into the saucer, balancing it precariously, delicately as though it could not possibly have spilt, as he shut the door with his ridiculous bottom. (Bailey, his name was. He was with me till he was killed at Dunkirk: no doubt that bottom was too good a target however sand-flat he lay, poor fellow.)

I asked Christina about the house we were going to see. She had discovered it by chance a few months earlier and

64

had been busy since making friends with the caretakers. "I could hardly wait till you came home to show it to you," she said, and I let this remark play happily over the warm surface of my enjoyment. We plunged into a maze of narrow lanes under the downs, where the greenery brushed the sides of the car. There was then a lodge where Christina had a successful colloquy and came back flourishing a large iron key. The house rose before me like something remembered from a dream, a great Palladian curve with pillars, niches, pilastered windows; its silver grey stone was mottled and pockmarked with age and neglect; window panes, splintered or empty gave it a *louche* aspect; the sun glittered blindingly on the remaining glass and the blistered paint. This one had obviously not remembered. The paving-stones beneath the once-splendid portico were mossy and tufted with flourishing weeds.

Empty houses have their own feelings of disaster and despair at all times; bare boards, empty hearths, the scars of pictures and furniture on faded walls, the hollow sound of footsteps on carpetless stairs, the echoing resonance of voices all contribute to this effect. It is difficult to remember comfort and warmth in an empty room. Certainly as we walked round, the shafts of sunlight served only to illuminate the dancing dust; there appeared to be no warmth to alleviate the chill of years. There was, I remember, still a trace of French blue in the oval drawing-room, a few toppled shelves in the library; the vast fireplaces were full of twigs and brushwood dropped by chimney-nesting birds. Upstairs great florescences of fungi grew out of the walls in pale and monstrous growths and birds flew in and out of rooms in distressed spasmodic bursts of flight. The nurseries were haunted by the ghost of a murdered heir, Christina told me, and the room in this wing, with the whipping-post still *in situ*, used by the monks, who had once temporarily occupied the house when ousted from France, as a penance room, had a concentration of violence in it which I can still conjure up.

I seem to have been involved with Christina in three, perhaps four, empty houses and wonder what significance there is in this, beyond her known tendency to romanticism. This was the first of the series. I was so happy that day that the sombre corrupt decay of a beautiful house was only a spice to my mood. We forgot to be a conventional subaltern and a girl in a cotton dress. She cast me as a refugee from the '45 waiting for a boat to France, a smuggler's boat in the cave below the house.

"And you're a good Scots lass married to an English lord, I suppose, hiding me, your brother, no, not I hope your brother."

She curtsied grandly to me in the hall. We made ridiculous conversation all the way round the house, except in that penance room.

"I brought the dogs last time I came and they wouldn't come in this room. They charged out, bellies down and howling."

"If we stay here a minute longer, I shall imitate them."

"Oh, David, I thought you were a nice, tough, simple soldier. That's why I brought you."

"No, it isn't. You wanted to see if I felt the same as you do, hating it, fascinated by it, romantic as always. I haven't changed, nor have you."

Christina, I love you, I said to myself, walking down the stairs again, where the banisters crumbled at a touch and the creaking of each step was like a gibbet in the wind (her simile). It was a strange place to have made the discovery but there was always something precluding reality where ever one was with Christina, so I only said this to myself. I babbled about redcoats and gratitude and fair winds to France; she babbled about Charles Edward and blood-dabbled heather and carnage at Culloden.

When the great front door was locked and we were out in the warmth of the afternoon, the house resumed its beauty. In the long grass of the forecourt lay broken stones toppled from their niches by weather or chance or the unfortunate soldiers billeted in the house in the Great War. There was a fountain filled with debris amidst the grass too; the pretty cherubic faces of its central group of statuary had blurred with time and moss to syphilitic leers. I undid the moss from one marble face while I ate sardine sandwiches and wondered whether I should ask Christina to marry me and whether she expected me to kiss her. I imagined that if I touched her cheek, as she sat now contemplatively in the sun by the tea-basket, it would have the feel of a peach or a nectarine. But I went on stripping the statue instead till its eyeballs stared, whitely cataracted, at the sky, under fashionable green lids.

"Will you marry me, Christina, when I'm able to, Army permitting, that is?"

She lit a cigarette and blew smoke rings with self-possession while I floundered amongst my thoughts.

"A chivalrous proposal with that diffident proviso. No, David, I want more passion than that."

"It's not passion you want, Christina, it's a past with some ancestral home as a shrine for it, preferably in Scotland. Aldengrove would never do for you or life in a cantonment."

67

"That sounds more like it. Bugles blowing and the funny noise camels make when they trot."

"Like hell they do."

"And the captain's wife borrowing the finger bowls because the colonel's lady is coming to dinner and sand blowing through the bead curtains and voices muffled by mosquito nets."

"There you go again. It wouldn't be like that in Catterick at all."

"I wouldn't be in Catterick."

"May I kiss you?"

"How could you ask me? What do you expect me to say? What do other girls say when you ask them?"

"I haven't. I mean, I don't . . ." my voice trailed away. My collection of kisses was not very extensive, but it included the dry and pecking and the wet and cloying, taken because the situation or alcohol demanded, rarely planned, rarely enjoyed. I had thought the request sophisticated. Did the men Christina went round with kiss and fondle her, did she expect them to stop their cars in lonely lanes? I saw her legs mixed up with the gears, half-comically, half-tantalis-ingly. Now it was too difficult to kiss her naturally and I was not sure that I wanted to. I could see Christina as my wife but I could not see us lying in the grass amongst the statues, like couples in London parks, anonymous in love. She handed me some gingerbread and refilled my cup; she had an unfussy, cool way of doing feminine things like that which made me watch her with pleasure.

I had discovered at Sandhurst that there were three kinds of women: (*a*) tarts – professional, (*b*) shopgirls, etc., sometimes of interesting amateur status (though their acceptance of gifts would have brought them into trouble with the M.C.C.) but mostly drawing rigid limits about behaviour and imposing them by giggles, threats and skilled naiveté, (c) officers' daughters, which covered most types not in the first two categories. Their mothers had to be reckoned with and a tribal background of taboos. The rebels from these were noted and asterisked in every station. Out of England, the middle amateur range tended to be harder to explore, particularly in the Middle East, but could yield fascinating byeways.

Christina did not seem to fit into (c), nor, of course, into (b) or (a). She was not a rebel because she would never have regarded any rule as applying to her. I watched her out of the corner of my eye, as I drank her tea, sucking milky grass stalks and gazing entranced at the house: a hollow, haunted, crumbling monument to imperturbable taste and the inroads of natural disaster. I wondered what backcloth it was supplying to what play for her? Some amateur dramatic company put on *Berkeley Square* somewhere I was stationed. I sat next to the adjutant who muttered, "Can't get the hang of this at all. What's it all about, eh?" at intervals while I was fascinated by the frustrations of time. But if *Berkeley Square* were the play for Christina, I saw only an Ian Hay comedy for myself. Only in Russian literature are subalterns of serious interest. When I said something to this effect to Christina, she only said,

"Good, I like men to be literate."

I pushed her over in the grass and struggled with her. She was as strong as I expected and when holding her down eventually, I kissed her but it was only a mouthful of hair I had, as she turned her face abruptly away.

"It's time we were going. There are people to dinner and I promised to help."

69

"I hoped you'd have dinner with me."

"Not tonight. Ask me again. Can you lend me a comb?"

We drove home the quick, dull way along the coast, already silting up with holiday crowds, through the desert tracts of boarding-houses and private hotels, past cinema hoardings and little newsagents and tobacconists with the more lurid of their Sunday posters still outside leaned against by small children eating ice-cream.

"What would it be like to be Sandra or Marlene or Mabel waiting for the change of programme? And would you be one of them?"

She pointed to a group of young men lounging at a corner, kicking a ball, slapping each other's backs, ringing bicycle bells, cycling a few yards, then slithering back to the group, idleness, lassitude and dejection apparent from every droop of their bodies.

"But my men were just like that. They can snap out of it easily."

"They're not like that in Scotland."

"Not even in Glasgow?"

"I've never been there."

"Snob."

"You like your men, don't you, David? You've become a proper soldier boy."

"I suppose I have. In a way I envy the men. I envy them all sorts of things like whistling after girls and kippers for tea and cosy Mums. But a lot of mine come from the North, oddly enough, and I don't envy them the depression. You should hear some of the stories they tell me. It's an insult to human dignity not to be able to work."

"Like the great evictions?"

"What were they?"

"Oh, David! I'll tell you sometime, when we've a lot of time on our hands."

Time on hand seemed to me then eternal in the summer light and when we came back to our village, to the green complete with goalposts, cricket stumps, three donkeys, two white horses and a miscellany of geese, it seemed that we should spend our lives coming back to it together. It would be wrong, at that age, to think one could be other than immortal and invulnerable. I am sure Antonia and Mark feel like that, particularly Antonia as she is in love and happy. Mark is merely hopeful but I am sure he wanted to go to Sandhurst more than I did. It seems ironic that my adopted son should have this keen family sense.

"Of course I want to do what you and your father and grandfather did. Yes, I know the South Dorsets are no more, but it's the same thing really."

Only it isn't, but one cannot disillusion one so bent. It was our regiment and my mother and my grandmother – and for that matter various great great aunts—had sacrificed themselves to it as well, whether they died of cholera or the Mutiny in India or boredom in Aldershot. Women are curious creatures. My old adjutant used to say when I first joined the regiment that it was a whiff of grapeshot rather than of orange blossom which brought the fillies up to the gate at a gallop. I never cared for the bloodier-minded ladies, those who wanted to hang the Kaiser in my infancy or strangle Germans or shoot pacifists or thrash criminals. There is something nauseating in the spectacle of women clamouring for violence; one sees them with little whips indulging in the odder perversions. When I read of a women's conference passing resolutions about flogging and hanging, I want to spew out of my mouth the taste of these ungentle, unnatural creatures. Army wives, committed to separation, exile and a succession of unlovely homes, are rarely bloodthirsty; they are too concerned with the aftermath of violence to want to pursue it personally. I remember my grandmother, a veritable mother and daughter of the Regiment, as a sloe-eyed, pure-browed old lady with a way of her own and an insistence on kindness and human dignity which even impressed me at five.

I am digressing in my thoughts, in themselves a digression. I was thinking of my family, now extinct in reality, except for Mark so determined to be a Kingsley and of my regiment, now extinct too. And of Christina and our son, neither of whom have I ever possessed in reality. *Je pense donc je suis*, said Descartes, but really one wants more proof than that. In reality, that is the key phrase. One needs more than a circuit of shadows to endorse one's existence; some people's lives are stamped like a frequently presented passport, they need only look back at events and people they were involved with to steady themselves. I feel I have lost that passport. I am stateless and a citizen of no world.

If I could explain this to Laura she would understand, for she fills up her diary with engagements to chart time. I have seen her look backwards at a blank week horrified and then pencil in something that she did each day, to make it more real, otherwise there was a week when she was not there. But Laura cannot bear explanations and blames my over-precise mind. She would not expect me, anyway, to discuss the problems of self-identification with her. So I take refuge in the plays I have no time to write, except when I am at Achranish and there, there is everything in the hollow of my hand, the words I want to use, the ideas I want them to express, cupped there, hard and sure, in all that solitude and beauty. All the rest is shadows and dilution now. And even at Achranish Aeneas has gone, grumbling, rasping, reminiscent, admonitory to the end. No doubt Christina was there to fold his hands and close his eyes. I am soothed with the contemplation of her tenderness.

That evening, so long ago, when we drove back into the village and I felt eternity before us, I was quite certain that I would both marry Christina and command the regiment, daring ambitions, arrogant perhaps, though I did not mean them to be so: I have done neither.

"Where did it first go wrong?" Rattigan made Alexander ask as his chain of conquest begins to rust and break. 'Where did it first go wrong?' we all ask ourselves when the taste has altered in our mouths. Why did I never marry Christina? There is no simple answer to that question, but it lies in our natures and circumstances. That day with her then was important for me but I doubt if she remembers it; she will remember the house and her feelings about it, oh yes, but not who she went with. It was important for me because I had seen the flash of love, like a kingfisher's wings disappearing into the reeds on Brading marshes, only a flash, but enough.

I did not meet Laura until nearly five years after that day: five good years of soldiering here and there, two spells abroad, one long, one short, a time in Dorset at the depôt, a most blessed time and then the posting to Chester. The whole time I was in Dorset Christina was abroad, doing some job in Italy. When I was home on leave, she was invariably either in Scotland or Ireland. We met sometimes in London, rather falsely, in the Savoy or the Berkeley. She

73

looked wonderful always, but was distrait. There were various people in love with her but she made light of them all, while drinking my gin, anyway. For a girl so immersed in the past and an esoteric section at that, she had become very perturbed about the present. She looked over her shoulder at the luxury-look of our meeting places and was critical of fellow-drinkers and diners.

"What do they care about hunger-marchers or Hitler?" she would ask in a fierce whisper and then consume smoked salmon with gloomy concentration.

She quarrelled with my mother, only temporarily, but it scarred the family friendship. What about? I suppose her views on politics, domestic and international. No one could really have thought my mother stuffy and opinionated but Christina was determined to find die-hards everywhere and insult them accordingly. Aeneas healed the quarrel, inevitably. Perhaps he quoted, "She's ower a lassie yet." Certainly he would have blamed her outbursts on her unmarried state, which at twenty-five or twenty-six he regarded as unnatural. I don't think Christina ever did anything more committing than subscribe in a temporary financial flush to the Left Book Club and to buy the *New Statesman* on railway book stalls. I associated her rebellion with her romantic championship of the underdog; she saw martyrs everywhere. Despair knows no nationality, she said to me once when I teased her.

Aeneas was always keen for me to go to Scotland in pursuit of her, but she never asked me and I was reluctant to chase her. Our mothers, despite the quarrel, were still keen for us to marry: no doubt both regarded it as a therapeutic process for her and a solution for me, who was regarded as being standoffish, shy, about girls. Aeneas was always warning me that I was the most 'eeligible baachelor' for miles, so mind now.

"Why should I mind? Christina won't have me."

"All in good time. She'll fall like fruit into your lap."

He was still hopefully pursuing that metaphor when I brought Laura home for him to be cross about. For once I had seen Christina at Christmas: I had some leave, but was going ski-ing with an Army party a day or two afterwards. We spent Christmas in and out of each other's houses as usual. Mr. Field had some new Civil Defence Commissar's job (which seemed unreal then, Lord bless us), Mrs. Field and my mother talked W.V.S. and Red Cross, Christina had joined the A.T.S. as a Territorial. She seemed content with everyone for once. Her hair, normally long and sweeping, had had to be cut for her Army uniform, which saddened me. On Boxing Day we went for a walk along the beach and the sea wall; it was one of those mild unreal Christmasses, with oppressive cloud about, giving one no appetite for turkey and cards. Even the sea curled gently on the sand and as we walked there was a tepid touch of distant sun. All the time we walked I was conscious that this would be my last chance to be alone with Christina for some time. The news from Europe was not good; it increased my sense of unease and impermanence. In varying ways I had asked her to marry me for years, had told her I loved her, perhaps rather as one would say one loved Oxford marmalade or the spring. (Noel Coward inspired both my understatements and the flat throwaway voice in which they were uttered.) I could not match her ever in mood now; I felt a dull plodding boy beside her. Presently we sat on a clump of rocks, smoking, watching the gulls swoop about in the sky.

"Will you marry me, Christina?" I said. "We could

75

now, you know. You'd be on the strength and I'm going to be in Chester for nearly a year. We could find a flat or a cottage somewhere outside. Couldn't you! It would be such fun.''

"Fun, David, fun?'' She turned her face to me and her eyes were tearstained. I don't think I had ever seen Christina cry before.

I suppose I lent her my handkerchief and said, "Darling, don't,'' and "I love you'' and a few such things and even perhaps kissed her, but she drew away from me, dried her eyes fiercely and asked me for another cigarette. "It's no good, it's too late now, David.''

"But why? I mean, we couldn't before.''

"Oh, damn that for a reason. I don't want to talk about it anyway.''

"Are you in love with someone else?''

"I've told you, the subject is closed, taboo, out.'' I was disappointed but not heart-broken. I remember walking back past the empty beach-huts, feeling something of the desolation of their boarded-up windows, but deliberately. The ski-ing was enjoyable; I drank more in the bar afterwards than I used to, and in Chester began looking about me at dances.

Perhaps I have always done what is easiest; nothing could have been easier than falling in love with Laura, pretty, pert, loving Laura. She was so anxious to be loved that it was impossible to resist the compliment. They were the happiest years of my life, up to Dunkirk, I suppose. Aeneas was inconsolable, but my mother coped with him. She stroked my feathers down very competently too:

"That's the worst of boy and girl friendship and managing mammas. If you'd met for the first time I expect you would have fallen in love and married, hey presto. But you've both become stale and self-conscious. And Laura's a sweetie. Aren't you lucky? Aren't I lucky? Christina, well, Christina has such a passion for being in the right, I doubt if she'll ever marry.''

III

LAURA

IN THE taxi David sat forward as if his life depended on catching the train. There was every kind of hold-up. In a narrow street, through which the driver was taking a short-cut, a man was collecting crates of empty bottles from a café, while nothing could move either way. He was cheerful, despite the rain, and wasted time trying to relight half a cigarette. Laura sat back, enjoying the scene, the turning leaves of the plane trees, the chalk scribbles on the blackboards of cafés and *épiceries* blurred with the wet, old women marketing, their black woollen stockings wrinkled and baggy round their ankles, and finally the unintelligible imprecations of their taxi-driver. David had shut his eyes with exasperation by this time; she knew that controlled expression by heart.

There would be other trains and other days, but David could never relax, be flexible. If she were ever in London with him, it always seemed their fate to be in some bus ahead of its schedule, sidling and crawling down Park Lane, recklessly disregarding beaconing green lights, lurching to a contented halt at the first glimmer of amber. David would begin to stiffen beside her, he would not speak but seize the seat in front until his knuckles whitened. "You're so neurotic, you bore me," she would say to him in an American accent, but not aloud, on these occasions.

Their path was eventually clear in the street and at speed they went on towards the Gare d'Austerlitz.

"I always forget how beautiful Paris is; the pale stucco frontages, the shutters, the trees."

"Yes," David said darting a lizard glance sideways for a moment, then back to his contemplation of the road ahead.

"There's a blue house now, it would look absurd in London. It's beautiful here. Do you see it, David?"

He nodded without looking. The rain, which had relented a little, danced down now with redoubled force and was splashed up against the sides of the taxi as they were hurled through pools by their driver who drove with hunched shoulders and stiffened neck.

"I remember rain like this in Nîmes," Laura said.

"We've never been to Nîmes; you're mixing it up with somewhere else."

She had never made such a slip before; unhappiness made one careless. It was a week slid from David's precise timetable when they were in Cyprus and she came home for two speech days, to bring the children back with her. She had got off the boat at Marseilles as planned, but instead of going straight home, she had met John in Arles and they had had one week after the long drought of a year apart. It had rained in Nîmes; steady, tropical rain, unremitting. She had been sliding round the shops, buying food for a picnic lunch, amused because, sheltering under awnings, other marooned bedraggled housewives greeted her as one of themselves. When the shower slackened a little, she envied their going home with yards of bread, bulging bags of *haricots verts*, artichokes and sliding sardines. *She* was only going back to John's car, stifling with shut windows because of the rain and the smell of oil paint and canvas, with the *pâté* and the peaches and the rolls. They had seen the Maison Carrée (infinitely beautiful in contemplation or recollection) and the Arena *before* it rained, and they went to the gardens and the Temple of Diana in the steamy, tropical aftermath of the storm. It was an extraordinarily green place, she remembered (or was that accentuated by the pistachio ice-cream they had bought from a kiosk at the gates?) with green runnels of water everywhere and the rain still splashing off the leaves. There was a Siamese cat on the steps of the temple who had come purring towards them; on her neck was a collar with her name, 'Nellie'. They had laughed at the Proustian snobbery of the name and her appropriateness in that setting. John had sat down on the steps too and talked to Nellie in his best French.

"*Que tu es mignonne, mignonne et chic, comme toutes les dévouées de Diane. Dévouées ou dévotes, Laura?*"

They had laughed at each other, with the leaves sprinkling her with icy drops and the seat of his trousers now wet and moss stained too. Nellie had walked between them, as proud as a priestess. John had wanted to give her a cat after that, so that she could be called Nellie too, but she disliked private jokes. Cats always took to David, anyway.

Perhaps rain in France was always different; intenser, more like rain and less like weather, just as food was more like food in France and less like nourishment or calories.

"We are more ourselves, in France," she had said to John.

"Do you think so, darling? Perhaps only like our image of ourselves, you know, bold at the Folies-Bergère, clever at little tables in the boulevards."

*　*　*　*　*

"It surely can't be far now. We've come miles. I wish I had looked at a map properly. There's only ten minutes before the train goes."

"If the taxi goes any faster I shall be sick."

"Nonsense, Laura. You haven't been in it long enough."

"Are we really travelling second class?"

"Yes. After that wedding we are. Anyway I would rather have more to spend on food and drink. It's only for a few hours and the people are more interesting."

John would never have let her travel other than first class. David had always been oblivious to his comfort or hers.

"Nîmes," said David reflectively. "You must mean Nantes; we spent a night there once when the children were very small but I am sure it didn't rain."

"You always had an atrocious memory, David."

"True. We're there at last, thank goodness."

The porter who collected their bags looked hysterical when they announced their intention of catching a train to Rocamadour. He looked at the clock, closed his eyes and went purple in the face when David groped for money.

"Oh, come on. Never mind *what* you give him. We haven't got our tickets."

"*You* get them."

At the booking office, the clerk seemed worried when she said Rocamadour, had a colloquy with someone invisible in which the word 'Brive' came and finally gave her the tickets with some injunction she did not stay to understand. The porter was behind her breathing heavily, and David by now, who seized her arm. They were bundled unceremoniously into the tall train, the porter pushing from behind, a passenger pulling from inside, and, as a door shut and David flung out some money, the train started. The man who had helped them get in found seats in his compartment, helped put their luggage up and smiled as he finally sat down, hands on knees.

"You nearly missed the train," he said, nodding warningly at them. One of the army of clerks, Laura decided, neat, shabby, well-fed. She smiled at him but could not speak; her heart thumped when she hurried and there was a piercing dryness in her throat. She turned to David and muttered,

"I hate running for trains. It isn't worth it and nearly kills me now."

"Well, what did I tell you? We should have started at least half an hour ago."

"I shall have a heart attack one day, hurrying."

"There's nothing wrong with your heart."

The Frenchman tapped David's knee and chuckled sympathetically.

"*Les femmes, hein, les femmes!* Always they have no sense of time and then they pant — like, like foxes in the chase."

Laura looked at his wife. She had that thin, oppressed, melancholy look one associates with women who are permanently ill and sorry for themselves. She said something to her husband and he shut the window with an apologetic look at David and herself.

"My wife feels the cold. I know you English like the fresh air."

"Do you know England at all?"

"Oh, yes, I have been in Wolverhampton," he said with enthusiasm.

Once David would have caught her eye; now he appeared

engrossed in the Paris suburbs. Laura sighed; it would be
her lot to have a long chat with the Frenchman whose wife
had their newspaper. David's profile expressed his tolerant
patience with a wife who could never leave well alone. He
was so able to escape into his fort of silence.

> *'Of what now I suffer*
> *She was not the prime cause, but I myself,*
> *Who vanquisht with a peal of words (O weakness)*
> *Gave up my fort of silence to a Woman.'*

Her grandfather, addicted to the rolling periods of
Milton, had taught her that; it was part of her upbringing.
He did not go all the way with Milton's views on women,
but he had quoted enough at her to make her cross. Milton
had a permanently Welsh accent for her, not the music-hall
kind but the rich, full-vowelled, resonant accent of a word-
loving people. Educated Welshmen do not say 'ooman' but
their pronunciation of 'woman' has a slightly twisted,
mocking lilt to it nevertheless.

Women can never have the freedom of that fort of
silence; they are always forced into politeness, persuasion,
agreement, anecdote, just as she was now forced to discuss
the delights of Wolverhampton where she once spent ten
minutes on the platform failing to buy a *Times*. Via Wolverhampton they discussed the economic position of France
today and thence to de Gaulle and Algeria.

"*Oui ou non*," the Frenchman said, slapping his knees.
"Life is never so simple, is it, Madame? It is an artificial
choice, *oui ou non*?"

"That's because you Frenchmen always want to say '*oui*'
or '*non*' with a shrug."

It took her some time to explain shrug; she felt David's

84

cool glance upon her as she imitated a Frenchman's shrug. The clerk laughed delightedly.

"Madame is a wit, *évidemment*," and he rolled his eyes and raised his eyebrows in enjoyment.

Laura liked being a success. But one has to say '*oui*' or '*non*' sometimes; the question may be complicated enough but there are often only two answers.

David came home with the news about his impending promotion with a look of the small boy concealing something splendid. Laura had not seen him look so young for a long time. She had become used to the jog-trot of his career and perhaps for the last three or four years had been so bent on the day when the children were old enough to leave that she had deliberately not contemplated David's future. He had been a captain when she married him, a major rapidly after that and had finished up as a lieutenant-colonel (acting). Back to major and then the slow climb again. As a captain's wife she had relished the distant prospect of his promotion; as it came, one was already prepared for it, well-rehearsed in the part. One spent years understudying senior wives and noting, with rapture, their occasional slips. There were wives who had headaches at important dinner parties, those who produced tepid tinned soup and tough chicken, those who forgot the G.O.C.'s name, others who name-dropped, produced hired maids and overdid the smoked salmon. Laura had seen them all; saluted the kind and patient who looked after another wife's children when necessary, had lonely wives to meals when their husbands were on courses, helped each other to move in and out of houses, commended them, thought no praise too high for them. Once, twenty years ago, she would have relished the thought of being a general's wife, now it was merely what there was for her if she stayed with David; one could call it neither a price nor a reward since to her now, it was valueless. But not to David. She had been paying for things for David for eighteen or nineteen years. This last prize demanded the highest price.

When he had told her of the new appointment, she had felt sick and cold and asked for a rapid drink to celebrate.

"It's a plume, a terrific plume," he said being generous with whisky which she hated. When he went out again half an hour later to the Mess (she suspected to spread the news), she rang up Dora who had shared military vicissitudes for years and was now also in Aldershot.

"Do you remember Jerry Drake?" she asked after polite preliminaries.

"You mean the man there was such a fuss over at the Services College? Yes, what about him?"

"Remind me why there was a fuss."

"Oh, heavens, darling, where were you? His wife left him and brought a suit for cruelty — such things. He had to go, of course. They're terribly choosy at the Services. You can get away with incest and mayhem some places, but not there. Why the interest in poor Jerry? I never believed half what his wife said. She could have enjoyed it all anyway if she'd just put her mind to it."

"Yes, Dora. Well, I wasn't really interested in Jerry Drake. It was the job. You see, David's got it."

Squeals of pleased incredulity and congratulation followed, in the flow of which Laura hoped Dora did not pause to analyse the peculiar angle her inquiry about the Services College had taken. It was not Dora's word alone she had taken; it is possible to acquire a great deal of information about the ambience of a posting if one puts one's mind to it. Laura had set about her task coldly and scrupulously, never, she hoped, allowing any of her informants to guess why she wanted such full information. After a day of dropping in around Aldershot and Camberley and another day in London, she was well primed.

She was driving back from London, a thing she rarely did, but her informants had been very scattered. It was a summer afternoon, agreeably warm; after the light industrial belt came the ribbons of houses, the hum of aircraft as she swept past the perimeter of London Airport, then the richer houses, the glimpses of portly red brick and black and white gable end through shrubberies, an occasional drape of climbing roses. The trees by the roadside were dusty, the bus-stops littered with ice-cream cartons, boys in prep school caps carried cricket bats. Everywhere was the smell of petrol fumes and diesel oil and warm dust. She had smoked too much all day and her mouth felt sour and parched which made the thought of the cigarette she wanted to light distasteful. And she had not seen John. She had telephoned twice and he was out, so she would now not see him till their usual Thursday. That was perhaps as well, for she wanted time to think, time to choose. Laura's referendum — *oui ou non*.

A stale summer evening breeds dissatisfaction, albeit of a different kind, as do the stirring, stretched cold lengthening twilights of spring; there was nowhere to stop and brood about this, only choked lay-bys and lanes off the main road to other even more desirable residences. Soon she would be through the gin and tonic belt and through the champagne cocktail belt and heading for Camberley. The trouble was that she had not had to choose before. Echoes of the day's conversations went on in her head as maddening as someone's transistor radio in a park.

"My dear, what a time you'll have. It's a good thing David has such a good wife; she has one ceaseless round of entertaining. They never appoint a bachelor for that reason."

"What an empire for you, Laura, all those foreign wives to look after. They must have picked David because you are so good with people. And he's wonderful, of course, so fair always and so honest."

"Of course, this is a *most* interesting appointment. Looks as if David might make the Top now. Jolly well deserves it too. If any one has given his life to the Army, he has."

"Jolly good show for you both. Of course it's as much your job as his, I hope you realise, my girl."

"What a mercy you and David seem set for keeps. There was that awful business with Jerry Drake. You *must* remember, sweetie. They're so stuffy in the Army now, sending directives round to second-lieutenants, so goodness knows what balloon goes up over a general. Even if he divorces *her*? My dear, that would be ungentlemanly as well as unofficer-like."

"He'll be missed, of course; the men like him. He seems cool but he's scrupulous and an old-type soldier, if you know what I mean."

The last stronghold, Laura thought, as she glanced at the great entrance gates to Sandhurst and wondered if she could catch a glimpse of Mark amongst that uniformed throng of blue blazers and grey flannels. And, ironically, it was a stronghold she approved of . . .

"*Oui ou non*," said the Frenchman again. "It remains to be seen."

They were through the suburbs now, in the rich, flat fields. It had stopped raining, but the sky was still dull.

88

David had stopped looking out of his window and was reading a Penguin. Laura forced herself to go on talking and tried to bring in Madame, who spoke no English; they exchanged some enthusiastic notes on the price of food. No persistent melancholy could restrain the flash in the French-woman's eye about food or its cost. Just as she was wondering for how long she must sustain this conversation, an attendant came by to announce lunch. David's thrift extended to second-class travel but not to food. He closed his book, marking his place pedantically and signalled her to follow him.

The Frenchman and his wife said goodbye ceremoniously; they would have reached their destination before luncheon was over. It was a long way to the restaurant car, through swaying corridors, past the inevitable grinning soldiers of any train. They were more appreciative of her as she lurched into their arms than their English brothers and this was consoling.

As they sat down eventually to have crumbs whisked away, a menu and wine list brought with rolls and butter and napkins, Laura could feel the first promptings of pleasure. She was in France after all and about to have lunch; some despised material hope stirred faintly.

"Our shoes are too good to travel second class, you know, David."

"Nonsense, these are old ones. Like my suit."

"Yes, but better quality than the most expensive abroad. It's a giveaway, makes me feel uncomfortable. We can't eat at workmen's cafés as we once did."

"*Ici on peut apporter son manger.*"

David was discussing what they would eat and drink; his French was up to matters of that sort. His hair had gone grey before she had time to register the transition stages; it was unsoldierly hair, stiff, moppish, poetic, which went well with his leonine face. Why leonine? A dominating face with a nose which age exaggerated. Some soldiers are dwarfed in mufti; their spell lies in the uniform and its associations. They acquire a pallor, a neutrality of personality in ordinary clothes; as civilians they become diminished. David could never be diminished, but he had a slightly fancy-dress look in tweeds or dark worsted. He looked tired and thoughtful: Aeneas's funeral.

"We should be drinking whisky for him, not this wine. Do you remember our giving Aeneas some claret when he came to stay after Jeannie died? 'Puir thin stuff that just goes wheespering doon'."

"You're a good mimic."

"It's the Welsh in me."

"You ought to go back to Llanyllty sometime."

"I'll take my grandchildren back for something to talk about."

"We'll probably end up there, buy Plas Newydd back. I could fish after all."

She took a backbone exquisitely out of a sardine while she concentrated on her reply.

"I don't think it would be the answer for either of us."

"Do you remember those black woods I courted you in? Woods without shadows or grass — extraordinary."

"Forestry commission," she said drily.

"I expected wolves or witches."

"I used to hurry the children past that summer we were there."

"I've never really understood why that went sour on you.

After all, it was *your* home. You'd lived there for years. We could have let the house until we wanted it."

"I *never* wanted it. It was different when it was grandfather's and when you were there with me."

David was in Egypt; she had had to come home. At first it was a relief not to be there. They had kept the house on for a while after her grandfather died, for just such an occasion. The nanny they had had in Egypt was French and wanted to stay there; Laura had depended on old servants rallying. It rained with all the hopelessness of Welsh rain and the skylights, of which there were many, leaked ceaselessly and noisily into the receptacles she rushed to place under them. Wherever she went in the house for days there was that endless drip, drip, implacably in her ears; below the house, under David's black woods, rushed a trout stream; now a raging torrent its roar, through the windows, was like that of a waterfall. The house smelt of damp and insidiously of neglect. Of these old servants, only Nans Evans remained and she seemed half-blind, but came back daily to oblige and provided a niece to wash the children's clothes and take them for walks; a niece, like a mouse, but a sulky one. It was June, so she felt exonerated from giving the children lessons till mid-September, apart from a little reading and writing and practical nature study. She made them listen to schools broadcasts and the thumps of 'Music and Movement' punctuated the dropping water and the sound of Nans Evans' noisy sweeping. She knocked brooms and brushes against furniture and doors which she did not see. The house stood alone, high up above the village and a bend of the hills made that invisible. Sometimes at night, regarding the dark valley, Laura thought it would have been different if she had been able to see a cluster of lights; as it was, there were a few foresters' cottages she could pick out and a farm and that was all.

A few people called and asked her and the children to tea. They were disappointed not to find David with her. "When your husband comes back you must both come over to dinner," they said, rubbing salt in her loneliness. The village people were kind, but so many old friends of her childhood were dead; their children and grandchildren had more casual ways. She found herself protracting her shopping so as to have someone to talk to and regarding her weekly expedition to the market town as an excitement. When the children went to bed, for a short time she was happy. She played her old piano in the drawing-room, knowing that the children liked to hear it. But as the sun moved round to gild finally the china figures on the mantelpiece, she knew that irrevocably another night was beginning. It was time to put on the lights and she stopped playing the piano. It was a dark house, embosomed by trees with two monkey puzzles to intrigue the children dominating the front lawn. But the trees brought an earlier darkness to the house and as it grew stiller and the sun's warmth faded from the old wood floor and doors and stairs, the creaking and tapping started, as the wood settled into another temperature. Bird songs diminished until the remaining songs had a hopeless, isolated clarity. The sheep, who surrounded the house, were then more audible; the crying of lambs, that most pleasing spring sound, could provoke the most despairing loneliness heard in an isolated house in the twilight. Laura would put on the wireless which engendered a certain false cosiness; so did supper on a tray and a Harrod's library book and the letters she intended to write. She lived in terror of the wireless batteries giving out or the electricity failing; it was generated by a sawmill up the valley and had an amateur flickering quality at best.

The fact that it was her childhood's home could not exorcise the chill that the house cast; she would sit remembering the pleasure of coming home for the holidays; the sheets of honey-sweet double daffodils edging the drive and on the steep banks to the house, Grandfather driving, his white moustache always slightly tea-stained, the house appearing through the trees, Grandmother on the doorstep, small and round and smelling of peppermints and in the background, the housemaid and the cook, promising food and comfort and ready ears. The kitchen had been a kind place then, with bustle and rattle and warmth; the postman coming in for a cup of tea and a newly-baked bun, their letters getting a little floury on the table unless Nans remembered to take them through as she was supposed to do, Dai Pentreath bringing some trout wrapped in ferns, chucking her under the chin, Bob the policeman, ludicrously de-helmeted passing the time of day, with his bicycle sprawled in the hedge outside and his legs sprawled over the kitchen flagstones. Myfanwy presided, behind some mixing bowl or chopping board or saucepan; unlike the cooks of legend, she was bony and dark-skinned with flashing eyes and gold gypsy earrings. She talked well and cooked well and cherished her row of plants in the window like children. Nans was plump and panting, prone to revivalist meetings and campaigns, for which she had a mortal and embarrassing weakness.

"How many times can you be saved, for heaven's sake, woman?" Grandfather would bellow. "Nine times like a cat. There must be a limit."

93

Nans would blush and twist her fingers and start to sweat; she left an odd smell behind on these occasions, faintly reminiscent of steak and kidney pudding.

But now the kitchen was a bleak place; the calor gas cooker replacing sensibly the range, the vast saucepans unused, the kitchen table scrubbed by Nans Evans and covered providently with clean newspaper. She liked to shroud everything decently in clean newspaper. Laura and the children used to play a lovely noisy whisking away game when she went off in the afternoon.

It was on a sheet of newspaper on the table that Laura had seen a reproduction of a picture of John's. She had never heard of him before. It was in some exhibition and had been accorded a photograph on the back page of *The Times*. Laura had a habit of never seeing newspaper photographs or headlines, having a prying eye for the sub-paragraph, the obscurer mention. This one caught her attention beyond the children's importunings; she was packing a picnic tea. Antonia came to look too, dark, serious-eyed. "I painted a picture like that yesterday."

"All I can say is," this was Mark suffering at that time from this portentous introduction to everything he said, "that I'm glad we never met horses like that."

The horses were nearer to Blake or Géricault than to Munnings. They were, indeed, the only horses John ever had painted, but it took Laura time to learn this about him.

John Ledcombe, the name meant nothing to her, but she even then thought, as one does, that inevitably in the next few days it would crop up. She cut out the photograph and stuffed it in her handbag and looked at it while they were having their picnic by some bleached, blown down trees and a sheep dipping pool with miraculous sunshine to soften her bleakness. She kept looking at her watch all the time with the distressing trick she was noticing in herself. It never seemed to get any later. The photograph of the horses, now crumpled, jostled David's last letter in her handbag. He was not a very accomplished letter-writer; in the early days, his laconic phrases had been endearing. He wrote that the decision about families might be rescinded in a few months, he might be able to get some leave in six months or so. What about the children's education? Did governesses exist now or in any case, what about a spell at the village school or was it entirely Welsh-speaking? And so on. Love was confined to the final salaam and had a perfunctory ring. Sometimes he said he missed her and went on to complain about the Mess. Once he said, 'this is a hell of a life', but she was not sure that it was to their personal situation that he was alluding. In this letter he had written something vague about a Captain Charlesworth and wife caravanning in Wales, possibly calling and being accommodated in the paddock. She remembered him with difficulty but would have been glad to welcome anyone.

They came a few days later, bursting with youth and love and the simple life. Laura could not now remember what they looked like: her past seemed stuffed sometimes with pleasant anonymous faces, as indistinguishable as sheep's. But the Charlesworths had remained as names if not faces because they brought John in their train: he was a cousin of hers. His name cropped up because, dutifully giving them supper, the conversation turned on painting. It emerged that John had been lent a cottage for the summer about twenty miles away.

"Do tell him to call if he's ever this way," she had said, thinking that he might have a wife she could talk to. They had talked of other things immediately and when a week or so later, a man had introduced himself on her doorstep as John Ledcombe, she had been astonished. She could always see him as that first time, because he looked so unlikely: stocky, fair-haired, short-legged, a hard, bony face.

"Why did you ever come?" she had asked him at intervals for the past twelve years as she asked him, "Why do you love me?"

"I was bored and painting badly and it rained and the roof leaked—."

"So did mine."

"And I wanted to talk to someone not out of a play or a novel."

"And I wasn't?"

"No."

She could dissolve that sort of conversation with a kiss, with an embrace, but not now, as it came back to her, eating veal on a train with David beside her and a prize-fighter opposite who had arrived during the last course, torn ears, misshapen nose, bruised jaws and all; he was unshaven and gorilla-like. Not now, never again. She could not taste what she was eating at all and could hardly swallow it.

"Why can they give one such superb lunches, even on trains, in France? Think of that last train lunch we had."

"Don't let's be tedious about comparisons, Laura."

The prize-fighter shovelled food in valiantly; Laura could not finish her veal; she pushed it under her knife and fork and cursed the waiter for taking an interest in her appetite. But David did not notice.

"You in your small corner and I in mine."

The prize-fighter's face was so large; so much acreage of

bristling purple jowl and veined cheek, a nose like a pulpy heap of flesh pushed up by an erratic hand, a mouth pink, rubbery and wet, eyes dim, cautious, watchful, out of which a man looked for every trick and racket; they moved a great deal but without animation. John, whose portraits of London life — dark, glowing Underground ladies, bursting exuberantly from their uniforms, barrow boys, hawk-eyed, cynical, cold, under their caps and their breezy slogans, commissionaires all braid and whiskers and rosy-blown, office cleaners in hats and overalls, keen-eyed and nosed, sharp-elbowed, had brought him as much fame as his horses and radiant French landscapes, might have enjoyed painting him. But John liked painting faces and places which were true to themselves; the bruised mask which hung over the table at her, outsized and maltreated as it was, would have appalled him. She had never sat for him; he had drawn her frequently, admiring her body, translating it lovingly in a few lines, but he had never painted her. He had wanted to; she had been afraid as if her portrait would become a hostage. Now she regretted it. One day a week leaves little mark on a place or a life. It would be as if she had never been.

Her coffee was bitter and hot; she refused a brandy, it would be easy these days to drink too much, to reach with a sigh that state of comfort and blur induced now by three large gins. John's arms, after a week, or month, or year of absence, had given her comfort and safety: "Home," she would say, closing her eyes. "Home again." She had never needed to trim her words with John; he had an accepting innocence which stripped away inhibition about cliché or sentiment. With David one needed to be smart and wary: he had a way of setting his mouth if one said anything fulsome and his nose seemed to grow thinner and bonier at what he considered false. He had turned a young man's irony into an older man's fastidiousness.

She and John had not fallen in love that wet Welsh summer. It had taken some time to do that, though she scrutinised afterwards every meeting, every thought, every winged desire of those years to see where the loving began. There was no thunderclap that first July. He was patient and serious with the children, drawing for them, painting great daubs for the nursery.

"Draw me a horse like the one on the kitchen table," Mark demanded and she had to explain. She still had that horse, bundled away in a sheaf of papers and drawings. They went over to his cottage more often than he came to Plas Newydd; Laura was afraid of gossip and minded the more because it was an innocent, fruitful friendship. She taught him the names of flowers; he was curiously un-particularised, botanically; 'that pink stuff', he would point vaguely at the hedgerow campion or foxgloves. Antonia had a passion for foxgloves; she would lay a sheaf of them in her arms reverently and process down a lane like a bride or someone in a cortege; they had some liturgical significance for her as finally she would lay them ceremoniously on a druidical-looking boulder with which that countryside abounded. 'That cream stuff. I want to paint that bank by the stream'; 'Meadowsweet. Can't you smell it?'

For her, afterwards, its scent was as evocative as the honeysuckle, buttery or clear pink and white, which flourished in those hedges. Then the scent stung her like a pain, its sweetness holding in it a loneliness, a purposeless-ness. She and John talked about the war; he had been in the R.A.F., a rear-gunner.

"And David, what about his war?"

"Dunkirk, then a long spell in England which he hated, then the Middle East and Italy. But he came back to train troops again before the Second Front and was in the Normandy landings."

"It must have been terrible to have been married then."

"I had the children."

"Where did you live?"

"Whenever I could, near David. But quite often I stayed with his mother, but then that became a Defence Area and rather dangerous, with Portsmouth and Southampton and all that. I had a cottage in Hampshire because we knew some people there."

"You didn't come here?"

"For holidays, yes. My mother was killed in the blitz on Liverpool in 1941; Grandfather became rather odd in the war; he could never understand rationing and had terrible arguments about petrol. People were very good and used to humour him, but it wasn't easy. Everyone sheltered him. He wouldn't believe my mother had been killed by a bomb because to him the blitz was beyond imagining. Odd, because he always talked about my father, killed in the Great War. He understood about wire and No-man's-land and mud and duckboards and trenches; they were part of the imagery of my childhood. But this war he could face in the terms of the last and that didn't include bombs on my mother's hospital. She was a doctor."

"You didn't think of doing something like that?"

"I married straight from the schoolroom, that's what I'm supposed to say, isn't it? In a way, I did. I was never clever enough for a university, anyway."

"It wasn't your grandfather who stopped you?"

"No, he was quite *au fait* with the world before the war. Indeed, I think he was vaguely disappointed that I wasn't going to be brilliant at something. The Welsh, when they're not cloud-capped, like success."

John had laughed immoderately; he always thought she was witty when she thought she was merely being discursive. She basked a little in the laughter she produced as in the occasional sunny lulls in the weather, when they would pause on a hillside and feel warmth on their backs and see its shine on Antonia and Mark. They went for childish picnics; it was on one of them that he told her about his wife and daughter, on holiday in the States; this was not the holiday they never returned from. They were due back in September. Somehow she had presumed his bachelorhood; she should have guessed from his skill in building castles and breakwaters.

It was a picnic by the sea, stormy and noisy with waves and gulls. All the way home she had an uneasy feeling which she kept remembering and then dismissing, a faint pang of disappointment which was always there when her probing tongue found the spot. She dreamed about him that night, amorously, and consigned the cause to her solitary life. It was ten days before she saw him again.

Looking back, she wondered how the children had not talked more about John to David, but the six months which elapsed made him seem no more to them than some institution connected with their stay in Wales. David came home to the War Office. Plas Newydd was sold; the children did not see John again. This was largely accidental and yet, perhaps, some omen had caused her to be careful. She mentioned him to David, who was not especially interested. She thought of having John and his wife to dinner and then thought that might be protracting an agreeable temporary friendship too far. The men would be hearty and wary, the women rattled and social. John telephoned her occasionally; she went to an exhibition he had, but not on the day when his wife was there and they had lunch afterwards, unpremeditated. She went to his studio to see some of his Welsh paintings and he gave her sherry and there was a faint unease about them; silence, then both talking at once.

It was a period in her life when she felt suspended like a leaf floating in the still air. They lived in a flat in St. John's Wood and saw few people. It was an anonymous time when she was released from her army-wife duties and only called her wandering thoughts to order for some occasional official cocktail party or when the horses clattered in the early morning down Ordnance Hill, rivalling the dairymen for noise and she remembered that that was the Army and it was her life. The children went to school and she had time on her hands and read voraciously books delivered in little boxes by Harrods. When she read about a character who lay about endlessly reading novels or biography or travel, she was relieved she was not alone. John and she regretted those wasted London years. David was working really hard and wanted only her dinner in the evening and to play 'scrabble' with her and then to fall heavily asleep in his chair and later in bed. He muttered in his sleep, at this time, talking names; they sounded like German, Willi, Ernst, Christof, and puzzled her. They were probably on some War Office file. Sometimes she wondered if he said 'Christina', but she could never be sure. She teased him once; never again. Sometimes she understood why David was feared and respected; he could produce a flash of wrath like a drawn sword.

"If you've finished your coffee, we may as well go back to our compartment. We have to change at Limoges anyway."

"Do we? How boring."

"I hope no one's come in since we left."

They had, an assortment of people, some of whom smiled and greeted them. In the corner opposite Laura sat a girl, heavy with peasant or gypsy blood; her dark hair was roughly twisted about her head and shoulders like a coarse curtain. What was extraordinary about her was that she was weeping, silently, uncontrollably, with great splashing, puddling tears which fell unheeded. It was raining again and her face was mirrored in the wet, streaming windows. At intervals she would scrub at her eyes with great fists and go on with the book that lay open on her lap. It was *Vanity Fair* in French and she was half way through it. Laura nudged David; he noticed the book and the tears and looked uneasy as if he might be asked for sympathy or a handkerchief, and then closed his eyes and firmly fell asleep, or looked like it.

The other passengers were ignoring the girl, reading, knitting or gossiping. Laura looked at her again, she was that ageless, strapping sort of woman who could be anything from fifteen to thirty-five, shy and aggressive, like an animal. There were no sobs, no shudder of grief, only a procession of great tears racing down to form pools on her coat, the seat and the floor. As Laura looked she turned fiercely to her book again. Her clothes were quite good; she was not in black. Laura speculated about the nature of her sorrow. A parting? An exile? A disappointment? or Thackeray?

There is no telling about the grief of others. The death of

a dog, the disappearance of a cat can cause a flood of sorrow which might not be allowed to be shown were it a husband who had died. She looked the sort of girl to whom both noisy emotion and stalwart endurance come easily. Laura could only remember crying in a train when she went away to school; she wanted to go, had been excited for weeks, but in the moment of parting dissolved into floods of tears which lasted all the way to Shrewsbury. There is nothing so shaming as brand-new uniform and red eyes; the humiliation stayed with her for a long time, particularly as the tears were seemingly not out of sorrow but from purely nervous and conventional reaction. Wartime partings had been poker-faced or breezy. She had wept when David came back from Dunkirk and on VE day and VJ day, the latter spent in the Island with her mother-in-law, thanksgiving in the mission church, judging children's fancy dress in a carnival on the village green, standing up in the drawing-room when they played the Queen, because David's mother always did (almost as embarrassing as falling on one's knees in the drawing-room).

To remember the depth and excitement of loving someone is as difficult to recall exactly as pain is. She looked at David, younger in sleep, beside her; she had agonised over the same face, the same body, through the war and after, until by that becalmed London period she had so schooled herself out of the habit of wanting him, out of the expectation of matched pleasure and excitement, that there was nothing left but the habit of affection. She had not fallen out of love with him because of John; John had filled that abhorred vacuum.

She had waded in through the shallows to loving John; the waters had deepened almost imperceptibly around her.

They had been cautious with each other, alert, nervously taking each step solemnly forward and yet realising that each step committed and involved them more irrevocably. John's wife and daughter left him for a long holiday. David went on a course. They started to go to exhibitions together, to Kew, to Hampton Court, to City churches. It was wonderful to look at pictures and architecture with John: the position over flowers was reversed. By the time John's wife started her delaying action letters, they knew that they were now in love. Whatever young, dizzy, ecstasies Laura had once experienced over David, this was different.

"That's what they all say. It's different. It's become a joke. My wife doesn't understand, my husband, etc. This is the real thing. This is bigger than either of us. Oh, what the hell! We've heard it all. We're not innocently, gorgeously in love; we're committing adultery; what is precious and loving and private is merely divorce court evidence. I don't *feel* sordid, but there are sordid names for me — for us."

"Laura, darling, get a divorce. Marry me. We've both made mistakes; let's start again."

"And my children? Your Elizabeth?"

"I've lost her now. At least I could have you. Your children aren't even yours."

"My God, John, what a thing to say. It wouldn't make it easier to leave them. Don't you see, it's impossible. I *chose* to have them, I contracted to look after them — I can't just leave them now like abandoned outgrown pets. I'm more responsible than if they *were* mine, because they're not David's either. What could he do with a couple of children travelling round?"

"They'll be old enough for boarding school. Mark's going to prep school next term anyway."

"It's holidays and letters and the sense of one's family being at home."

"Even though home changes all the time?"

"It's no good, John. I've known this all the time. So long as the children need me, I'm staying with them."

"How long will that be?"

"Till Antonia marries or starts a career. Ten years. Can you wait ten years? No, I can't ask that."

"I love you so much now I can't believe in any future that doesn't include loving you."

"Is there any future anyway for any of us?"

She had asked herself that for the whole of their lives with her and incredibly now they were grown up; she had not dared look beyond their childhood and they had grown out of it.

After that conversation with John, she had gone back to the flat. Françoise, their *au pair* girl, was playing New-market with them, surrounded by toffee papers. They had had coffee for tea, their height of sophistication. Hearing her come in, they rushed to pull her into the game; she was soon sitting on her heels counting poker chips, listening to asides about their day at school. She could never quite believe that two quite separate women had borne them and they were not hers.

The weeping girl was at it again and David was still asleep. Weep for me, shed tears for me. Live? Our servants will do that for us. There are no tears bitter or bright enough to salve my sorrow.

That summer night she drove home to Aldershot from London she had wept, on the Farnborough road – soldiers, cinemas, canteens, glossy cars – she had turned the wind-screen wipers on because her vision was so blurred. How mad can you get? she had said, taking a handkerchief to her eyes. David was out; it was a Mess night and he would sleep in his dressing-room. The house would be blessedly empty, Antonia was away. She looked at it blearily as she drove in. It was red brick with curious port-holes and looked like a dropped off portion of Victorian barrack. They took round with them a selection of Aldengrove and Plas Newydd furniture which softened the standard Army look inside and most of the curtains were hers too. The drawing-room smelt of cigarette smoke. His glass stood on a table; she smelt it; whisky and soda. She poured herself out a generous glass and choked over it; hateful medicinal stuff.

The room had the stale silence of a summer evening indoors, a fly buzzed on the window panes. In six months she had seen herself with John in France, in a little stone house with walnut trees and a view of maquis-covered hills. They had chosen one often: she had seen life as simple and as perfect as lunch there in the sun, spread out on a checked tablecloth: a long loaf, a pat of white butter, a bowl of salad, a bottle of wine, round goats' cheeses wrapped in chestnut leaves or rosemary, sliced cold meat shaded from white to rose, a basket of greengages. And John would be sitting opposite her, legs stretched out, tired from his session at the easel, fingers still stained with paint, holding her hand as he almost always did at their meals together. For ten years he had held her hand like that and she had teased him. He had waited a long time.

Tears; let them fall for me. You are my hired weeper, my mourner.

Somewhere over the hills to the left as this train travelled, there was a little town where she met John once: a stolen weekend from a week officially in Paris, staying with a schoolfriend now in UNESCO. He had driven north to meet her: it had been a warm evening in September with the smell of the south in the dust, in the heat that remained in the stones when the sun had set. They sat in the small courtyard of a restaurant, dimly lit by lights in iron *torchères*, the leaves of the trees round them were yellow and unreal, an unseen wireless played Mozart, inevitably the Jupiter. It was a simple little place and they had eaten well and watched soldiers strolling in the square outside through the railings and dogs on their last walks and young girls giggling and hovering and then suddenly walking off with proud flounces. John held her hand and made it difficult for them both to eat. It had been a longish absence. That was four years ago: she had seen the end of their sentence that night. The world she knew faded away when she was with John: the real world was the fantasy they created for themselves, the private jokes and allusions and reminiscences, the tenderness and concern they had for each other, the rich reality of their closeness.

Now it was France again, but with David; all would be the same, the food, the radiance of landscape, the kindness and richness and style of the people, and yet how it would all be different for ever now.

She looked again at the girl opposite, who was now reading with fierce concentration. What would she make of Becky Sharp? If she were of good acquisitive peasant stock she would comprehend her entirely, perhaps. David was still asleep, but the carriage was rustling to life with the approach to Limoges. She woke him apologetically.

"I wasn't asleep, anyway. Limoges, is it? Damned

nuisance having to change, I thought the train went right through to Brive.''

''You mean we have to change again?''

''No, according to the timetable it goes through to Rocamadour too, with luck, but I may have misread it. Now for goodness sake don't leave anything behind.''

''I never have done.''

''You always look as if you were going to.''

''*That* look is the result of years of practice. Helplessness is a woman's capital asset, somewhat forgotten nowadays.''

''Do you think Antonia realises it?''

''Oh yes, she's much better than I am, as a result of my early training.''

David looked at her and laughed appreciatively. Perhaps it would not be so bad after all; she would survive this next fortnight and then the next, till gradually all was a habit again and when they moved to the Allied Services she would have no time to be other than the Commandant's wife. Antonia and Mark would not be far away and they both, astonishingly, enjoyed David's and her company. Mid-twentieth century parents are such modest, diffident, amateur creatures that such a discovery is as agreeable as it is surprising.

Limoges station was cold and rainswept.

''You ask about the Brive train or the Rocamadour train, or something, Laura.''

''For heaven's sake.''

''Your French sounds better than mine and they all gabble on stations. It's bad enough trying to hear train announcements in England.''

Laura attacked a passing official, who seemed dismayed and nonplussed by her question. She repeated it. He immediately button-holed a colleague and they had a rapid conversation which she could not understand. Then he turned round to her and with a shrug of his shoulders indicated a nearby train, labelled 'Brive' indeed.

"What did the fellow say?"

"That's the train over there. The rest I didn't follow. He seemed astounded that I wanted to go to Brive, let alone Rocamadour. Goodness knows why. I don't know whether the other colloquy was about trains or my hairstyle or the madness of the English. They both seemed unhappy about something."

"The weather, I should think. Let's get into the train."

IV

DAVID

IN MY mind's eye I can see the long trail of mourners behind the coffin. If one were up on the hills, one would see black figures moving down the fields and tracks down to the road to join the growing dark serpent of people there. It is a long way to the kirkyard and the wind will be coming off the water, salty and cold, and there will be golden leaves from the birch and beech trees drifting on to the coffin. James will be there (the Oxford term will not yet have begun) but not Christina, according to custom. And so Aeneas will join Jeannie. In his last years, Aeneas lost all traces of having been a gardener all his life and seemed like an old sailor, trim, tidy, self-sufficient; perhaps it was the seaman's jerseys he had taken to wearing over his diminishing frame, perhaps living again in the family home, old facial characteristics asserted themselves.

Jeannie never took kindly to returning to Achranish; like some other wandering Scots, a visit home every few years was one thing, residence there quite another. She liked the south; she liked buses at the door and the cheerful clack of trippers past her garden gate, shopping round the village green or further afield to Ryde. My mother's death hastened their retirement because we decided to sell Aldengrove and Aeneas would not stay with new people. During the war he and my mother became closer than ever. It was a curious, fractious relationship. My mother began to have

heart trouble about the middle of the war and had to drop
her Red Cross and W.V.S. commitments and stop working
in the garden to help Aeneas out as there was no one else
available. The cook and maids went early on and there was
only a morning woman from the village. Mother fretted
about the state of the house and garden and hated her
enforced sessions on the sofa. Nights were bad with con-
stant German planes and there was the feeling, I suppose for
the first real time, that this was indeed an island, easily
severed from the mainland. She and Aeneas used to discuss
the war, its strategy and repercussions endlessly, like two
retired generals in a club. They had maps to pore over,
three newspapers a day and listened to all the news bulletins.
The nine o'clock news at night they always heard together
over a cup of tea; Aeneas's ostensible reason for the visit
was seeing to the shutting of windows and doors, getting in
coal, seeing that the fire was all right and my mother safe
for the night. After the news they would discuss it all in
detail and if there had been a letter from me or from any
friend or relative in the services, that was read aloud. They
were very cosy, the two of them, and sustained each other
admirably. What Jeannie thought, I don't know; she was
what they call a 'douce' woman; gentle, patient and
enduring, she was also uncommonly stupid. Fortunately,
her stupidity was not malevolent or jealous, but the nicest
kind of sheep-like silliness. Aeneas suffered her, not in
silence by any means, and she never minded or even heeded
him, I don't think. But a woman's simplicity becomes less
bearable as her prettiness goes. I expect she knitted and
listened to the Forces' programme and thought what long
hours her husband worked. When I spent a day or two at
Aldengrove on leave, Aeneas would leave my mother and

me tactfully alone, but I was committed to long technical sessions with him in the garden on the conduct of the war. Then I went off to Italy. In a way, I would have liked Laura and the children to have lived at Aldengrove: fruit and vegetables and good air and lots of space, but the Island was not a very safe place. My mother was either extraordinarily busy or later, unwell, and perhaps, though both were tactful, it would never have been an ideal arrangement.

The years after the war were confused. Mother seemed no worse but no better and resented shortages and restrictions in a true-blue way which she had gladly taken with enthusiastic martyrdom during the war. Aeneas and she had head-wagging sessions now; she withdrew more and more from people, even from the Fields. I was tired and worried and nagged and constantly hard-up. My father's investments went the way of many others because of the war; there was enough money for my mother's lifetime and precious little but the house after that. I had always had an allowance which had to go: Laura minded about that, as she minded about Aeneas's pension later, which, of course, we had to pay him. In a way it was because of the pension that I came to have the cottage at Achranish near to Aeneas: he refused to take money for nothing, so he was my caretaker and my factotum, when the children and I were there, chopping wood, making fires, digging holes for rubbish, advising on fishing.

When Mother died, Aeneas dwindled: they had sharpened their tongues and their wits on each other, blaming plants which failed to do well or lapses of armies or governments on each other. He was, as it were, appalled at the silence which fell and talking to Jeannie was like eating bread and milk; he told me so once. The spice, the flavour and the salt had gone. No one could have mourned my mother more nor loved her better. Jeannie plodded through the *Daily Mail* at intervals all day: he missed my mother's skimming through *The Times*, her resumés of opinion, her tart comments. He had enjoyed the brisk air of the heights for a long time; now the air on the lower levels seemed flaccid and exhausted. My decision even to sell the house and the garden he had tended so long did not rouse him.

"Ay, Colonel David, I thought you'd not be wanting the house now."

"I'd keep it if it didn't eat money and I could live in it, but there's no hope of my doing that for years, Aeneas."

"My elder brother George has left me his cottage in Achranish. Jeannie and I will away there as soon as the house is gone."

"Find me a cottage too, there, will you?" He brightened at that.

"I will. I will. You're serious, Colonel David?"

"Yes, I think perhaps Scotland would do me very well."

"Christina could mebbe find you one."

"I'd rather be near the sea where you are."

"Did you ever pass Aberkindle when you were there in the war?"

"Yes, I did once. A great pile in the trees near Perth."

"Ay, I mind that. I saw a picture."

Neither of us thought then that there was any possibility of Christina having the Buchanan's house, owned now by a bachelor uncle. It came to her eventually not by inheritance, but by mutual agreement. One of her brothers went to Rhodesia and another to New Zealand, both affected possibly by the temporary atmosphere in which they had been brought up. They wanted Christina to have the house she had always adored. Aberkindle, her husband's house, was only a staging post on her road back to her forebears.

I went to Aberkindle once, the day it was being auctioned. Empty houses seem to have been a constantly recurring background for the events of our lives. Perhaps there is something symbolic in this. Christina would once have thought so. I have never been close enough to her for years to know. There was the house on the Island when summer and love were so immortal that they hardly mattered. And there was the house in London where I last saw her alone (not literally true, but metaphorically true) in a north-west suburb. Laura teases me because I never know whether it's Tuesday or Thursday, but women never grasp that memory is a sifter of the important and unimportant. Everything swims about happily in that overcrowded aquarium of a woman's mind; they have only to scoop out an elusive fish and they know the day of the week and what hat they wore five years ago on Friday. Back goes the fish to swim about till next required. There is something alarmingly simultaneous about women; not (*a*), (*b*) and (*c*) but '*cba*' all together jumbled at the same time. I can remember with the clarity of yesterday some things that have happened. That last night with Christina has remained, partly because I have gone over it in my mind so often and partly because it was the start of a chain of events.

The years to Dunkirk were the happiest of my life – two of them – phoney war included. We *were* happy, despite the war and separation and anxiety. Dunkirk was Dunkirk and I won't go into that; I think it was a greater blow to the professional soldier trained to consider such things than to the amateur, the bottom of whose world would have fallen out anyway the day he joined the Army. Amateurs and professionals, distinctions blurred by sand and patience and blood and fear and misery, struggled into those long survival lines in the sea. Bailey bought it at Dunkirk and that saddened me too and others too. The regiment was not in a happy state after Dunkirk. Laura had been living in Wales, doing some canteen work locally; she came to live near by where I was stationed, in the Midlands. All we could find to live in was a dreary, semi-detached house in a road of them. Accommodation was scarce, we were lucky, but I think living in a hotel which some of my officers did, would have been a better idea. I had to leave her alone a great deal obviously. She worked in one of the Services' canteens in the town for long hours and she brooded over our childlessness. She had expected a baby in the statutory time, straight off; there was a slight crisis every month which started as a joke, but by 1941 had assumed other dimensions. She started a round of doctors and clinics, growing more intense about it all the time. It seems incredible now, looking back, how young she was and how intolerant I was. Nervous, overworked, hounded by a particularly bloody C.O. who might have posed for the original Blimp. I was doing a staff job, away from the regiment. *We* did not have Blimps, we considered them ungentlemanly. He carried his stomach before him, like Falstaff, and there the resemblance ended except that his *bonhomie* was that artificial sort induced by drink and attendant conviviality.

He had tiny eyes which he pretended he narrowed shrewdly, a capacity of absorbing other men's ideas and the credit for them, a malignant view of humanity and a gigantic view of his own importance. When, as I have risen to his rank and beyond it, I have been tempted to shout or bang the table, I have remembered him to my own and my subordinates' advantage. The hierarchy of the Army was specially designed, according to some of its officers, for the express purpose of licensing rudeness from the top down. One clicked one's heels and said 'Yes, Sir' knowing one could go out and glory in the same sense of articulate or semi-articulate power now purpling the wattles of one's immediate senior officer. I have never subscribed to this state of affairs which reminds me only of school. Only the immature or perverted put up with things themselves solely in order that they may in turn inflict them on others.

So, what with this man spoiling every living day for me and Laura, weepy, dismal and discouraged at home and the war going from bad to worse everywhere, it was a dreary time. I failed to comfort Laura because I was tired and because a weeping woman irrationally makes me cross. I wanted children too, but there did not seem any terrible hurry. Once I told her she was only so het-up because she was sure I was going to be killed and that in view of the derisory pension she would have, it would be better for her not to have a child to bring up on it. She cried the more, but I think I was right. Women have these primitive instincts about the survival of the race; it took time for me to take much the same view.

Finally, Laura came back one night and told me quite briskly that it was hopeless. We could never have children. The doctor she had been most concerned with had suggested adoption. I was not very enthusiastic, but I was relieved that no one had suggested that I should go along to one of the clinics too. It would be so like going through the un-marked door to the V.D. Department of a hospital; every-one knows why it isn't marked. I could imagine sitting in a row of unproductive fathers, feeling like failed stallions. Perhaps it isn't like that. I was spared that anyway. Laura never even discussed the technical details of what was wrong with her. She was aggressively reticent about it. "We can't have children and that's that; it's no good going into the whys and wherefores, let's forget it — and decide what to do next."

Wartime seemed a hell of a time to me to adopt children, though I supposed it increases the number of unwanted ones. Laura nagged endlessly: she seemed to think she had some inalienable right to children.

"Have you ever thought that it might be ordained that you *shouldn't* have children and that you're flouting Providence?"

"It wasn't, and don't be so stuffy and pompous. It sounds unreal even if you are only teasing me. Oh, dear, David darling, I *am* being tedious, aren't I, and I do go on so."

We were staying at Aldengrove for the weekend, carrying on a relentless argument the minute my mother and Aeneas were out of earshot.

"You had a happy childhood here. I want our children to, too. Don't you *feel* anything about children?"

Ironically, I did not, except in an abstract way. I was sad for Laura, sad for the family, but so many horrors crowded upon us that spring of '42 that personal disappointments seemed almost things one promised oneself one would feel about later. Adopted children with someone else's lineaments of gratified desire and an unknown background stuffed with events, opinions and people one knows nothing of, slightly appalled me. I am not a very class-conscious man and what class they would come from would not concern me all that much, except that there are some faces so utterly plebian as to be difficult to see mirrored as one's family. I told my mother about it and discovered that Laura had too.

"She loves you very much, David. I'm not keen on some ready-made grandchildren myself, but I think she is in such a state that something will have to be done."

"After the war."

"No, now, she's feeling insecure and upset and frightened."

"So are millions of women."

"David, you're being heartless and it isn't like you."

I think perhaps that I was jealous of the love and care Laura wanted to bestow other than on me; I recognised the pang but that didn't help me to quell or to bear it. Aeneas, ever the one for tactless questioning would say:

"Well, now, Mistress Laura, it's time you settled down and were thinking about a family forbye. Time's going past and I want to see Major David's children here."

She made me tell him after that, stamping her foot about it.

"I won't be lectured and hectored by that dreadful old man. I don't care what you tell him, but he's never to mention the subject again to me."

Perhaps she found the compassionate looks he directed at her after that even harder to bear; to me he made only scriptural references. There had never been many children in my father's family anyway. I had not been brought up in the warming atmosphere of loving cousins and I could not honestly claim that I had a comfortable vision of teeming family life. Laura, an only child herself, since her father was killed about six months after her birth, had an envy of large happy families which I hadn't.

When all the complications of adoption were over I liked the two children. I had not realised that even when in bed asleep, what another dimension babies added to a family. They were not young babies when we had them; it seemed less hazardous so. Laura who had gone thin and sallow, bloomed again with their coming. When I was sent abroad again they would be a comfort for her, I thought. My mother was delighted with them and even Aeneas unbent. But it was Phase III of our married life and I could hear the click of change as we moved into it.

I was moved back to the regiment, part of it anyway, in a curious training depôt, dominated by its H.Q., Hexington Hall. All wartime camps and H.Q.s in retrospect now seemed confused with those so admirably described by Mr. Evelyn Waugh, and indeed, I cannot now adequately remember which was mine and which his.

It was a relief to be away from the staff job, my terrible C.O. and unexciting subordinates and back among friends even though their numbers were now swelled with new faces. There was an A.T.S. unit attached to us and after I had been there a few weeks, along some muddy path of the unkempt woods surrounding the Hall, I met Christina.

"*Major* Kingsley."

"*Junior Commander* Field."

We shook hands formally under the dripping trees, explaining our presence to each other. I had hardly seen her since Dunkirk, when we quarrelled violently about France; I suppose I was angry all through that summer, an anger of the nerves and the blood. Since the outbreak of war, when my regiment had gone dramatically to France, I had not heard a shot fired, except by my men poaching partridges during that waiting winter, until all hell's noises had been let loose in May and June in an endless head-splitting burst. I was haunted by that noise; almost I welcomed a few nights of blitz, it was less uncanny than the silence of waiting. In Hexington that autumn particularly, I found the leaden silence forbidding, and even when fractured by shouted orders, marching feet, the click of weapons and the distant thuds of the range, each sound sank back into the sleepy, sodden fields around us. For the first time in my life I found myself looking forward to the first drink of the evening. I had not yet been able to find anywhere for Laura to live. A house was to be vacant at Christmas, but by then I might be far away. Temporarily, she was with her grandfather.

Finding Christina was like finding a boon companion in a desert; the setting, her clothes, our work, gave me a crisper consciousness of her. I had never seen her except in the Island or in London; out of context and yet familiar, she was exciting as she never had been before. We talked endlessly that afternoon till solid rain and a resumption of duties drove us back. It was difficult to find things to do together at Hexington: Christina was tired of the sort of jokes our friendship would produce. We could have an occasional meal together in nearby pubs, go to the cinema, walk over an unrewarding countryside. Diversions were limited and occasional. Perhaps it was that that fanned my feelings for her. I liked watching her at a distance, picking her out from khaki anonymity. Sometimes I heard her voice as I passed between Nissen huts, clear, penetrating and unanswerable. Like the rest of the Mess I found it easy to be ribald or querulous about the A.T.S.; unlike the others, perhaps I minded that they were indeed competent. The gusts of femininity that blew out of their hut doors compounded of the Forces' Programme, talcum powder, underwear drying, schoolgirl giggles and snappy voices in authority, made me resentful of their existence. In fairness, I had to admit that I was equally resentful of the cosiness some soldiers contrived to make blossom in military austerity; socks drying, patches of ground sown with flowers and vegetables by hut doors, sessions of sweet tea and letters from home. I liked my worlds separate. But I could reconcile Christina to both. I never cared for meeting other people from school or home, sometimes some of them drifted across my path and I was brusque and reserved with them. I remembered them eating ice-cream on the fringes of garden parties; my mother called one of them 'darling' by mistake at some cricket match tea. His ears flamed still in my imagination: he had been my senior at prep school; he was only a captain when he appeared at Hexington and called me 'Sir' with pointed flat-footedness.

What brought Christina and me so close together was not really the shared past but a tacit recognition of alikeness and a timeless affection. That was in the quiet beginning. As the leaves dwindled from the trees we walked under and the days shortened, an affection for each other had spurted like a matchflame – Christina even declared that she could catch the whiff of sulphur. It was she who produced the simile as we stood nervously and intensely embraced in some scrabbled rhododendron bushes.

"And you think it will go out as quickly? What a gloombird you are, darling Christina."

"It's my Celtic incapacity to accept happiness. And how thankful one is sometimes for a matchflame in the dark."

"Talking of Celtic incapacity, we have a countryman of yours in the Mess now – Andrew Grant."

"If he's a Grant from Aberkindle, I know him. Why don't you like him?"

"I didn't mean incapacity to apply to him, idiot. He's all right and I expect he looks gorgeous in the kilt."

"Yes, I've seen him at some Games with Grandfather. They live about eighty miles or so away – quite near."

I quenched the laugh she expected and kissed her again. It was a little like Christina's simile; I felt strangely incandescent amidst the coarse, rank evergreen smell of the shrubbery on a damp, cold night. I remembered the huddled clasped couples I had avoided in my boyhood: they could never have felt anyway as I did then. Embraces in the shrubbery or in the tangled avenues and copses of the neglected park were exciting but limited. In the beginning I liked the novelty of subterfuge, the swift brush of our hands or hips, the glimpses I had of her. Another dimension had been added to ordinary life. But it was not enough; war makes one greedy, impatient. The fruit may fall before it can be gathered. The idea of a weekend together grew without being planned. George had helped with his continual offer of "bed-stroke-beds, old boy". Even schedules for leave had not had to be manipulated.

This had contributed to the naturalness of my feeling about Christina. I suppose I pondered a little about deceiving Laura, but she gave me every excuse that November, fussing about the children, refusing to leave them for a weekend in Hexington or London. It was as if my marriage to Laura had never taken place; loving Christina and being with her was something that had been with me all my life. I did not scrutinise very carefully her feelings for me; I hoped that she loved me and that I excited her even though she viewed it all as a match lit in a dark cupboard. Christina had always made me feel humble or uncertain. I had always been the follower in her games, but she had never wanted anyone else but me to play them.

George (perhaps it wasn't his name, but I've always thought of him as George) was not, of course, in the regiment. He had an expansive laugh and nature and I was uncomfortably grateful to him; it was easier to become a man of the world with George than with smoother, shrewder types: he had the jargon without the scrutiny of experience. One did not have to explain, only suggest in broad, very broad outline. George supplied the rest with nods, nudges and winks. He was not yet old enough to dig an elbow into one's ribs, but he would come to that. Naturally enough he was devotedly, faithfully married and had been known to produce photographs. His wife and children were safely away from London: the house was shut up.

"There are candles there, old boy; electricity shut off but not water in case of a fire. There's a ruddy great divan bed in the drawing-room: I always camp out there when I'm passing through London. There's a primus there too. Don't set the house on fire, ha ha."

The house was in some northern suburb. Christina and I planned to meet there since she was not free as soon as I was, and it seemed safer so. I bought violets from an old woman in Leicester Square; it was an embarrassing purchase for I found myself clutching wet bunches with nowhere to put them. Military regulations forbade the carrying of parcels when in uniform: no mention was made of flowers. I had too my gloves, stick and valise and no prospect of a taxi. Cinema queues shuffling by in the wintry light regarded me, seemingly as dispassionately as they regarded the passing soldiers of every nationality and the loitering girls. Some curious suspension of activity and interest came over every sort of queue. Nevertheless, I felt their incurious stares as I unzipped my valise, willy-nilly stuffing the violets on top of the paper bags from Fortnum's. My pleas for odd, unrationed foodstuffs there had met with dignified sympathy. It was difficult to do up the zip again; a helpful girl or two hovered, but when I stood pink-faced and upright again I declined their offers of present help and future comfort and made off towards the Underground. It would be better to arrive at this unknown house before total darkness fell, I thought. The journey, even, I remember; unknown stations on an unknown line; arriving in the anonymity of paper stalls, empty chocolate machines, shuttered tobacco kiosks labelled 'sorry'. It was almost dark, with the cold absoluteness of early December. In the blackout it was always difficult to remember the charm of earlier lamplit winter twilights with shopwindow radiance reflected on pavements. There were no taxis again; I had to ask my way several times and I was exhausted when I finally put my bag down in the dark hall. I found my torch and went round the house; it was larger than I had expected, Victorian and rambling; some of the furniture and pictures had obviously gone to safety. It took time to find kindling and coal and I used every paper bag and scrap of newspaper before any fire was established. The blaze that eventually warmed my hands was for Christina. I wanted to present her with a room lighted and leaping with flames and smelling of violets. I had heaped them in the first bowl I could find and their bruised scent struck occasionally across the smell of charred wood and paper. I lingered over the unpacking, trying to set the room to rights, stumbling over unfamiliar furniture in the shadows. Finally, supper was laid; there was even something to drink, triumphantly cajoled from the Mess, and the fire was burning brilliantly.

I hoped she would come at the peak of its beauty; it was certainly time. The silence of the house which I had not noticed before, began to overwhelm me; there was only occasionally a footfall on the pavements outside; each time I decided it was Christina, but the sounds died away. Sometimes in the distance, I could hear a bus changing gear or the rumble of a train; their sounds emphasised the quiet they interrupted. I sat, thinking of all the possible delays; trains, air-raids, every complication and mishap. I had never wanted anything so much as for Christina to come. One can never quite recall the fever of the blood as one waits for the loved one, I only know now that waiting there was before I made love to Christina and that all the past is after that.

How could it be important, anyway? I have no romantic ideas about love-making changing the world. To be honest, I remember that firelit room and waiting in a disquieted, disturbed, tremulous way for her, more than the feel of her in my arms.

I had not seen much of her for a fortnight or so before the weekend; we had a new intake and some new re-organisation; there was a conference and a V.I.P. or two and much the same for Christina's outfit, I thought, wrongly. Christina had that rare capacity for understanding absences, of body or mind; or was it indifference? Laura has always minded if I were preoccupied, forgetful or plain busy. She sees the Army and herself in close combat for my attention and has never understood that I see them as things apart.

Did I think of Laura at all as I waited, even in contrast

to Christina? I was to see her in the next day or so and perhaps absently I thought of her and Mark and Antonia, in the way that I thought of the familiar: Aldengrove and Aeneas for instance. I had news for them all: I was posted at last to the Middle East. Christina I intended to keep it from for the moment: she might see in this carefully arranged weekend a dramatic finale, whereas in my mind it was only the beginning. But the posting had closed my mind to considerations of having to do something positive about the future. All things personal had to wait.

The sirens sounded and increased my anxiety about Christina. She would either be killed or injured or pushed into a shelter by an officious warden and be kept there all night. The latter seemed most likely: some ironic tilt of Fortune was to be expected rather than a lethal shaft! I was waiting for the door bell, forgetting about the electricity and discounted the thumping as some outside noise.

"I thought I was wrong after all," she said when finally I let her in. "I've been blundering about in the dark and lots of crumps off stage. Darling, what a *place*." She shone a torch over the hall furniture and pictures and on the bare boards where the carpet had been taken up. I was proud of the drawing-room and led her in there quickly. She flung off her greatcoat and hat, sweeping a hand through hair which just contrived to pass the regulations about length.

"Give me a cigarette, David, for God's sake, and is there anything to drink?"

She kicked off her shoes by the fire and stood absurdly on tiptoe as she drank; I watched her face, rose-gold and bronze in candle and firelight.

"That's better. It was a fearful journey. The train crawled; there were two alerts, no heating and lighting like a brothel — or do you like your women illuminated? Do you feel very wicked, David?''

"Only serious, as if a hand had been laid upon me."

"A hand? Oh David."

"A sort of prophetic hand."

"You mean this night is fraught with Fate! Oh, David, don't be serious about it. That would spoil everything. We've always had the most gorgeous games: this is one of them. Very curious romantic setting too."

"We seem to go in for empty houses."

"That house has soldiers in it now; cold and haunted, poor bastards. I'm sorry. You don't like my rough language, too imitative, I'll try to be gentle and ladylike. That bang was distinctly nearer. What would our mothers say if we were killed here?"

I caught her hand and felt its slight tremor as I put it to my cheek.

"Darling Christina, I've been posted."

"When did you hear?"

"Last night. I suppose it's the Middle East. Does it make any difference? I wasn't going to tell you yet."

"And now you've shouted it out with fearful honesty? Would there be any more gin? David, I'm glad for you. You've been longing to get away."

"Will you mind?"

"I'll miss you. But it doesn't make any difference to this — and us."

"I can't — I can't think of a divorce now."

"You haven't mentioned one before."

"Not in so many words."

"Not in any words, my love. Scrub it, scrub it. God, I'm tired. I want comforting and I'm going home after this,

128

which is like a services canteen now organised on a very voluntary basis.''

I should have talked about divorce then and not been diverted by inward speculation about the Field's house. The moment never came again so naturally. We had supper and we went to bed and the next day we went out on a foray for food and that was all. It was that time of December when there is only a brief span of daylight, grey and foggy at that, between stretches of darkness. We talked and made love and the candles burned down in their sockets and time seemed to have stopped. But when I woke on the Monday morning to the murk of seven o'clock and the winter coldness of the room, with the sense of an empty, alien house pressing round me, I could hear the tick of the clock again. Christina was still asleep, I thought; I could barely see her face and I put out my hand gently to feel her cheek bone and the line of her brow and jaw. Her face was wet with tears. I had never known Christina cry, except once before. I even remembered Aeneas at that moment when he found me howling in a hothouse the day before going back to school. ''She doesn't shed a tear.'' I didn't comfort her. I lay in the darkness beside her, holding her hand affectionately as if we were on a seat in the park. Perhaps I was a little diffident about her tears.

She turned to me eventually.

''Ridiculous, darling, isn't it? A swashbuckler's tears.''

(We had always made jokes about her 'swashing' at Hexington.)

I put my arms round her.

''What is it, Christina?''

''Nothing. Nothing anyway that I can or intend to communicate. What about some coffee?

"Whose turn is it to get up to make it?"

I had opened a window and a curtain and had to shut them before putting on a light: it was still fairly dark, but as I looked out of the window I could see the tall rank grass and weeds of the garden, plumy and torpid in the first grey light. Perhaps it had once been a tennis court; old George probably wielded a pretty racket and a nice line in court banalities. It was cold and I shivered.

"You'd better hurry with the coffee before you get pneumonia. It might interfere with your posting."

Christina seemed to have recovered. I boiled some water, shook out the remaining dregs of tinned milk and made a pot of coffee. We had it in bed and drank out of each other's cup. Then we were brisk and dressed and washed in cupfuls of hot water and tidied the room. I raked out the ashes of the fire and added the violets to our small collection of rubbish to put in the dust bin. I wanted to take some away pressed in a book: I only had a Penguin thriller which seemed inappropriate and the whole idea very faintly comic. Perhaps in the last war men went off with violets in their Thucydides and Horace; there was an innocent nobility about those young soldiers.

It was time to go; Christina to Waterloo and I to Paddington. We parted in Piccadilly Underground; it was crowded and we did not linger.

To take one's leave in an anonymous crowd is curious: one moment it is not there at all, a swirl of blankness and the next all one can see are face upon face, meaningless, measureless. One is braced for the moment of solitude but unprepared for the rush of ordinary life into the vacuum, jostling, touching. Of my week's leave with Laura, nothing remains but a recollection of plans made and a heaviness of spirit and body. The machinery of war swallowed me again and I was thankful.

Post and papers went through times of irregularity in the desert: it was three or four weeks before the news of Christina's marriage to Andrew Grant reached me and then it was in a letter from my mother. Aeneas was delighted, she wrote: a cousin of his had been assistant keeper to an uncle of Captain Grant twenty years ago. The Fields had been stirred into surprised enthusiasm; none of them was at the wedding by a miscalculation of leaves and timetables, but photographs, gossip and tit-bits had floated through the village. A little of this silted debris appeared from time to time in all my letters from Aldengrove.

There are some states of being which detach one curiously from reality. Love or anger can sometimes well up to suffuse one in an oblivion of passion. Fear can draw one into some separate enclave, the processes of killing or being killed are only possible because one has crossed by then some dark barrier. The news of Christina's marriage was, therefore, only a fact, as I had registered deaths of friends beside me at Dunkirk as fact, but as fact valid only in the compass of the fictitious world in which I found myself. I had no time to brood and sleep was as important as food or drink to remain alive. *She* did not write and I didn't, though I had done so before the news of her marriage and regretted it. Christina had never been a girl for pen and paper. Aeneas wrote me a letter in his crabbed tight hand; news of my mother, of the garden and finally, "You will always have known that she would do this, David. Captain Grant is a very suitable man; you cannot allow otherwise."

She had married within a couple of weeks of our weekend together and I had known nothing of the relationship which

131

must have already existed. Like the sand and the flies, this thought was constantly with me. I had not seen much of her for the week or so before: I had made the wrong assumption about this.

The Italian landings, bloody, triumphant, unexpected were made. It was very different from the Italy presented to me decoratively on a silver platter by my mother years ago. Then, I suppose, I had had a boy's glimpse of beauty and violence, but it was mingled with smiles and *cassata* and boring paintings and cypresses like warning fingers. The southern landscape of the zones of heat and poverty was a better setting for war. In the winter which came it was easy to forget the heat but not the poverty. The weather, as always, provided an endless endurable subject for the men to grate their humour against. Even the advantages of education had not prepared me for snow and ice; it seemed a contravention of immutable laws, such as other people's aunts had made in going to Italy every year on the first of December. It was so cold that it was reckless to do up one's flies on going out: one's hands would always be too cold to manage them again.

But the weather for me was the ice which contained the horror. When I was very young I found a book of (was it?) Conan Doyle's in the library at home. I don't remember its name, only the blue binding with deep gilt lettering and the illustration. The story (some Polar adventure?) must have concerned, in a horrifying way, dead men preserved in their freshness and youth, in ice, for there were drawings of gigantic fishmonger's blocks neatly containing corpses. In the cold, under strain, I had fantasies about this ice: ridiculous, improbable fantasies unbefitting my rank and responsibilities.

Christina's son, mine, was born in late August. The news did not reach me till the autumn. The vital letter from my mother must have been lost, as several were: I only read headlines in what newspapers came my way. Laura was wrapped in the children and rationing, in her grandfather's illness and in concealing my mother's from me. Aeneas, for the latter reason, sent me cigarettes and shortbread baked by Jeannie (depriving themselves of their butter ration) but did not write.

It was, of course, clear now why Christina had married Andrew, although even to my sketchy male information, it would have seemed that she had made a rash, if accurate, assumption in a particularly short space of time. It explained why she had not written; she might have been afraid of what I would do.

As it was, I became foolhardy in my world of cold and insulated misery. I got an M.C. that winter. The discipline of years made me scrupulous for the lives of others, but I was past caring about my own, except in those sudden flushes of life which came to torment me with hope when I had glimpses of Christina and me and our son, gilded by firelight and safety. I had never cared as urgently as Laura apparently did for the necessity of children; in time, yes, but I had no passion for fatherhood, even when she told me that we couldn't have children. It was a statement of fact for me. But now, the thought of Christina having borne my child and in deceit and unhappiness, filled me with a burning tenderness for her and our son. She had called him James and was living in Scotland with Andrew's father. I have never found it easy to be devious: deceiving Laura was more of a sin of omission and loving Christina too deep a state to be anything but simple. Therefore, I found it difficult to imagine how she could bring our son up as Andrew's heir. That was the beginning of my hatred for Andrew.

I was recalled to England with my battalion in the spring: some battle-seasoned troops were to be added to those who had trained for the Second Front. I had some leave and there was an investiture at Buckingham Palace. My mother was not well enough to come by then. Laura looked pretty and radiant in the photographs, though she made fun of herself in her becoming but not *recherché* hat and diamond regimental brooch as the perfect Army wife. We have all become unsteady and self-conscious in our rôles in the last twenty years, however well we fill them. We spent that leave at Aldengrove and there was always some reason why I could not call on the Fields. Aeneas and I had long sessions together; he had no help now and there was so much he had to do for my mother in the house, that the garden was becoming neglected and he was glad to have me working with him, if only for a few days. I asked him, with difficulty, whether he had seen Christina and Andrew.

"She brought him here a year ago and then she was away to Scotland. They've a fine house, with a library and pictures, tho' the shooting's not much good these days. Old Major Grant has the arthritis. They'll be company for him, she and the child."

He darted a glance at me.

"Mistress Laura brings hers up well. It's not easy for a woman with her man away, as well I know from your mother, Colonel David. You'll be proud of them."

It was the kindest thing he had ever said about Laura and the children – the cunning old man chose his moment well.

My mother's routine was upset by our visit. No doubt she and Aeneas talked longingly about me in my absence, but the four of us interrupted all the household tranquillity. She made only the barest reference, at first, to Christina. Mrs. Field was apparently delighted, boringly so.

"We always hoped you two would make a go of it," she said to me, however, the afternoon before I left. "I'm sorry you didn't, but she was too much of a swashbuckler. Mary never did have an idea about bringing up children. Sometimes I've thought you had still a notion or two about her—"

I shrugged my shoulders and looked out at the daffodils in the orchard and the grass starred with pear and plum blossom. Laura was standing there with Mark and Antonia; it was a pause in some game, they were all breathless and laughing, and then I watched Laura's face grow distant and abstracted as she stared up, apparently at my mother's windows. She hated reunions and partings: was afraid of what was in store.

Oddly enough what was in store was my return to the Island for those assembling days in June when the vast invasion fleet moved along the coast and no one could stir in or out of the Defence area. It was odd to be along that familiar coast, once so thick with paddlers and bathers and now given over to khaki and weapons, bristling like a belt of rusty reeds swaying in the tide. There was that day's delay which meant that the stiffened sinews had painfully to uncurl. The weather was cool and unkind, the prospect of sea uninviting, but there were diffident sorties of local inhabitants pressing hot drinks and even sausages and pies upon us. We were strictly under orders not to move. I hoped that someone would get word to Aldengrove that I was about and contemplated creeping along the sea wall when it was dark. Christina and I had so often tried to reach the house, banished men, outlaws trying to establish contact with their families, find money or treasure, rescue prisoners. Looking at the house shrouded distantly in trees and weather, it was hard to separate those games of romance from the reality of tossing boats and bloody landing-prospects. We had made ourselves very frightened once, Christina and I, as we hid from Aeneas or Jeannie or the kitchenmaid hanging clothes out at the back of the garages. I could recognise from that apprenticeship to imaginary fears, the alternation of cold heaviness in the stomach with a lurching dizziness of the blood and bowels which now beset me.

Aeneas came down to talk to me, peering amongst the boats, bringing a flask of coffee and a cherished dram of whisky with him. I watched him finding his way to me in the twilight, like some searcher amongst the camp fires.

"Colonel David, can ye not come up to the house?"

I shook my head.

"Ye'll be waiting for the signal and the tide."

"How is Mother?"

"Well, the excitement hasna been good for her and she's fretting, though she'd not say so."

"Give her my love and tell her not to worry."

Aeneas nodded as if I had said something sage.

"I canna telephone young Mistress Kingsley: it wouldna be safe?"

"No, better not. Perhaps in a day or two just to tell her you saw me."

I wanted to send a message to Christina; I even fumbled in my pocket to tear a sheet off my notebook. But Aeneas was eyeing me with that shrewd beadiness which had always prevented my doing what I wanted. To please him I drank the coffee and pocketed the whisky for later.

"Do you know that I've never been to Scotland yet, Aeneas; I meant you to take me."

The sardonic lines deepened.

"I will, Colonel David, there's plenty of time."

"I suppose so."

It was Christina who was to take me to Scotland and we both knew it and no doubt, dramatically and gloomily we both thought that trips to Scotland were now too late anyway, with the water slapping on the boats in the bitter little night wind and in the darkness beyond that unseen French coast.

"I'll be saying goodbye, then, Colonel David, and away back to your mother. She likes me to shut the windows and make her some tea and have a wee crack about now."

"I know. You're very good, Aeneas. Look after her."

We shook hands and he looked for the first time an old man to me as he wound his way back along the beach. Some hours later we moved off thankfully: anything was better than shuffling in the shallows and making interminable jokes or reciting privately what had to be done when we reached the other side. It was almost impossible to distinguish Aldengrove from the mass of darkness as we slipped past: I suppose I thought that I might never see it again, but it was Christina and James who occupied the undercurrents of my mind as the first lightening of the sky made my heart beat louder. But I could not claim, as our boats moved in, that they occupied much of my attention. I had passed beyond the barriers of unreality once more.

It was some weeks later, I suppose (or in the horrible Algebra of the time, D Day+x) that I found Andrew in our Mess. I had heard that he had been posted to our Divisional H.Q. and in the mêlée, my battalion was looking after some of the rear divisional troops. War is full of coincidences beyond fiction. I accepted his presence as I would have done a bullet, with a sour, dulled resignation, in which, in my more self-dramatising moments I might have detected a gleam of heroism. I set myself out to be irritated by him and succeeded. He was a good-looking young man (too young for Christina) with a great deal of golden, carrotty hair which grew on his arms and the backs of his fingers. I used to watch his hands bristling in the sun (like gilt-wired caterpillars to crawl over her) and imagine his muscular hairy legs and his undoubtedly hairy chest. He had a way of whistling about the place, a tuneless, shrill sound, which particularly maddened me, and told funny stories, slowly, thickly accented and bluntly pointed. There was a snap in his eye and a whip to his tongue and temper which made him respected by the mixed bunch that we were at that time; it did not take people long to discern an asperity in my attitude and I regretted this. It is difficult to hate someone for no other reason than that he is married to the woman one loves; difficult because one sees them frequently as human and not diabolical. They disarm one, the people one hates, so often by a gesture, a look or revelation. And if one hates for the rôle and not the person it is difficult to sustain the emotion without a shame which exacerbates one's anger. I laid traps for Andrew and he annoyed me either by avoiding them or falling into them. I teased him about Scotland and watched the fair skin flush and the tongue bite back what he would have said. I betrayed Christina at every turn. It never occurred to me that he would have known about us; the bare facts of our shared childhood he knew and never presumed on, except that perhaps that would have accounted for a certain hurt surprise occasionally perceived in a twist of his mouth. He was essentially an innocent young man; how otherwise indeed could Christina have married him in the circumstances? His innocence, his naïveté, his hopefulness affronted me. In the battered terrain of war which surrounded us, his whistling, his jokes, his pride were a banner I could not bear to see flying.

He had a letter the day he was killed from Christina. Our H.Q. was in one of those farmhouses which took one back to our fathers' war; not very beautiful or interesting, but possessing in its grouping of trees and farm-buildings a certain curious charm. We messed in a long, low-raftered room, which was very cold in the mornings in a dour northern light. Andrew opened and read his letters with maddening slowness. He had several that morning and left the one from Christina to the last so that it lay on the table upside down before me. The large, sprawling, affected handwriting danced. I tried to read the postmark. I could count on one hand the letters she had ever written to me and I don't think that I had kept them. Did she tell him what James was looking like, noting the first smile, the first eager lift of the head? Andrew parried some breakfast wit, frowned at an injudicious bill and finally with old-maidenish care, slit Christina's envelope with a knife. For one so young, he had a curious collection of niggling habits like that. I watched him draw the letter out and read it with concentration at last.

"The little woman, eh?" It had to be George who said that.

"Ach away," Andrew said as he did, and smiled at something Christina had written. There was a signal for me from Brigade H.Q. at this point and I left.

Half an hour later I was with my driver on a quick dash to liaise with Ronny Fortescue, whose forward unit was reported to be in a disagreeable muddle, having suffered heavy casualties, particularly amongst his officers. Brigade H.Q. wanted me to see personally what could be done for him. Fortescue was a cool type, an imperturbable maiden-aunt type I always thought (he had a lean, bespectacled face with an anxious look), conscientious and hidebound, worried by infringement of rules rather than by danger. This was a period in the Normandy fighting where nothing was clear, except our undoubted invasion. There was a swirl of troops, pincer movements, beleaguered enemy and thrusting allies. In a way, Fortescue's queries should perhaps have been settled by wireless communication, but Brigade wanted a consultation and report.

We drove up in an armoured car, through orchards of summer dullness; sometimes there was a mile or two of devastation; sometimes from the small pastures cows with very French faces (amiable and slightly coquettish) looked up with surprise at anything passing them more noisy than one of those clop-clopping carts with the reins slack in the dozing driver's hand. I rather envied those troops who would land later and inherit possible desolation. There is something inhibiting about the confrontation occasionally with a smiling and passive countryside. The towns and the villages were a different story, where there had been house to house fighting. Even our farmhouse H.Q. bore traces of skirmishing and bullet holes. But here, amongst the orchards and farms on a side road, if one did not listen too hard for the sounds of war above the noisy engine of the car, one had the unnerving illusion of peace.

We had just passed one small farm, timbered brown and

white with a garden full of untidy roses and peonies flopping over the fence. I was looking hard at the road ahead in fact, seeing landscape and garden only out of the corner of my eye, when I saw in a coppice some distance down the road, a momentary blink of steel. There were thick coppices frequently along the roads in that part of Normandy, perfect for ambushes. Just at the moment that I saw the flash, there was a swoop of aircraft, low flying, ours, which almost seemed to disturb the white dust of the road. What they did, of course, was to obscure our approach. The Germans in their, as yet, imperfectly made ambush, flung themselves through the bushes to dive into the ditch. We were on them before they had time to be ready for us; I shot the three of them with my Sten. My driver had not had time hardly to stop the car to help me. He was an eager little Welshman from Cardiff, with an aroma of the dogs and the dancehalls about him, rather than Cwm Rhondda and sheep.

"Now what would three Germans be doing here, sir, miles from any others and waiting for us, so it seems?"

He just managed to refrain from calling me 'bach'.

"Don't stop the engine, Jones. We'd better get on. There may be some more up the road. They can't just have been strays."

All I could think of was that we had escaped being killed, that I must get a few miles on and then safely back, that I must make the right decisions with Ronny Fortescue. I had a brief interview with him, listening to his woes, which were many and related in a damp aunt-like way. We evolved some fresh plans between us and I promised to let him have an officer to replace a dead company commander. He suggested Andrew and I agreed to fix this with Division on my return. I knew that going back to his regiment would please Andrew and I would be rid of him.

"Same road, sir, or shall we try another one in case there are any more of those Germans? I was looking at a map, sir."

This phrase of Jones' was a bye-word amongst us; "I was looking at a map, sir," in his eager sing-song voice was a signal for automatic disbelief in whoever he was driving. Old George maintained that it was one of those pink, Empire-patched maps in his infants' school to which Jones was alluding; he could just about pick out different countries and the sea.

"No, we'll go back the same way. The chances are even that if it was an official ambush, that it won't have been checked or relieved yet."

I saw us otherwise lost in a dusty knot of twisting lanes with precious time lost and, apart from considering the resumption of an ambush, forgot the men I had shot as one forgets the wasp crushed on the breakfast table. Then suddenly we were on them again and I asked Jones to stop so that I could check their regiment, etc.

They were the first men I had ever shot: modern warfare is very impersonal unless one is a Commando or in the jungle: and they had been alive twenty minutes before. Now they had the ungainly look of a group of dishevelled statuary: I remembered the stone heads in the grass in Christina's empty mansion: here death, not moss and time had given their faces a greenish pallor which reflected the leaves and grass as no living flesh does. Their mouths and eyes were open, not like statues, with a sort of hysterical surprise. I noted their regiment and then looked at their identification discs and noted down their numbers. Jones had started by making a wisecrack or two:

"There's no good German like a dead German, that's what my Dad always said. You certainly didn't give them time to say their prayers, did you, sir? — *if* they ever say their prayers."

But as I began to turn out their pockets, his complexion began to resemble that of the Germans and I suggested he should remain in the car with the engine running. I was possessed by some fearful impulse of curiosity: I cleared out a letter or two which each had, leaving, in a calculating way, enough sentimental clutter for their relatives. It was very still and rather warm in the little copse; there had been sounds of firing but now in a lull I could only hear the purl of a stream near by, the steady chewing of some cows, the inevitable damned larks soaring in song. I set myself to remember their faces by their letters and numbers; Ernst, blue-eyed, long-lashed, unfortunate chinned, with a New Testament and some vulgar French postcards of the seaside/lavatory sort; Willi, older and creased, sallow face which showed anxiety about his family and perhaps about his cause, eyes dark without being brown, glazing over now, newspaper cuttings, letters, photographs, sugar lumps, toffees in his pockets, an avid collector and assessor squirelling through the dark winter of war. Christof, younger than anyone in uniform should be, or perhaps it was death that had effaced any experience of life from that schoolboy face, a growing, uneven, immature face not yet settled into expressions and shaving, letters, photographs, a Bible and some poetry given him by a girl: this was as unfair as the larks, if as accountable. There they were, my three victims, never to go home or make love or worry about bills. One never thinks of oneself as a murderer in war. That way lies insanity. Kill or be killed, if one must use the word; there are a number of modern euphemisms. I recalled the episode; in so far as they had time to have reactions their hands had been on the way up; only one had been about to shoot. That would have been Ernst – an automatic killer. I could have taken them prisoner; surprise would have given me the advantage of the two against three situation; Jones, anyway, hardly counted; his aggressiveness was verbal only. I *could* have. Jones revved up the engine a little more shrilly to remind me that we should be getting on. I had no desire to go on. I wanted to sit with my corpses in a numbed but receptive way and wait for my mounting sense of guilt to recede and leave me a soldier with responsibilities. But I closed their eyes, which seemed difficult, picked up my collection of mementoes and climbed out of the copse. My boots had crushed the campion and foxgloves I had trodden over in the ditch. Jones looked at me and the letters I clutched with surprise and distaste, but he said nothing.

It was when we were almost back that I remembered that I had wasted ten minutes, at a time when every second was vital to new operational plans and that I could get it back no more than Ernst, Willi and Christof could their lives. If I could have had that last hour again, I would have given almost any price, even then, and that was before Andrew was killed.

For I got on the 'blower' to Main Division and then sent an order to Andrew to report to Fortescue at once. He was killed at precisely the spot where I had killed the Germans. Willi's, Ernst's and Christof's reliefs had arrived; it was an important strategic point, as we learned later, and near a massing point for German troops about to attack Fortescue and break out of our encirclement. It was not for some time that I realised that Andrew was killed at precisely that point, but there was no doubt about it, just as there was no doubt that I had failed to warn him of possible ambushes along the road. I should have realised that the road was interesting the Germans anyway and reported this, which in the flurry of organising other reinforcements for Fortescue and the deployment of a company on to his left flank to reinforce the curve of our troops which would contain some of the alternately fighting and retreating Germans, I omitted to do.

The fact that I remembered about the three Germans and sent a message to Andrew three minutes after he left did not salve my conscience. I had been incompetent and careless, involved in larger considerations than Andrew's journey; possibly taking a longer view, my plans saved lives and expedited an advance. But it seemed to me that I was wholly responsible for Andrew's death. As a soldier one has to exercise some rational blindness about one's activities. In the end, however, one cannot escape guilt for mistakes. The burden may be removed by court-martial and official reprimand; in my case there was only myself to know about it all. Guilt is a curious thing; one cannot push it away into an inadequately shutting cupboard, one cannot be entirely diminished by it, recklessly giving it pride of place to placate it. It would have been better for me to have been blamed officially. Then my private guilt would have been dwarfed. As it was, my subsequent account of shooting the three Germans provoked only approval. "You couldn't possibly have brought them in. It would have caused untold delay and been very risky."

That sop didn't work, however accurate a comment it was. I had shot them without working out why; perhaps intuitive action is what training of any kind in any profession produces, but when the intuitive action is to kill, one is concerned.

I was not Andrew's C.O. so I was spared having to write officially to Christina. Friends sent off his possessions. I wrote, of course, but not truthfully; although Christina alone would have understood. If I had written "I was seized with curiosity and remorse about the first Germans I had killed and therefore wasted ten minutes which meant that Andrew was sent to his death", I think she would have comforted me. But was I sure that subconsciously I had not intended Andrew to be killed and involuntarily produced those circumstances which meant that he most likely would be? I had hated Andrew as her husband; what more natural? so I could not beg comfort or forgiveness from Christina.

The German letters I buried amongst my possessions; I knew a little German and read a line or two desultorily. If one is sensible, one knows when to stop. Some instinct of self-preservation coupled with a sense of duty and a surrender to one's professional skills kept me as a responsible, even quite good, officer till the war ended. I even collected a D.S.O.

By that time I had seen enough of the German's handiwork to make me pat in self-justification. We had to fight them and beat them; there never was any decent alternative to that; whatever any silly young man may say now. "What good did it do? The world isn't any better off." They never smelt the concentration camps or saw the slimy trail of blood across Europe. But knowing we were right doesn't wash one's own hands. One has to accept that as the price one pays. That is something that civilians and the backroom boys don't know; they paid in hard work and discomfort and privation, but they didn't have the kick in their guts as they killed someone or the long ache afterwards.

I have never wanted to go back to Normandy, preferring my phantasmagoria of recollection. I suppose the roads are just as straight where the armour once snaked under the poplars, that the roadsides are now peaceful margins where thrifty old women in black gather baskets of sorrel and dandelion leaves for themselves or herbage for their goats. I suppose the proud little towns, Coutances, Avranches, Argentan, Lisieux have rebuilt themselves and are still grouped round their indestructible churches and that their steep cobbled streets now only strike sparks from a passing horse's hoofs and bump the car tyres. We were welcomed by most with tears and joy and buried bottles of cognac; I made a few speeches from balconies (sweating at my accent and the fatuity of sincerity), was spat at by one or two peasants whose land and crops were ruined, experienced black terror at air strafing, poker-faced grief at 'Last Posts', pleasure at a quiet meal and the odd night's sleep, admiration and respect for bravery and endurance and kindness. There is nothing more touching than a soldier's kindness, those gestures both rough and tender towards his comrades and hungry children and frightened, confused old people.

There were leaves, of course; I spent New Year at Aldengrove with Laura and the children and my mother, visibly and indomitably frail. Laura was tactful about my moodiness and sickness. The Fields were all away in Scotland and overseas. Then I was not home again until after the end of the war, both in Europe and the Far East, in September. I let everyone else go on leave until my regiment came home.

My mother died the next winter in that iron weather

when there was hardly any fuel or electricity. The first months of 1947 were extraordinary. We were stationed at Aldershot with no quarters available (I had, of course, lost my half-colonelcy by then) and living in a cottage ten miles away with no electricity in the depths of the country. We had barely enough paraffin for cooking and lighting and enough wood for one fire in the enormous living-room. The children practically had frostbite, but they loved the eternal snow. Laura, revived by life together, endured everything relentlessly and we enjoyed ourselves.

The summer after my mother died we spent a lot of time at Aldengrove, knowing we would sell it. I saw James once, groping in a rock pool, four years old, plump-legged, intent. Christina had left him with her mother while she went abroad with a brother. Sometimes that year I thought, on bright mornings, that if Laura would divorce me I could marry her, but when I thought about it at night the impossibilities became distinct. There was no future in thinking about Christina, in terms of reality again. Unfortunately, I began thinking about James.

It must be a relief to be so far gone that one does not realise how obsessive one is. I have always been aware of my obsessions; keeping them from Laura has become about as much of an obsession. Laura would be gentle and comprehending, suggest doctors, holidays, hobbies, and withdraw even more than she has done over the past years. In a way, I suppose I have been fortunate. I have seen various marriages in the close quarters of Army life and all kinds of wives who have ruined their husbands. Laura has been perfect and I am grateful, although this means that now I have to repay her by being the General whose wife she always hoped to be. For years I have wanted to leave the

Army; after the war, when I was tempted to make Alden-grove pay: flats, market gardening, etc.; when the regiment was amalgamated and the old colours laid away (pointless to go on mechanically); when Antonia announced her engagement and Mark was safely into Sandhurst. We would have enough money for me to live at Achranish and for Laura to live somewhere else quietly. We could have made some civilised arrangement; neither of us has many friends; we could have had each other's company now and then and done what we wanted in life. I have wanted nothing but Achranish for years and Laura hankers for galleries and concerts and theatres and dress shows.

But Achranish perhaps is an obsession too, although to me it is the cure for all ills and frets. Perhaps I should not continue in the Army, disillusioned with it, hankering after the mystique or the status and the solidarity that have gone, disliking the occasional 'cave' survivors one meets, all tusks, pomposity and triviality; disliking equally the new young men whose leisure is entirely captured either by wives or television. The Box and the Mess are antipathetic. The men rush off in buses for weekends; for them the Army has become a job like any other. One cannot blame them in this new society, only regret. What? That we bought them body and soul only when unemployment gave them the queues and chips without fish. This college I am to administer, to guide the senior officers of the Commonwealth and put them in touch with NATO, to keep them out of the hot fingers of the Communists, I can believe in it in the abstract. I shall do my best with it, but inevitably one will be fighting continual small nagging time-absorbing battles with the Treasury, the War Office, the Foreign Office, etc. It has become impossible to do anything simply and well.

But I shall be a major-general and Laura will be in the star rôle at last. (Was it Orwell who once said that the mark of the middle classes was uselessly learning what to do in a variety of improbable circumstances, like the Queen suddenly coming to lunch?) Mark will like it; he could not be identified more closely with me or with Laura. She has been unfailingly good, except in never coming to share Achranish.

Perhaps she has always had some sixth sense about Christina and James.

It's odd to think now how close I have come to James, now continually in and out of the cottage when I am there and with Aeneas when I'm not. Aeneas no more. For years I haunted the place he was at prep. school (it was only forty miles from London and various War Office duties took me past frequently). Christina sent him away to school very young and in the South, which was out of character, but it was Andrew's old school. I think he was happier there than he would have been at mine, although boys everywhere have mercifully changed. It is difficult to lurk in the vicinity of a prep. school nowadays; not only are one's motives suspected, but by everybody now from the postman to the old spinster knitting in her cottage window. However, I used to see him sometimes, returning from a walk before tea or playing football manfully on the fortunately visible playing fields. It became a detective game and I was very good at it. The thing was to have something to do in the immediate neighbourhood, which was a small village. Shopkeepers and the tea shop perhaps thought me a parent. Christina used to send Aeneas photographs of James at Christmas. He had sent one to me with a few dry lines, so that I found it easy to recognise him. He was a dark-haired little boy with a serious face; at least I hardly ever saw him smile. I suppose that skulking round school shrubberies or the departure platform at Waterloo was unseemly but it gave me great pleasure and excitement. There was a man at the War Office Legal Branch who had a boy at the same school; finding this out was a kind act of Providence; I used to produce curious posers for him regularly towards the end of term and bring the conversation round heartily to the holidays. Mark by this time was at his prep. school too, so it was fairly easy. First the day and then the train, which I could discover from the railway people. Planning well ahead I would contrive to be on the platform or by the barrier, but this was a chancy business because Christina or a Field or some known friend might be meeting him. But usually I was safe and absorbed either in reading *The Times* or looking for some non-existent traveller and able to survey him as he passed intent on the holidays and the problems of being met, growing larger and more confident, carrying a case and some fearful unpackable object in wood or canework. I came face to face with Christina once, not mercifully by the train, but by a bookstall. That was the time I wouldn't meet him, for I did not want to be recognised in future. Christina was wistful about my refusal to meet the train with her; she was on her way to the Island. She looked handsome and rather fine-drawn with a little grey in her hair. Life at Aberkindle looked a little thistly I thought, but did not ask. She left her sentences unfinished, asked questions which she thought better of.

"Darling David, you and Laura must come and stay with us sometime. Heaps of room for the children too. Wouldn't it be a good idea?"

I shook my head.

"Laura is allergic to Scotland and when I go it must be to see Aeneas. I haven't been yet and he's negotiating for a cottage for me."

"Ah yes, Aeneas, I see him when I go over to Achranish, but that's not often. I . . ." she sighed, for the fourth or fifth time in our conversation, then looked at her watch.

"Another five minutes. I wonder what the craze these hols. is. I wish—. David, did you—?"

"Did I what?"

"Oh, goodness, I've forgotten what I was going to ask. Forgive me, my mind was on the time."

She was beautiful and restless and uneasy and I wasn't in love with her, so I told myself as I went off to the Underground, foiled of seeing James.

But I changed my mind and doubled back up the escalator and went to stand where I could watch the nearest taxi queue. She stood rather abstractedly with him, they both seemed detached from each other; I wondered if she overdid the non-possessiveness as my mother did. I could have told her it was a mistake; James looked to me the sort of boy, who, once the barriers were down, would like to bury his face in warm, maternal fur.

I used to work out future activities for James and me; ridiculous, fatherly daydreams of fishing and walking. At least they did not include cricket, but in those days anyway I wasn't much of a fisherman though Aeneas has done his best since. So every aspect of the dream was ridiculous, and I had Mark and Antonia. It was as though James touched some deep welling spring of love in me; I wanted to spoil him and to cherish him. James was myself at his age and I knew all about him accordingly. Mark was quite different; I liked him, was proud and touched by him, but there was no bond of flesh. When I thought of anything happening to James, I could feel myself shuddering and shaking in my flesh, whether it was a beating or a railway accident I contemplated.

An obsession with fatherhood is a curious thing to confess to, and occasionally I had to tell myself that it was a punishment for having treated Laura's urge to motherhood with affectionate detachment. But it was not punishing. It coloured those sliding London days with files instead of men and interminable committees. The General I worked for was a fool and I had to concentrate when he was on his feet, instead of drifting into a Jamesean fantasy, otherwise he would promise men and arms which didn't exist, reverse judgments of the Army Council or read out notes from his brief meant for his eyes alone, such as 'Do not raise this unless forced', etc. He was fond of Laura and used to send her flowers every time he made a gaffe and I covered for him. I have nearly always admired Generals with their simple, saintly faces; this one was a stray. I can't claim to have the sort of face for the job; sobering to rise and to know one's inferiority.

Other Generals must have killed in their time; they cannot always have been spared the finger on the trigger, the grenade hot in the hand. But I associate them with the big guns; with the cannons sending, in lazy arcs, the iron shells of other wars. As young men, they had peacetime soldiering; in the war they were too senior, except for me.

It was, I suppose, while I was at the War Office that I began to be haunted by Ernst, Willi and Christof, long since tidied into war graves from their improbable toppled statuary grouping (do they have iron crosses with steel helmets tipped crazily over them or was that another war?). When I was tired or cross, and circumstances made this frequent, three figures in *feldgrau* jostled me, nudged me. Their eyes were open again and their lolling mouths tight now with mirth, mirth of a skeletal kind, the unholy joy of the skull.

"You killed us," they said, "so we are yours now." I surprised Laura and myself by suddenly being vehement and enraged at a dinner party in a conversation about West Germany, growing richer and more organised and more coherent every year.

"There *are* no good Germans. I wouldn't have a German under my roof at any price," I went on boringly, like some old man out of my childhood, while people blinked and one or two argumentative liberal-minded ladies remonstrated. Laura sat fidgeting with her bread. She always rolls it into grey pellets if she's disquieted; her only social peculiarity. I could see Ernst and Christof and Willi march in when the ladies left. They did not sprawl at the table with their boots out, but sat neatly on three chairs, like evidence before a committee. I began to sweat with fear; I had never seen them so closely before. It was easy to excuse myself, to splash water over my face, light a cigarette, but they were still there when I went back. After my outburst, I hardly spoke again, 'haw-hawed' at a story or two, could think of none relevant to exchange, was a loss to the company. My guests leered and grinned at me. "We are the three good Germans, because we're dead Germans," they said.

I took Laura away after coffee and a decent interval. Driving across the Park we were silent; I thought she was being critical or appalled at finding herself married to an antique Colonel Blimp. (The Colonel Blimps of this generation are now too busy praising the industry of the German workman.) But presently she put out her hand and touched mine.

"Dear David," she said. "I understand. If you mind about people, you have to hate a nation to justify having fought it, otherwise what are you but a murderer — long-range, of course?" she added hastily.

I pressed her hand and returned it to her lap. I regretted that I didn't tell her then, but she went on briskly.

"I think it's time you had a holiday, away from me and the children. Go and see the cottage. Aeneas will be dying to show it to you. Then you can take the children on a proper holiday in the summer."

"What about you?"

"I thought I might go and look at some pictures in Paris or explore around a bit. There are one or two people I could look up."

"You wouldn't come to Achranish with me?"

"No, thank you very much, darling. Aeneas and Jeannie would like to have you to themselves and I've had enough Celtic-logged landscape for a lifetime."

It had been a trying time: selling Aldengrove first, and then Plas Newydd. There seemed no end to the amount of work and detail involved in both transactions. Perhaps my hauntings were attributable to fatigue and anxiety; we were so eager to disclaim our ghosts and our responsibilities for them.

I drove up to Scotland because there were only a few steamers weekly from Oban to Achranish and no other way in except a road Aeneas had warned me about. It was May and I had ten days overdue leave and the Great North Road was spread in front of me if I looked beyond the choke of diesel trucks and cars. But I drove remorselessly and my three companions sat beside me. I was thankful for that, remembering wryly ghost stories where figures have beckoned the unwary on to precipices or raging torrents. A ghostly hand waving one on right into some unseen oncoming Jaguar would be appropriate these days. I reasoned with them patiently as I drove on.

"You're lucky anyway, remembered as heroes by your families, all the trying things about you forgotten, no new Germany to come to terms with, no third war looming for your children. Anyway, what else could I have done? You would have killed me and Jones. He wouldn't be running a fish and chip shop in Cardiff — highly successful at it too. I wouldn't be grooved into seniority and approaching middle-age and the dissatisfactions of both. Let's face it, we haven't done each other any good at all. I stopped you living and you've interfered in my life ever since, practically. What do you want with me, anyway? I'm tired. Leave me alone for a bit. It's all over and done with now."

I didn't raise my voice to them but talked amiably, tractably, persuasively.

"If anyone should haunt me, why not Andrew, nothing like a really 'braw' ghost? I can't be nice about him even now, poor Andrew, and he had the worst of everything. But he took Christina away and my son. Shut up," I said to myself as I lost my equable tones.

But Willi, Ernst and Christof weren't at all interested in Andrew. They were entirely self-centred apart from their *idée fixe* about me.

I had chosen to drive into Scotland over Carter Bar, because I had an agreeable if hazy memory of the road on my only other visit there. By now, I don't know which I would choose. The overnight sleeper which conveys one from Euston to waking in the Highlands with the suddenness of a dream and projects one startlingly from one life to another, the road from Carlisle to Gretna which translates one from one country to another in a state of anti-climax for both (anyone who can conjure romance from Gretna must have had a very hard life), and there, at one's lowest ebb, draws one into the imperceptible softness of the first hills, the other from Scotch Corner takes one swiftly into a more and more northern territory, straight roads looping remorselessly through the woods and the smooth high curves of the landscape till Scotland lies before one, seemingly unpeopled and endless. No other country gives me such a sense of stretching to infinity. I have always the feeling of fold upon fold of moor and hill and water behind and in front of me.

In a way I approached Scotland that May resentfully. This was Aeneas's home and Christina's paradise: indirectly perhaps why she had always refused to marry me. Also the English who rave about Scotland and find excuses for wearing the kilt bored me. Aldengrove and the Island, with the microcosm it presents of every glory and gentleness of England, were what I thought I liked and wanted. So I was wary of the beauty that unfolded and relieved when it rained, as it soon did, because I could curse the Scottish weather and look at the blurred hillsides with pity. Towards Glencoe the weather changed dramatically for the worse. Rannoch Moor is, as I have since learned, a tedious stretch of undistinguished barrenness at the best of times − if one does not look on at the great hills. The road across it that day alternately glittered in burst of hard sunshine or was drenched in rain and the hills it approached were dark with the storm I was driving towards. One had, for an hour or two, the sensations of earlier travellers, less securely and warmly enclosed and borne onwards than nowadays, more prone to regard mountains with awe and horror. Primitive terrors pricked mysteriously; the twentieth century seemed to fall away in the black rain that was hurled down and the wind that sighed and shrieked as I drove through the narrowing pass. The ferry, of course, was not working because of the storm and I had to drive round the head of Loch Leven, where the weather became less fierce and the impact of the rain and wind dulled by banks of evergreens. Corran Ferry was working and there was a silver lightness in the west as I turned the car towards Achranish on the other side. Aeneas had not exaggerated the state of the road; great holes and cracks and high ridges of grass made progress as slow as a horse and carriage; one might be more comfortable, one was certainly no faster. There seemed to be a wilderness to cross; Aeneas had also referred tersely to this; he had not quite prepared me for the mile upon mile of uninhabited land stretching as far as eye could see, still scorched with frost, the new green only discernible among the roadside rocks where the bracken was shooting. The road went on with implacable hope; sheep reluctantly heaved themselves off as I approached and lambs ran bleating and uncertain from side to side. I quite welcomed the sheep and the curlews; they relieved the stillness of the scene. For occasional stretches one had the feeling that some civilisation was at hand; there would be old gnarled moss-grown trees at the roadside, a trace of shrubbery, a tidier, closer grass, even a glimpse of ruined stones under the nettles of domesticity, then the wilderness again. I remembered that Christina had once promised to tell me about the evictions.

Then the landscape changed completely. There was a smell of the sea and the air lightened and crispened. The road dipped to the side of the loch, a heron fished amongst the reeds, waves slapped seaweed against lichened stones. On the left of the road the land rose steeply and there were cascades of primroses among the moss and the ribbons of water winding down to cross the road and tipple into the loch. Enormous trees grew precipitously out of the crags, many had fallen and the still living branches grew out of the moss and the fern that now decorated their trunks. There was a curious air of ruined, spilled splendour; an old boat-house covered with ivy, toppled gateposts, a flowering shrub. Great indistinguishable stone beasts sat on the gate posts of the Achranish House invisible behind its azaleas and rhododendrons. The landmarks Aeneas had described I began to identify, and it was with mounting excitement that I reached the first cottage. Aeneas came out of the door at the sound of the engine; I had been driving slowly anyway; the road surface, if it could, had worsened.

He looked subtly different from what I remembered and he shook my hand fiercely through the window.

"Ye're late, Colonel David, I expected you hours ago. The fire will be out and the kettle off the boil if Jeannie has dozed off waiting. Now come along now."

The people at the cottage came out to be introduced and Aeneas dealt with this matter briskly.

"Now come away, come away, we'll be going now. Another mile or so up the road, ye mind."

It was now a richer and softer landscape with Mull rising an evening lilac from the sea to the right, avenues of great trees bordering the road which curved and dipped amongst the pastures and cultivated fields, to circle, finally, around the sheltered bay under the high, beech-hung cliffs where plumes of waterfalls spouted down. Aeneas's cottage was down near the sea, mine, a field or two above, with only a path to it. It was an old keeper's cottage, furnished roughly with what was available by Aeneas and Jeannie. I have never altered anything, even the curtains and patterned linoleum which Laura would hate. It is a typical two up, two down but and ben, but it has a bathroom and a water supply, no electricity, no telephone. The deer come down through the woods at the back of the house as tamely as if it were still deserted and from the windows I can see the puffers and MacBraynes and the occasional naval vessel or a yacht making their way up the Sound of Mull.

Aeneas took me home for supper that first day and I was almost too tired to listen, let alone talk, not just from the journey but as though here I could feel the burden of fatigue exquisitely because it was at the moment of sloughing it off. I went to bed almost straight away in my own cottage, by unnecessary candlelight: in the long luminous nights of May and June it hardly ever seems to get dark at Achranish. I fell asleep at once, which is usually difficult to do when one is so tired. At about four, I awoke to hear the stamping and shouting and snuffling of horses. Through the tiny skylight I saw them, three ghostly white garrons in the cottage garden, grazing on Aeneas's tenderly nurtured grass, so I went down to get them out. They had leaned so heavily and with such determination on the field gate, that it had come adrift from its fastenings. In the milky glow of the twilight blending imperceptibly with the dawn, they stood before me like fairy horses, strayed from Celtic mythology. I went to find some sugar lumps and began the long task of coaxing the mare out of the gate, hoping that the other two would follow. There was no sound but the deep breathing and occasional whinnying of the horses, fetlock deep in the white mist which bathed the landscape. I was a little afraid that they might rear and strike out at me; there was no room for manœuvre in the pocket-handkerchief garden and no escape if I were pinned against the walls of the cottage. But finally, after much patience, the second horse left and then the third and I shut the gate as firmly as possible behind them. I could hear them whickering gently like supernatural creatures as they crunched through the bracken and under-growth behind the house on their way back to the hills, as I stood, trying to assess the damage to the garden in the half-light. Apart from some hoof-marks and one or two dishevelled groups of peonies and pinks, all seemed well.

It was possible to see quite a long way now; the mist only lay like a coverlet at ground level, above it there was the shadow of Mull and nearer, the tilt of the fields down to the sea, darkened in patches by trees and the occasional stead-ing. The light was extraordinary, a pallor unlike moonlight because it was thicker and whiter, almost as if one was seeing the world through a veil of muslin. I could see some deer moving swiftly and confidently across one field and a seabird or two cried in the silence. There seemed to be no one but myself in this place; no one, not Willi, not Ernst nor Christof. I accorded them a brief surprised thought and went back to bed to hours of deep and peaceful sleep.

Aeneas was cross but resigned about the garrons; he took me fishing, showed me where to go for walks, administered briskly to household and garden needs, but otherwise left me, surprisingly, very much to myself for three or four days. There was a good deal to see, out of the Achranish treasure hoard; bullet-headed seals bumbling in the sea, eider duck skimming the water, ravens croaking above the cliffs, eagles' feathers on the sheep tracks of the hills and above all, perhaps, it is the flowers I remember that May; primroses, violets, wood anemones and bluebells, growing lushly and brilliantly among the clenched fists of the budding bracken and the new rich grass, gorse like no other gorse I've seen, in coruscations of clotted yellow and the air powdery and sweet with blown bird-cherry blossom and the mealy bloom of the rowans. There was no one to distract me as I walked about, watching it all, discovering a new vista at every turn, then returning to see again diffidently some haunting beauty for the fourth or fifth time as though looking might diminish it.

After that period of solitude, Aeneas began to introduce me to the few people who lived round about, to the shepherds and crofters and those working still on the Buchanan land. They had all of them the dignity and quietness of their surroundings. Laura and I have always laughed at the 'simple lifers'; because they obviously have to devote all their energies to maintaining life, however simple. A lack of electricity, shops, telephone or water soon makes for difficulties so laborious that hardly any time or energy is left for the complications of an easier or more sophisticated life. This had always seemed ridiculous. It was not that life at Achranish was simple, but it was uncluttered and clean and quiet. One could shop in Oban by boat once a week, one could row over the loch to the shop by the ferry, one could walk a mile or two to the travelling shop which lumbered its way weekly over the terrible road. The postman called, one could not think of telephoning and I could get no sound on my wireless above a whisper.

Aeneas and I decided to put the wood stove in order, sawing logs and stacking them in an outhouse, cutting kindling: there was plenty of fallen timber about. I liked doing things for the future of the cottage.

"I'll bring the children here in September. I shall be having some leave then. To tell you the truth, I'd like to come to live here, altogether, Aeneas."

He paused grimly in his sawing.

"And leave the Army, Colonel David? You'll surely not be thinking of doing that?"

"I want to write a play, about war, a good play. And I'm tired. And with the regiment about to be merged, what does it matter any more?"

"Ay, I can understand that. And you'd like it fine here, but it's no life by yourself, and what would Mistress Kingsley say about it?"

"That's the rub, Aeneas. She wouldn't care for it at all."

"It comes over men – and women too, mebbe, at your age, that they're doing the wrong thing and not caring for life in the way they have it. It's common enough, I doubt. There's all these books about getting away from it all," there was a depth of mockery in his voice, "but you must do what your hand findeth to do and do it with all your might."

There was a silence between us.

"Aeneas, I killed three Germans in the war."

"Was that all, three?" he said reprovingly.

"I mean, I shot them myself, in a sort of ambush in Normandy – I could have taken them prisoner. I can't forget them, at least I couldn't till this week. I'd begun to be obsessed by them. They'd never leave me."

Aeneas went on sawing rhythmically.

163

"And then there was Captain Grant, in a way I caused his death too, because of these Germans. Think what I have done to Christina."

Aeneas paused again.

"That's not what you did to Christina. You broke her heart by not marrying her when you could have done."

"I couldn't as a subaltern."

Aeneas spat derisively.

"There were other things you could have done — aye, it would have been difficult but you would have had her."

"She always turned me down."

"Because she knew you had your doubts. Christina wanted you only to want her. She's a proud woman. You never understood that, mebbe."

"She wanted some Scotch laird and she got one and I killed him."

"She'll have the big house one day, mark my words. Her brother will never settle to live there. You could have had it together."

"You don't understand about Andrew and the Germans."

"No, mebbe I don't. You're a soldier and you must do as bid and have others do likewise. There's risks you all take and blood on your hands is one of them, there's no denying that, Colonel David. You're not the first soldier, nor please God the last, to mind about the lives you take. We're no bad at remembering the dead but we forget, forbye, what we made the living do for us."

"I could forget here."

"So you think now, and I'm glad of it. But if you'll take my advice, you'll not try to forget those Germans. Would you be remembering their names, now, or anything about them? You'll be sent to Germany one day — maybe you

164

could be finding out about them, what sort of men they were."

"What would my father have done?" I ignored what he said in my embarrassed anxiety to ask this question.

"The Colonel — he lived in happier times. But he worried about the Great War, don't think he didn't. He had to see the young men killed and himself come back."

"I wish to God Andrew Grant had come back anyway."

"Aye, I wish that too. But it was doubtless not meant."

"It wasn't a question of being meant. I could have stopped him from being killed."

"That's verra interesting, Colonel David, but the Ways of Providence are inscrutable."

"For heaven's sake, Aeneas."

"Now we'll just get on with the two-handled saw, Colonel David, or we'll never finish these logs."

His mouth was set with a determination to say no more and he didn't, until he was saying goodbye. I had given him and Jeannie a lift down to the travelling shop.

"Now feel his kippers now, lassie. I like them firm and juicy. Well, it's goodbye for now, Colonel David, and we'll be seeing you and Mark and Antonia in September. You'll be able to taste Achranish in London, I'm promising you, and as for that other business, don't be forever fretting and fidgeting about it, like a woman. It's a grand day for you. I hope the rain keeps off."

As I drove regretfully back towards the borders, I thought about Christina and began to understand why she wanted to live in Scotland. Even away from the peculiar beauty of Achranish, I was still aware of the sense of space and time everywhere; the roads seemed bare of traffic to an Englishman; the villages far apart, not ribboning together to merge in one suburban unison of bungalow and villa. The architecture, at first glance, was deplorable, but even the miniature Balmorals of the Victorian age with their yellow sunblinds firmly down to the requisite level and their solid fronts stoutly breasting weather and change, had a certain appeal and those flat-fronted tall gaunt village streets by their outright ugliness had none of the cosy hypocrisy of a row of pebbledashed and gabled contemporary houses. And there was Edinburgh as I came up, incomparably beautiful with its curving terraces and squares, and Glasgow, on the return road, warm, tram-noisy, cobbled, sooty and starling-stained. I crossed the border with love and regret.

Laura was affable and polite about Achranish and eager for the children to spend holidays there with me; I had anticipated difficulties about that because she worried interminably about them always, from wet feet to drowning, more than any normal mother nowadays.

Our holidays were always a triumphant success; for me and the children Achranish began to be home more than anywhere else. Laura minded less about this too than I had expected, though she was tart about 'Grandfather' Aeneas.

"Just because he utters wise saws in broad Scots makes Antonia and Mark think he is some kind of ancient prophet; there's nothing like dialect for making clichés seem clever."

"It isn't a dialect."

"Oh, David, really, you'll be looking out a tartan next."

We were indeed posted to Germany that winter. I was thankful that she came back to England or went to France fairly frequently, to see the children and friends. Germany was recovering fast, but there was still a smell of ruin about. It was difficult to make friends with them, and at the same time one was stifled by the cantonment atmosphere of the

British settlements. When Laura was away, I could live in the Mess, which I liked; my small talk has diminished with age; in the Mess, I could get by. What I missed was seeing James, though he had been staying at Achranish House and Aeneas wrote about him with pride. There was nothing I could do about him. I resisted the books I wanted to buy for him, the presents I yearned to give. With stealth and cunning I took Aeneas's advice and began to find out about my Germans. I had their wartime addresses, at least I had addresses from which parents and wives had written to them. Ernst was first. He had had a letter from his mother in Berlin. When I was sent there on duty I went to find the flat, but it was in a block that had been demolished. It was too easy to think that all his family had been killed. I began to look at the records, not easy, and found that indeed a Herr and Frau Krebs had been killed in an air-raid. From further research it appeared that Ernst was their only son. This information cost me a great deal in patience and explanation (not strictly truthful), and by one of those odd coincidences I was supplied with the information about there being no other children by a clerk in a German equivalent of Somerset House who looked it up for me and volunteered the information that he was married to an aunt of the family. I tried not to be too eager.

"Had he known them?"

"No, I had only met my wife three years after the war."

"Could I come and see her?"

He was wary, but I took her some tea and coffee and an explanation so veiled in my garbled German that she was willing to talk about her sister and husband and son. She was in her forties, unhealthily fat and pale and the little room where we talked was brilliantly lit and sparsely furnished, giving an impression of chromium plate everywhere. She had not cared for her sister's husband, who was, I gathered, an ardent Nazi, over-eager with information about his neighbours in the flats whom he thought listened to English news broadcasts or had Jewish relatives. Ernst had been a good boy at school but there had been some scandal, not involving him, of course, but which he had brought on. The master had been sent away, "to one of those camps, sir, though of course we knew nothing of what went on at the time". Ernst had been thought quite the little hero by some; his aunt was old-fashioned enough to use the word 'sneak' about him. Then he was in the Army and killed. "Which is just as well," she said in her housewifely voice. "There is hardly room or time for us who were not so nearly concerned with it all. Hitlerism came out of the disgruntled soldiers of the last war, to a great part; better have fewer soldiers left this time." She thanked me for the tea and coffee and hoped she had been of use, "though why you should have ever known anyone who knew Ernst, I cannot imagine". She envied my suit with her eyes as she said this and saw it on the little clerk.

I went away curiously put out by her acceptance of death and disaster and Nazism as something unhygienic and untidy. She had not approved of Ernst. I could not feel sorry for him now, though I wondered whether it was eagerness for his fierce father's approval that had made him tell tales out of school; I remembered his weak chin; he would have connived not to be bullied and not been scrupulous about the methods of keeping out of harm's way.

Willi had lived in one of those sleepy towns on the Rhine one sees from the train. I had to visit Austria: it was easy to skip a day's trains and visit his wife. The house was indeed still there, a tiny cement horror of the 'thirties but with a wonderful view of the barges and boats going by and the soft vineyards rising. There was a streaking of snow about but it was sunny and hopeful. One could have been happy in his village, I thought. I asked at the post-office about the house before I went, choosing an elderly official. Indeed the house was still there, yes, it belonged to Frau Ebern, but now she had re-married and was Frau Schmitt. Thus armed, I went on. She was prettier than I had expected, Willi's photograph of her had been a bad one, and she seemed younger. There were children too, of the second marriage. I raised Willi's name diffidently: told her half the truth: that I had found some letters (I had indeed brought them with me) and had always meant to return them. I apologised for the delay.

She asked me in to the polished and clean house where the wood crackled in the shining stove and there was a smell of soup and coffee. There were photographs about, but none of Willi: a laughing man dominated most of them; his successor, I imagined. Talking about Willi did not come easily to her. I held the letters in my hand and she eyed them uneasily across the room.

"I was very young when we were married. I didn't know him very well."

"Do you come from round here?"

"Oh yes, my father has a farm a few kilometres away."

"And Willi was brought up in this village?"

"Oh yes, he was in the office of Herr Gimpel — these are the Gimpel vineyards."

I wanted to know what he was like, but she seemed disinclined to remember him.

"How long were you married before the war?"

"A year, I think. Willi bought this house; he had been saving up and then an aunt died."

"It must have been very hard being left so young. I mean, when he went into the Army."

"He was on leave sometimes; he brought things back from France. Then he was in Norway with the ski-troops. He was a good skier; it was his hobby."

He hadn't looked like that to me.

"Norway, eh?"

"He liked that very much. The people were so nice. He liked them very much. It was the best place he was."

"And after that?"

"There was the terrible Eastern front for a while; then he was ill and his parents were killed in an air-raid. It was hard then when he was home. He had always been serious, even when he was young. They did not promote him either; he was always ill or unlucky. I expect his being killed was just unlucky too."

She pouted a little now; being married to Willi was something of a misadventure.

"Did he have many friends here?"

She shrugged her shoulders.

"Willi lost his friends. He argued and he was a bit mean, careful of his money, you know. He did not like to waste it on drinking. They kept themselves to themselves, his parents, so they say."

"Is Herr Gimpel still here—the man Willi worked for?"

"His son. He would not remember Willi. You are very curious about this writer of the letters you found."

She flashed her eyes at me a little at this point. I could

imagine her dealing briskly with door-to-door salesmen. I smiled at her.

"You have been very patient. I am a soldier; we are always anxious about other soldiers."

"A morbid anxiety, perhaps." She glanced at the photograph of the laughing man.

"Let the dead rest. It is we who matter now. It was you who killed him, wasn't it?"

I had not expected this. The pretty blue eyes were shrewd.

I nodded.

"Don't tell me it was all a mistake. It was bound to be where Willi was concerned. As I've told you, he was like that. You cannot have killed many men or you would not have time to go round finding out about them."

"Perhaps not. Does it seem very odd to you that I should?"

She got up from her chair, one of a pair of elaborately carved old-fashioned chairs with arms.

"You should go now, my husband will be back. It would be difficult to explain."

She showed me to the door.

"It is a beautiful view; you have a comfortable home," I said pacifyingly.

"Yes, at least I got something out of him. Don't let him lie on your conscience. You did me a good turn anyway."

She shut the door on the last sentence and left me gaping as I walked down the neat path between the well-dug garden beds. It was as if our interview had driven her to a climax of resentment that I should be interested in Willi.

Christof had come from Heidelberg. The ink and the

171

paper of the two letters I had were good; the address sounded prosperous. It was May before I could go there. I arrived in the evening, surprised from the stream-lined scenery of the autobahn to find myself suddenly in a medieval town, walking old streets under pink flowering chestnuts. There was an unmistakable feeling of the old Germany here; a country one recognised from books with pleasure; I even saluted the statue of Bunsen with enthusiasm. As I had little time to spare, I went to the address after dinner; I checked with the telephone directory; his parents still lived there, his father was a professor. This was the interview I would prefer not to have, the most difficult.

They were both there, his father looking older than he probably was, his mother with an unmistakable air of academic dowdiness. It was a beautiful room; Persian rugs, good pictures and furniture. They heard me out, only interrupting my halting introduction to suggest that I talked in English instead; the Professor sat, finger tips together, a man of judgment. She frowned slightly and went on with her sewing, which looked like a piece of stiff church embroidery. I had not really intended to tell them the truth, but, playing by ear, confronted with the sort of people they were, it seemed improper to evade the real reason why I was there.

"And what do you expect to get from us, Herr Colonel?" she said with a harsh voice, almost as if she were stifling a laugh, "Absolution? Politeness? We could not bear you to be worried because you killed our son."

I took heart from the Professor saying, "Hilde!" reprovingly. There was a pause which none of us seemed anxious to interrupt. She bit a thread off with her teeth and raised her eyebrows.

"Well?" she said at last.

"I did not find it easy to come to see you," I began.

"Perhaps you exaggerate the social embarrassments of calling on the bereaved. By now you would not expect us still to be wearing mourning."

Her English was enunciated with precision. The Professor took his hands away from each other.

"You must forgive us," he said. "After all, this is an unusual situation and we are none of us sure how to behave in it. Perhaps it is a situation not to be encouraged."

"I like Heidelberg," I said irrelevantly. He nodded judicially.

"You have been to other – er – victim's homes?"

"Two."

"I see. Did you offer them any compensation?" she asked.

My mouth was drying and I shook my head. Perhaps Willi's widow would have liked a bonus for Willi: it would have confirmed her last laugh.

"A lump sum or a pension can sometimes do wonders. But not, unfortunately, for us."

Looking at the carpet I was inclined to agree with her.

"Perhaps the Herr Colonel has some last words to tell us?" There was a vibrating sarcasm in her voice that put me completely on edge.

The Professor straightened himself.

"If there is anything you think we should be told, we should, of course, be most grateful."

"Death was instantaneous."

"Ah, yes," they said almost in harmony and with equal incredulity.

"But it was."

"The Herr Colonel is doubtless a good shot," this was the Frau Professor again.

Outside in the garden, I could see the chestnuts and lilac nodding in the lamplight; there was a glow of flowers.

"Was he your — only son?"

"Yes, we have three married daughters, however, and eight grandchildren."

"So you must not think, Herr Colonel, that you have made us lonely in any way."

"I am sorry." The words were wrung from me, though I had almost vowed not to utter them.

"That you came or that you were such a good shot?"

There seemed no answer to that. I thought at the last minute that he would relent and make some gesture, but he didn't. She asked me whether there was anything else they could do for me and then rang for the maid to show me out, giving me a stiff little bow as I went. He stood up and bowed too, outside in the street. I felt relieved rather than sad; I hated them; I almost danced with rage on the chestnut blossoms on the pavement outside their gate.

I should have left Heidelberg next morning, but in the middle of my predictably disturbed night, I remembered a boy at the University whose parents I had come across because his father held some civic position and I had to see him from time to time. He had always been agreeable and helpful and I had met the son at his house. Finding him that morning was not easy, but I ran him to earth in his lodgings finally, hearing that he went back there to eat at midday.

"Professor Erhard? Yes, of course I know him. His wife is notorious; she eats students for breakfast."

"They had a son, a young son, who was killed in the war."

174

"Oh yes, Christof the hero. I had a cousin who was at school with him. That's really why I know the Erhards."

"Why — 'hero'?"

"He ran away to join the Army when he was fifteen. He was the apple of his mother's eye. He was mad about the Army and Hitler and saving the Fatherland — a real Nazi boy, you know."

"He *was* very young."

"Yes, younger than I am when he was killed. His parents never spoke of him again — they only kept safe by a miracle, you know. Old Erhard was against the Nazis, so was she. They thought Christof was a traitor to them, as well as a young fool, at least so my cousin always said."

"They talked about him quite differently to me."

"Did they? Well, they are proud, you know, it wouldn't be easy to get Ma Erhard to climb off her dignity."

I sorted over the interview in my mind and finally I went to a florist and ordered some flowers to be sent to her. I pitied her.

What I had now were three case histories, incomplete, half-guessed, but perhaps enough; in a way I almost preferred my ghosts. Finding out about them may have exorcised them; it did not change my feeling of guilt, but it altered my attitude towards it. It also left me with inevitable uneasiness about my own importance; only Christof of those three had left any dent, and if I read the signs aright, his parents were perhaps glad that he was dead and ashamed.

I did not particularly enjoy being in Germany, and neither did Laura. The insularity of the Army and its dependants has always annoyed us; the number of eccentrics it harbours has diminished sadly, so has the number of those who believe in getting to know the natives; living overseas has always seemed to me pointless if one is insulated against foreigners. And, at the stage we were at, it was difficult to get to know any Germans in the right atmosphere and circumstances. Laura seemed to have given up making friends; I blamed her restlessness on her apparent boredom with people, admirably concealed in running wives' clubs and having dinner parties. I began to play bridge again, after a lapse of years, but Laura shuddered at the thought, so this meant she was alone more evenings than I liked: she said she enjoyed going to bed early to write letters and read: Laura has always been generous about my activities. There were always a number of exercises which involved my being away for long periods: she used to go back to England or to France then. In a way I was sorry that our life together had fallen into such grooves and ashamed that it suited me; Laura was undemanding in every way: my solitariness was beginning to envelop me safely like a shell so I appreciated her perhaps austere companionship.

When we came back to a posting on Salisbury Plain, Mark was just going to his public school, my old one, and fifteen miles away from James. It would have been easy to have arranged to take him out from time to time, but I was worried lest Laura, with awful intuition, saw a resemblance. I did not want any relationship with him except the true one and had to accept that I could have as much as I liked of Mark's company and affection and nothing of James's. I tried scrupulously to be fair to Mark over this and, I hope, succeeded; he was, anyway, good-natured and amusing; Laura and I had been lucky. Antonia was a wisp of a girl at this stage, dwindled by the enormities of the school felt hat and overcoat, a pale smudgy-faced girl, endearing too. We lived in a red brick barracks of a house, Plain type, and I wondered how Laura managed to fill her days, apart from her weekly visit to London. She would be reading someone's memoirs by the fire when I came back in the evening, yawning, looking lost in another world, pause to ask perfunctorily about my day and then slowly drift back to her book in the middle of my answers. Perhaps other marriages were like this too; ours was at least tranquil and well organised. Despite Laura's apparent abandon to literature on the sofa, the house looked as good as it could (we had withdrawn furniture and carpets and pictures from store to soften the Army's fatal furnishings), a good dinner was cooking, the flowers were well-arranged, letters to the children written. She was as unobtrusive a housekeeper as she was now a wife. I sometimes caught her looking at me searchingly, unexpectedly as if trying to solve a riddle about me; she had the bothered but absent air of someone with an elusive crossword puzzle clue. If I told her about James, about Andrew's death, the three Germans, would it solve any mystery for her? Revelations tend to increase fissures, not repair them. The spilling of a confidence between one man and another frequently chills a friendship: perhaps it is different for women. I did not want to be vulnerable to her tenderness over me.

That summer, Jeannie died, and instead of my going north with the children, Aeneas came to stay with us, disrupting plans and for once toppling Laura from her pedestal of calm. She was furious, though her proposed holiday had not sounded very exciting to me. Aeneas was not himself and not at all well; he stayed reluctantly in bed part of the time, was moping and critical, though we took him to see gardens everywhere. Jeannie had been a comfortable woman and if she had bored him with her soft ways after my mother's plangent personality, he had sunk into her cushioning a little and missed it at last. Laura was icily scrupulous about looking after him; he teased her in a remorseless Scots fashion and told the children long stories in front of her: she did not enjoy that peculiar pawky humour (I remembered Andrew's) and as many of them seemed to be about funerals or whisky-stills she did not consider either in good taste. Occasionally he varied this with a golfing story, a game of which she knew little and cared less. A story which the children adored was a blend of a golfing and funeral story.

"Tell us about the man raising his cap on the ninth tee, Aeneas," they would clamour, "when he saw the hearse pass on the road."

Laura would sigh and bite her lip.

"All his stories are so dreadfully unfeeling. Are all the Scots like that?"

"You mustn't take him so literally. Surely your Welsh blood helps."

"The Welsh have *quite* different stories. And I'm too Anglicised by now to remember. David, how *can* you . . ."

"How can I what?"

"Oh, I don't know—put up with him, I suppose, like him."

"He's part of my life. He means as much to me as anyone."

She looked stricken and I was sorry for her and grateful for all she had done for Aeneas, for which he was unlikely to thank her.

The next February I had to go to Scottish Command, to Glasgow, Edinburgh and Perth. When I had finished in Perth it was Thursday morning and the sun shone and on impulse I sent my driver back to Edinburgh with the Army car and hired one instead. I would go to Achranish for the weekend and get a sleeper back. Looking at a map I saw that one road would lead me past Aberkindle, so I chose to go that way. I saw the posters about it up in the village before it, where I had stopped for cigarettes. There was a three-day auction sale, which had started the day before. Then I remembered that Aeneas had told me that the old Major was very ill: I had missed the announcement of his death evidently, not being one for the front page of *The Times* which I leave to Laura. It seemed strange that Christina was selling the ancestral home. Inevitably I drove in at the great gates as I passed.

It was a vast house of no beauty at all, either of colour or proportion; a gaunt, Victorian dwelling indicating a certain date and a certain status and that was all. But around it was beauty all right, woods and lawns and hills and, cupped in the middle of the prospect, a lake, now frozen over. James must enjoy that, I thought. It had been snowing in the night and the trees were plumy with it and the ground streaked with black and white like an engraving. There were a number of cars and an air of *bonhomie* and bustle about the people clustered round them or going in and out. It was nearly lunch-time and there were flasks and luncheon-baskets visible. It was like a point-to-point, with women in sheepskin jackets and headscarves and men looking rosy with cold in British warms and tweeds. I resented the jolly crowd, the pet names, the entreaties and the ripostes that issued from it as its breath smoked through the freezing air. A few looked at me as I walked away from my car, straining to think who I was and disappointed at a stranger. I made my way into the house through another gay group on the steps.

The entrance hall was formidable with pillars marbled like haggis and the first of the house's dark portraits staring down; 'warts and all' he had been painted, some unknown ancestor of Andrew's and the bristling little hairs in the warts too. I bought a catalogue and was told they were selling the dining-room, so I walked into the drawing-room. It was a vast, neglected, peeling room with a good plaster ceiling fretted with flowers and birds and intricate knots. Pictures had been taken down and the dark places stared from the faded wall-paper. The furniture was good, the upholstery shabby. Through the great uncurtained windows I looked out to see what Christina and James had seen. There was a film of sunshine over the landscape now. I wished I had a whisky flask like some of them outside. The house was cold and I was shivering.

"I might as well be thorough," I said to myself and started off all round the house. They were bidding for china in the dining-room; there was a great deal of it on tables, not, from what I could see, in very good condition. There was a library, with some handsome books and a study, all blue plush and rugs with holes and old photographs which I avoided. The gun room and the billiard-room I avoided too. Upstairs it was even colder; great unheated bedrooms with handsome furniture and all the washhand-stand equipment of our grandmothers, including flower-patterned footbaths which some women would doubtless buy for bulbs. Then there was the nursery wing, through a tattered green baize door. The Victorians certainly never spoilt their children. The room faced north and looked on to a prospect of dark trees but there was one bedroom with a view of the lake and I hoped it had been James's. In the day nursery there was an old upright piano with candlesticks on it; one

had been wrenched loose and dangled; there was music still
on the piano and books lay haphazardly on the shelves. It was
very much a neglected room someone had just walked out of.
There was an old rocking horse in a corner; it still rocked in
a squeaky way. As I pushed it idly, Christina stood behind me.

"I've been following you from a discreet distance. Design
or coincidence?"

"Coincidence."

We shook hands with a mutual twitch of the mouth. Her
hair was greyer and it gave an ashen pallor to her face; she
was bundled up in assorted tweeds, jerseys and scarves, but
appeared gaunt.

"You look tired out. Have you been ill?"

"Goodness, no. *You'd* be tired with all this going on.
It's been driving me mad, what with everyone telling me
what to do and what to keep, etc."

She touched her hair in a reminiscent way and sat on the
arm of a chair with her old casualness and lit a cigarette.

"It says, 'No Smoking' everywhere, but who cares? It's
still my house."

"Is it? I wondered whether it wasn't and that's why
you're selling."

"Ask the bank why I'm selling. This place eats money
and doesn't produce a penny. I've tried for years to make
something pay; the fruit and vegetable garden – no, no one
would buy round here; the game – no, it wouldn't do, it's
always been given away, there's the 'list', Andrew's father
lived on 'lists' – you know, for the garden parties and the
shooting and visits. I may say that most of our neighbours
have more sense; land has to pay these days. Anyway, look
at it all; a moth-eaten house and policies – thank God no
entail, a sensible will. The old man wouldn't let me have

my way while he was alive, but he trusted me to do the best for James."

"And what will you do? Stay round here in a smaller house? You don't want James to lose touch I suppose?"

There must have been an ironic note in my voice because she looked at me levelly and raised an eyebrow.

"No, I don't. What else has he got but the family name?"

I lit a cigarette too then and let the pause continue.

"This wasn't his nursery, it was Andrew's. James had a couple of rooms near me. I hate this now. Sheltered is another name for 'shut away'. They shut away everything in those days."

"Was there an older house here once?"

"Oh yes, burned down, not romantically in the '15 but at some houseparty in the 1850's and then was stylishly erected – everything interesting went in that fire."

"So you've no locks of Charlie's hair?"

"Not a wisp, David. Let's go and have some lunch. I've got a hide-out in the old housekeeper's room. Will sandwiches and whisky do?"

We went through a maze of old kitchens to a small room marked 'Private' with a fire. "This is better. Have some whisky."

"I've been needing some."

She drank hers fast and looked brighter after it.

"Laura never likes the taste."

"Another thing we haven't in common," she said. "Dear Laura, are you being nice to her?"

"Not particularly."

"Girl friends?"

"No, I'm very faithful. You've never thought of remarrying?"

"No."

She poured out some more whisky for us both and gave me a sandwich.

"This is our third empty house, Christina."

"Do you think it's symbolic? Perhaps it is. 'Here is no abiding city'. Did you know I am coming to live at Achranish. Don't look so horrified. I won't disturb you."

There had been rumours about Achranish House for some time. Christina's grandfather had died, a very old man, only just before I had my cottage there: the house passed to Christina's surviving uncle who occupied it occasionally and then died. Aeneas, prone to speculation, had assumed that it had passed to his son, an unknown quantity, a lawyer in New Zealand and that it might therefore be sold or worse, fall into desuetude as so many houses have in the Highlands.

"But Christina . . ."

"There's been a great family conclave about it. Cousin Nigel doesn't want to live there and has lots of money. He quarrelled with his father years ago about the woman he married and regards his inheritance as a ridiculous accident, so he wanted to hand it over to my brothers and *they* certainly don't want to come home from Rhodesia. So I'm to run the estate and the house as profitably as possible and try to give them some money from it. I can put all my ideas for this place into practice much more successfully at Achranish. I'm thrilled to bits and so is James. You're my tenant now, David. Ha ha!" and she dug me in the ribs.

"You should take the old name."

"I'm not such a romantic. The place will be good enough for me. Your children are there quite often, they tell me; they'll be company for Jamie. We shan't be there this summer, I'm afraid, I'm taking him abroad—away from school for a term even, his chest's been bad this winter and I want a lot done to the house before I move in. I'm turning part of it into flats for holiday letting and putting in proper heating."

"Is he all right?"

"James? Not too bad. There's been a bit of a fuss, but I think he's all right really. A long dose of sun will do the trick, I hope. Another sandwich?"

She was brisk enough. I wanted to talk to her, but it was no good. In a way I was a little frightened of her. She looked dark-eyed with restless fatigue. No doubt James had given her more anxiety than she had confessed to and I could imagine the trouble over the house.

"Will it sell? This house I mean?"

"I doubt it, but the land will. We'll take the roof off and that will be that. Cheaper in the long run."

"The roof of your house on the Island is off too, so I believe."

"And did the London house survive the bombing?"

I shook my head.

"A V2 finished it off. No one there. George has some stockbrokers' dream in Claygate. We went to a party there: Laura complained she was the only one without a bit of mink."

I was rather proud of myself for getting through that coolly. I went to see the gap in the road one day; jagged fencing and willow herb and curiously extant, a fireplace which must have been in the drawing-room. I was better at lighting fires now, with much practice, but that was my proudest fire. In a way I was glad the house was destroyed.

"Do you regret selling Aldengrove?"

I shook my head.

"No, I miss it but it wasn't practicable and anyway it wasn't the family house. The house in Wales was sold too. We've nowhere now except Achranish and that's not Laura's idea of home."

"No, it wouldn't be. But that's because she doesn't love you. Oh, David, don't look stricken. You don't love her either, so it would be a pity if she did. You're just living out a comfortable notion of matrimony."

"You haven't seen us for years."

She smiled her old arrogant smile.

"Dear David, how conventional you are. That's the last of the sandwiches. Are you planning to bid for anything?"

I wondered whether she expected me to kiss her. We were both standing now before the fire. There was an alarm clock on the mantelpiece, tilted, with a leg broken, ticking loudly and ridiculously, and an hour fast. It reminded me of cottage clocks in Achranish which record an alien and always incorrect time. If I had taken her in my arms then, could I have kissed away time and accomplished for both of us some golden miracle? But the taste of my mistakes, of Andrew's death and of Christina's treachery was in my mouth. Treachery is a melodramatic word, but we are constantly involved in it. We betray ourselves and each other all the time and then are betrayed by time. It crossed my mind that I would give up the idea of the snowy dash to Achranish and stay seeing Christina. She read my thoughts and shook her head.

"You'd best be getting on, David. It will be dark early. Have you any idea whether the road is passable?"

"I've got chains – the snow never lies on that road anyway, does it?"

"No. Aeneas will be longing to break the news to you so don't spoil it by telling him you saw me."

Her eyes, amused and compelling, held mine for a second or two and then she saw me to my car, exchanging a word or two with people as she passed.

It was not a happy weekend. The journey was slow and trying. I was haunted by James and by my sense of failure and inadequacy. Rumour had reached Scottish Command about the submerging of my regiment. There seemed little point in my staying in the Army: I seemed to have done what I had to do, none too well, but uncannily successfully, which was embittering. Aeneas had lit fires and paraffin stoves all over my cottage and there was food and drink there (the children and I always amuse ourselves laying in the emergency stores). It was cold and magnificent outside and I could not bear the thought of going away. Aeneas danced about with his secret, choosing his moment to tell me, until I could bear it no longer and dragged it out of him, feigning surprise and incredulity.

"Now the place will be itself again."

"I didn't bargain to have Achranish with Christina."

"It'll be so good for the children."

"So she thinks."

I had privately raged against the manœuvring necessary in the future to prevent their meeting. The innocence or cunning of Aeneas, in his seaman's jersey, smoking his pipe by my fire, infuriated me.

"I'll get Laura to knit you a little round cap with a tassel, Aeneas."

He smoothed his jersey down over his corduroys with a certain pleased self-consciousness.

"Och away, Colonel David. It's convenient here, wearing these. D'ye expect me to wear a baize apron and bring the vegetables to the back door?''

"Perhaps Mrs. Grant will want you to work for her.''

"She'll want her money's worth; I'm too old to give that.''

"I'm still thinking of leaving the Army and coming to live here. I still want to write that play, but it wouldn't be the same with people here.''

"Mistress Kingsley will never want that. She won't come here for a week, let alone years.''

"There mightn't be years and I'm tired.''

"Aye, you have your problems, Colonel David, and Mistress Grant will have hers.''

Aeneas was stately: he disapproved of self-pity.

"I must leave before lunch tomorrow to catch the night train.''

"Aye. I'll bring you two eggs for breakfast if the hens lay this afternoon.''

I took a turn up to Achranish House, never a favourite haunt of mine. It stood high up over the loch, Gothic in style, as uninteresting architecturally as Aberkindle. The low wintry sun made the windows wink blindly; the drive needed weeding and the steps, on which my father had been photographed I remembered, were covered with the droppings of white fantails which, despite the attractions of their dovecot near by, haunted with cooing caresses the massively shut front door. I had never been inside. Looking up at the windows I wondered what James would think.

That night, in my sleeper, Christof, Willi and Ernst came back to me after a peaceful absence: I had been expecting them. Laura complained about my tiredness when I got home.

"Achranish indeed – all that way for a couple of days."

I told her about Christina and she looked thoughtful.

"Goodness knows why she doesn't marry. Is it you she always wanted, David?"

"You don't marry people you've known since their cradles."

"I don't know the statistics."

And she changed the conversation.

The children and I spent our usual fortnight at Achranish and then I was sent to Cyprus and avoided the hazards of Christina and James for two years. When I was first confronted with James he was sixteen.

He walked into the cottage to see me, introducing himself gracefully for his age. We shook hands and liked each other, and from that moment I felt that Christina had given him back to me. I did not see much of her; she was always busy with some scheme and in addition to the flats she energetically rented out, she had paying guests. The stalking was let and the fishing and shooting, except for a little she kept to divert her visitors. It was a new aspect of Christina, whom I had always considered, like all the Fields, a dabbler. She wore corduroy trousers and drove a Land Rover with considerable dash.

"I don't have dinner parties; come in for a drink when you feel like it. You're not on the telephone so I can't ask you specially. James seems to be haunting you. Do you mind? It's good for him to have masculine company in the holidays."

I said gravely that I didn't mind; I could have added various remarks including the fact that Antonia and Mark behaved towards James with all the truculent sulkiness that adolescents are capable of. They had, perhaps, because adopted children have a tightly knotted need of their security, no desire to enlarge the bonds of family life in the holidays. Unlike their contemporaries, while willing sometimes to go to stay with school-friends, they rarely wanted them to stay with us. Achranish was to them sacred to the three of us, with reluctant affectionate backward glances at Laura. They closed up when James came near, invented excuses to be elsewhere, resented the claims he made on my attention and interest. Antonia, now taking her looks seriously, looked down on him for his age and none of James's darting looks of admiration would melt her. Mark, adopting a would-be simple subaltern attitude, was boisterously incredulous about James's grave demeanour and slightly dandified casualness: he talked too much about music and pictures. He was hoping to go up to Cambridge and to go into the Foreign Office. I wondered how he would react to any dissertation of mine on what he had looked like as a small boy and whether the sophisticated surface would ripple. But I was so immensely touched by his evident friendship I had no desire to say anything out of place. It was a relationship I was determined to preserve however the children felt about it. I brought James increasingly into our activities, or, because Antonia and Mark had something else on hand, walked and fished with him or sat about on the rocks watching the dolphins roll in the sun and MacBrayne's weave busily in and out of the islands. Up on the high cliffs, one had a God-like view of a universe for once altogether pleasing. We would lie there in the heather, with the ravens croaking above us, watching that misty panorama of Lismore and Mull and Oban, with the lighthouse glinting in the sun; there was always a sense there of the edge of another world. Curiously, it is a characteristic which I think is shared by the West of Scotland with Greece and Sicily, a sense of another civilisation, of an ancient order of things, of turf worn down by other feet, of unseen bones whitening under immemorial grass and stone. I don't know whether James shared this fully or not; however sophisticated, he was as inarticulate about his feelings as Mark was. But we would be silent together or talk of trivial things in a companionable way; he never demanded anything of me; he assumed with nonchalance that I liked being with him. In fact, he took me for granted in a way that might have annoyed me in someone else, but with him, only confirmed the deep link there was between us. He was tall for his age but it was a well managed height; the chest trouble had left him a little hollow and bony, I thought, but that was passing now. He had very faint eyebrows, dark hair and eyes like Christina. I could see no resemblance to me, but sometimes I did see a look of my parents in him. It is always hard to see oneself mirrored anyway. He was more intelligent than Mark and in a curious way perhaps I minded this. Christina was proud of him in her off-hand way and indeed rather tactless about him.

For the last two years I have been very happy with James; something of the Achranish relationship spilled over into ordinary life. Once or twice I have met him in London and taken him out to lunch and occasionally I have been to his school, at Christina's request (she found it difficult now to get away from the estate), and had long conversations with his housemaster. Nothing could have given me greater pleasure than this. I have had enough sense to keep such meetings from the children and even from Laura who tends invariably to side with them always. Perhaps also my decision to leave the Army and retire to Achranish, giving Laura most of what money I would have, made me feel serene at last. Until I did this, I knew that I should have no lasting respite from my guilt over the three Germans and Andrew. On any level, I felt by now I was a failure, living the charmed life of one who had got by. However competently and successfully I had served, in my own eyes, I had blundered fatally and bloodily. In other ways, more selfishly, I had no taste for the sharp rigours of competition, the endless subtle studying promotion prospects. Aldershot had a whiff or two of the past; one could shut one's eyes in some of those dusty tree-lined avenues of red barracks and quarters and forget Bingo, bedside lamps and the rights of man as interpreted by T.V. But I could never reconcile myself to the fact that the subalterns crouched moodily over the "Box" in Mess ante-rooms and the soldiers disguised as black Italianate teddy boys in the coffee-bars in the High Street were the same stuff as those who sailed with me up the Channel with blackened faces and irresistible confidence. This is a middle-aged man's difficulty.

So I wanted to leave it all, with only the hurdle of telling Laura between me and daily contemplation of the Sound of Mull. Retrospectively, perhaps, I was right in not broaching to her the subject which would have destroyed that tenuous yet soothing relationship between us. She had an armour of self-sufficiency which tempted me to think that she might reconcile herself to a life partly on her own, partly at Achranish. But I had not allowed for events.

In May I was told that I was to be posted to the Allied Services College, with the rank of Major-General. I knew at once that this was something I would like to do and in that pang of recognition and pleasure, the realisation that I was going to have to decide and renounce. There never really was any decision to make: I deluded myself that there was and went to Achranish to think and to see Aeneas who had not been well that winter. He seemed thinner, more brittle and alternated between being irascible and tender — I can think of no better word. I would find him leaning on a gate looking at lambs convulsively sucking their mothers as if he had never seen such a thing before or looking at the deer trooping down through the trees as if he had never cursed them for ruining the bark and the young growth. Other times when he came to tidy up, bring eggs or do the fires and trim the lamps, he would hardly have a word for me and a black silence would descend or he would complain to me that Mark had left a fishing-line snarled and tangled in the bottom of a cupboard and Antonia had thrown tins out into the burn instead of burying them neatly. This kind of grumbling had infinite expressions and in the end was muddled with my boyhood misdemeanours and his grievances of forty years' standing. I should have realised he was a dying man, but better for us both that I didn't.

May was always my favourite month for Achranish and for the first few days it was enfolded in the sunny, still weather of legend and recollection and had all the gold and blue of a cornucopian springtime. I went to dine with Christina, a rare occurrence, because she had acquaintances from the Island staying in one of the flats and some people driving over for the night. Her house had a much-loved air now; the fantails still cooed around the front door and our dinner-table talk was punctuated continuously with the clap of their wings outside the open windows. There were stocks growing in the beds below and their sweetness seemed to blend with the soothing stir of the pigeons. It was a comfortable party: we all knew each other just enough for conversation to be allusive and oblique without being too general or too trivial. The silver shone, there would be a clap of wings, some slight sally of wit, a trembling of candle-flames in the wind. Christina's wine was good; there was a home made pâté, trout fried with almonds, roast lamb and an old-fashioned candied peel tart, rich with rum and butter. Achranish had given Christina back her beauty. It made me ache to look at her, in some black gauzy dress she claimed was years old, with the firelight and candlelight making the familiar line of bone and curve of hair mysterious and shadowing her face with the amber and rose I remembered from our other candlelit evening. She was flirting a little with the men with the teasing audacity she had always excelled at and then sliding into dignified and rather intimidating composure with their wives. We were discussing, as I looked at her with wonder, as I remember, the Scottish face.

"Scones or sheep, I always think," Mrs. Whatever-her-name-was, from the Island, said, "You know, wholesome doughy or that long white shiny look sheep have."

"But they have such historical faces." This was the man from near by. "Go to the Perth Bull Sales or a point-to-point in the Borders or the Northern Meeting, and you'll see any number of Raeburn's and Naismith's. You could put any of them in the dress of any period of history and they'd look right in it, which is more than you can say of us English. It's what puzzled me when we first came to live in Scotland; their faces just didn't fit with the Oxford Street shoppers or the Underground rush and the queues at the cash desks of supermarkets. And then I realised that it's because they are the faces of history."

"Old-fashioned," Christina said smugly.

"Oh no, there's a difference."

"Inbreeding," someone said.

"Whatever it is, I like it," I said.

Christina smiled at me down the length of the table, a smile of complicity and affection. Perhaps it was that smile which made me linger with her till her guests had gone and ignore any suppositions they might make. We stood in the great drawing-room windows; there was the unromantic chug-chug of the electricity plant mingling with the cry of the curlews and oyster-catchers. The pigeons were silent now and a stir of sea wind which rustled through the garden brought with it the scent of the wild yellow azaleas from the shrubbery to add to the sweetness of the stocks below. I told Christina about the milk-white fairy horses of my first night at Achranish; there was something about the light which reminded me. She was amused.

"My old garrons now, I suppose. You were lucky not to be kicked by the stallion — they're shod with spikes for the hill, too. Dear David, you must have been very brave, and you not a horsey man either."

"No, I've been the unhorsed adjutant in my time."

"You might have to ride a horse through the streets of London yet."

"God forbid."

"Do you hear the cuckoos at dawn, David? They seem to fly out to sea each morning — it must be a trick of sound. I wake up and wonder."

I had heard them too, fracturing the first dawn chorus with cool, mocking calls, dying away as they flew as if in chase.

"Are you happy here, Christina?"

"What a question." She put her hand over mine for a

moment. "To have what I always wanted – how could I be otherwise?"

"You may not have wanted it by yourself."

"I have James and I'm used to being by myself."

Mull was now only an indistinct mass in the sky, so streaked and barred with silver and purple clouds that it was difficult to separate it from the sky it had sunk into. The moon was rising, the earth blanching.

"Christina, I love you."

"I know, David. We haven't been very clever with our lives, have we?"

She laid her cheek against mine as we stood there and I put my arms round her. It was as if there were no problems to solve, no knots to untie, only an islanded peace between us.

"Christina, can't we do something about it now?"

She stood, still resting her cheek on mine; an owl hooted and she pressed her fingers against my arm as if to prevent my talking any more. It was as if twenty years had never existed; I was dizzy with a newfound, new-minted love. I brought her face round to mine and kissed her and she was warm and yielding. Then she unfolded herself and slipped from me, went over to the fireplace and lit a cigarette, kicking a log into place as she bent over the fire.

"And that's the end of that, David."

"Will you marry me, Christina? Laura will give me a divorce. There's nothing to keep us together."

"You've never given Laura anything, have you, David? Love or children or your thoughts? She doesn't know what devours you. She's never even come to Achranish to see what you love."

"That's her own fault."

"Why should you give me anything either, David? I'm a demanding woman. And I've learned not to demand what I can't have."

"Christina, I promise you . . ."

"No, no promises. I think I love you, David, but I'm not sure quite how. You were part of my life. You've become part of it again. But it's too late."

I tried to bluster her cheerfully, reasonably, out of the sad set of her face.

"You make it seem so simple and so ordinary, David, and it's neither. You mustn't make it difficult for us both to go on living here."

"I'm trying to make it easier by marrying you."

"And leaving the Army?"

I had told her about the new job.

"I don't have to take the College job."

"Don't you think you might give something to Laura? She's been about the best sort of wife you could have had—everyone says that. I bet the War Office mentioned her when the whole thing was mooted to you—they did, didn't they?"

They had. I nodded.

"It's Laura's reward as well as yours. She'll adore being the queen bee and entertaining and all the foreign parties and saying "No, the General is in Paris till Thursday." It's the least you can do for her, after all those ghastly years in Tidworth and Camberley: having the memsahibs to bridge and wondering how soon your rank would be substantive and not just acting."

"She's never played bridge. I do that."

"Poor girl. Worse and worse. I'm serious, David. You haven't been very generous to Laura."

"We've been quite happy together."

"Sulky, darling? Have some more whisky. We both need it. And then you'd better go, before I start explaining about happiness."

I drove home in a dream of loving Christina; the moon had never shone so brightly nor the sea glinted so brilliantly in its light. There were a hundred scents and sounds in the air. I put the car in its usual place and stood in the cottage garden. There were various aspects of the situation Christina had not mentioned; if Laura divorced me, I should most likely have to resign my commission and certainly would never get the new job. I could not afford to support Laura and Christina and the children. And there was Andrew. I went to bed and woke in a sweat an hour later with the moon blazing on my face and the faceless ones in *feldgrau* leaning on the bottom bed-board.

"All right. So you've come back to remind me — what of? Error, frailty, mortality? Killing people like you or being killed by you is what war is about, or used to be. Two of you knew what went on, anyway. Willi, perhaps, didn't. Which is Willi now? I've forgotten. Ernst and Christof — Nazis both — sinned against certainly, but also sinning. I killed two Nazis, so what? And Andrew. That doesn't make me any less fit to run the Allied Defence College, does it? One must be blooded surely? One cannot be part of the theory of teaching how to kill without some practical experience, my friends. You were part of my experience. Don't grin at me. Just go away and leave me to sleep. It's all a trick of moonlight and fatigue anyway. You're only a trick of light now, how do you like that? You who crouched so hopefully in a coppice once in summer with the larks singing and letters in your pockets and relief due shortly

197

and the distant pound of battle. She was right, that pretty, plump wife of yours, Willi. 'You cannot have killed many men or you would not be so curious.' If it had happened daily, I would hardly have noticed you, except as an entry in the Game Book. But, it only happened once and it killed Andrew. *I* killed Andrew. And I shall have to tell Christina that, if I want to marry her. You've come to remind me of that, haven't you, my unbeautiful tricks of light? if I blink or move my head or pull the curtain, you will vanish, so don't be too arrogant or obstinate, will you?''

But they stayed there and I stared at them and the night wore on and the wind rose and rain spattered on the roof and the skylights and when it was dawn at last, the cuckoos sounded valedictory and admonitory. I wondered whether Christina was listening to them too. Then I fell asleep.

Next day was one of brewing storm and continual rain. When I awoke the day after, it was to the shriek of wind. It was late, but Aeneas had not come up as he usually did, bringing a jug of milk from the cow he shared with two other families. When I went down I could hardly open the front door or stand upright outside. It was a cruel wind, the worse for being so powerful, it had none of the gusty touch of an ordinary high wind, only implacable frontal force of absolute power. As I walked round the cottage, looking to see where tiles had blown off and the orchard and wood full of fallen branches and toppled trees, I thought I had never encountered quite such a wind before. The cottage, fortunately, was not in the path of any tree which might fall, but I eyed one or two of the oaks and beeches with misgiving. After eating some breakfast, I thought I had better find Aeneas and set off across the field by a short-cut. Climbing over the fence I was laid flat on my back like a ninepin: it was a disconcerting experience to be felled silently by the wind like some trick punch by an invisible opponent. In the sheltered crook of the bay several ships were anchored; even so, they did not look too happy. The sea had a churned-up, muddy look as if it had been stirred to its depths. There was a curious silence in the trees and then a whistle and a sibilant rush of hardly audible sound and a tree would come up by its roots and fall cracking down, bringing with it branches and twigs from adjoining trees. New green leaves were scorched with salt spray and hung blackened and limp as if they had been in the path of some fiery frost.

There was nothing ordinary about the walk to Aeneas's cottage; what was beloved and familiar had suddenly assumed a strange disordered aspect, like a rifled room or a friend in some unknown rage. The great trees, admired, respected, were now only menacing and in some almost cataclysmic way, the waterfalls which normally smoked, thundering down the steep, wood-hung cliffs, now stood erect in the air on the cliff tops like pillars. The reversal of natural order is one of the most primitively alarming things in the world. Looking at those formidable pillars of water, I tried to run to Aeneas's cottage. But it was like the dreams of my childhood; heavy-limbed I could only move at a shackled pace.

Aeneas was sitting like a ghost by his fire; trees had fallen near by and had miraculously missed the cottage, but the sea had risen. At first I did not notice the significance of the high-lapping tide.

"I'm no very well the day, David. It's my head and my limbs; some kind of a chill, maybe."

I felt his head, which was burning, and heard his teeth

chatter a little; his eyes were sunk darkly in a face that suddenly seemed semi-transparent.

"Would you take a good look at the sea now for me? It'll be a gey high tide in this storm."

"The waterfalls are standing on end."

"Are they now? It has happened before. I have heard about them and I mind once — but go and look at the water."

It was a beach where marine life was always mixed with the pastoral and woodland; hens foraged in the seaweed and seagulls vied with them for edible scraps; the grass where the shared cow occasionally grazed was fringed with reeds, the dipping branches of alder and willow were washed by the tides. Aeneas's garden hung over a steep bank which gave on to the shore; I could see that one would be thankful for that bank today, although looking along, where the turgid yellow sea now roared over grass and drowned bushes, it seemed flimsy enough as a bulwark. I went back to Aeneas.

"It's a fairly high tide and an odd colour."

"Yellow, is it?"

"In a way."

"Ay, that would be the colour today."

"Have you a thermometer?"

"There's one Jeannie had, maybe, though I put out most of the medicines. I canna remember."

I knew where the medicine chest was and found one and poked it under an unwilling tongue. I was no good with illness. Laura always accused me of being helpless and brusque, as if illness were an unnecessary untidiness. If she or the children were ill, I left them alone, feeling awkward and abashed, as if my feet and hands were too large and my voice too loud. I could hardly bear to sit with my mother when she was ill, even when she was dying. It seemed to me that one should be allowed to be ill alone in proper privacy. As for hospital visiting, I have had to go and see my men, of course, sometimes, but the mutual embarrassment has helped visits to be short and formal. Even I could see Aeneas was ill. Mrs. McDonald, the shepherd's wife, was as far in another direction as my cottage was and next door to her were the other McDonalds and the wife was in hospital in Fort William. When I took the thermometer out, I was appalled by his temperature.

"I'm going back to get the car and take you to Christina."

"There's no call for you to be doing that, David. It's just a wee sort of chill I've caught."

I made him some hot milk and put coal on the fire. It was all very well for me to talk about getting the car, but I could see all the difficulties; I could also see the water creeping up along the grassy margins of the beach. This was no place to be left in any state of health.

The walk back was easier because for some of the time I was not facing into the wind, but nevertheless it was difficult to be sure from what direction the wind was coming. It was morning, but there was a timeless murk, the light was opaque and shadowy.

I cleared fallen branches from the entrance to the shed where I kept the car and drove it out through the gate, feeling it lift and lurch in the silent gusts that shook it. Sometimes there was a convulsive jerk and I expected it to be blown on its side or upside down, but the balance held; down across the field path, sticking once in the sodden grass with a fearful scream of whizzing tyres; I had brought sacks with me and eventually extricated it. Then I could not get the gate open and it was a long fight, during which my arm was almost broken. By the time I drove the car triumphantly through, all my bones ached with effort and tension. There was then the gauntlet of trees to be run. I tried not to think of their falling while being alert to the danger; it seemed to take an age to pass under the dark avenue and then as I turned the corner, by a bruised stretch of bluebells, I could hear above the racing engine the whistle and rustle, the sucking up of a great tree by the roots, the fierce plucking as by a giant, the convulsive final lift before the crash to earth. I put my foot on the accelerator, almost overturned the car as it hit the ruts too fast and the tree came down just behind me. I could feel that cold, sick, dizzy lurch of relief as I broke out in sweat at the escape and then realised that, on the other hand, I was now trapped with Aeneas on the wrong side of the tree. I stopped the car and went back to test the tree's weight. It was immovable by me. I drove down to the cottage, whirling various plans in my head.

"I've been dozing here, David and dreaming. It's very cold. How's the sea?"

It was much nearer and made my only coherent plan for rescuing Aeneas the more improbable. Round the curve of the cove, leading down to a now disused boathouse was a track going up through the trees. It might just be passable by a car and would bring us out the other side of the fallen tree, but to reach the track meant driving along the sea's edge and whether one would get sufficiently firm sand was unlikely. I packed a small case rapidly with some odds and ends of Aeneas's and closed and bolted the shutters, providently outside the windows. Then I went down to the beach to investigate. Fate seemed with me; the tide had come in high at both arms, but the stretch between the cottage and the boathouse, though licked and splashed, was still the sand and not the grass.

"Come on, we're going by another route." I explained about the tree, while bundling him up in rugs.

"Ye're just raving mad, David. The waves will catch us and you'll lose your car."

"So what? It's our only chance."

"I could just go to bed with a dram or two and you could wait with me. There's enough food for us both and a bottle."

His words came with difficulty and ran into one another as they do when one is tired. I practically carried him into the car and felt as feverish as he did as I started the engine and turned the car down towards the boiling sea. The waves were enormous now and hurled great stones and clattering showers of stone and shingle landwards. I worked out a technique of letting a wave crash, then racing forward as it was sucked back, then pausing as another came, to take the brunt motionless. The sand was hard and the thrown shingle helped; there were a few times when I thought the waves particularly engulfing and the engine stopped once, flooded, I feared, but started miraculously. Eventually we reached the boathouse. The track seemed narrower, rougher and steeper than I had remembered. I left the car at the bottom, behind the boathouse and ran up to clear away branches and rolled stones. With one great strained run I brought the car up on to the road. Never had its potholes, fissures and great central belt of grass seemed smoother or more welcome.

The rest of the journey was by no means easy but after the shore all seemed possible. We met the full fury of the wind occasionally as if it paused in its task of universal devastation to frolic cruelly with a trifle like a car. No trees blew down in our path and we managed to skirt branches. I stopped at the first cottages to see whether all was well with them and the children there and to explain about Aeneas in case anyone went to find him and to tell about the tree across the road; one boat had broken from its moorings and vanished; a sheep or two had been blown to death, a stag had been hurled off a crag, but the children were safe and rejoicing in no school and the excitement. A great deal of Christina's drive had been washed away and a torrential stream channelled down the gravel. Aeneas had been silent all through the journey, closing his eyes sometimes, sighing a little, moving his hands restlessly in his lap; as we drove up he stretched out one hot trembling hand and touched mine on the steering wheel.

"You're a good man, David."

Christina was at the door as I drove up looking anxious and about to launch on her tale of disasters when I explained about Aeneas. She had him out of the car and into bed with hot-water bottles and aspirin before I had time to explain any more. The telephone wires were down, but the doctor from fifteen miles away was expected because the lodge-keeper's mother was due for an injection and it was his day. Someone was despatched to the lodge with instructions that any car bound eastwards was to be stopped and the message reinforced.

"Do you think I ought to go for the doctor?"

"It's not life and death. 'Flu and a high temperature; I can cope. I've various things here; one can't keep expecting Dr. MacLean to come this far all the time. Don't worry, I'll manage. But don't go back, I need a man here. The chimney on the north side is going to fall any moment and I can't bear the suspense."

Christina had her swashbuckling look; the crash of masonry was an imaginary terror. She went off to Aeneas again and then we toured the outside of the house perilously to check on the state of things. There were trees down, slates shivered into black splinters on the path, climbing roses had been torn off the walls and lay straggled on the ground, a window had been blown out, the fantails were invisible and silent in the dovecot.

The rest of the day passed nervously. There was a message brought by a breathless boy that one of the bridges on the only road out had collapsed under the combined forces of the high tide and a swollen stream; now the doctor could not come. But I had growing confidence in Christina's ability, watching her deal with the cases that came to her for first-aid in the course of the day. She dealt calmly with every emergency, marshalled her men to do what was immediately necessary on the estate and found time to look after Aeneas's needs. The gale did not abate at all; we could get no weather forecasts because the wireless, which at the best of times was fickle, was now completely silent. The sea came on and on, swallowing tongues of land, crumbling banks, throwing up pieces of wreckage.

But eventually, the tide turned and that was comforting. Almost one believed that the entire natural world was disordered but at least the waters eventually receded, snarling, amber and opaque. One grew accustomed to the alternate silence and roar, to the crash of things falling, to the pauses broken by the agitated murmur of birds and the hysterical bleating of lambs on the hill, to the howling of Christina's dogs which bayed continuously at the weather.

But by early evening there were signs that the storm was abating a little.

Christina and I had a moment to relax. We took our whisky to the drawing-room fire, which burned uneasily and smokily. The day had stripped me a little; anxiety over Aeneas, the journey, the storm, forages into the fields to gather up injured sheep: I was exhausted and unnerved. Christina looked untouched by it all. The whisky was, I suppose, my final undoing.

"Christina, you will marry me?"

She looked startled at my vehemence and shook her head.

"For James's sake."

"James?"

"After all, he is our son."

Watching her, it was as if she did not at first grasp what I had said. She looked unmoved and then suddenly all her colour went and came again in a mounting flush.

"What on earth do you mean, David?"

I was impatient with her, impelled by whisky and fatigue to be clumsy.

"James — of course he's our son. That's why you married Andrew. Though why, for God's sake, I've never known. I wanted to marry you. You didn't tell me about James. It's taken me years to forgive you for that."

She stood up.

"I married Andrew because I was in love with him. And James is his son. You must be mad or drunk."

"You married Andrew in a hurry because you were having a baby."

She strode over to me and slapped my face hard.

"You fool, David. Oh, I'm sorry. No, I'm not sorry, not at all. Wake up, sober up. James is Andrew's son."

"You married Andrew only two weeks after that weekend."

"I was in love with him for weeks before that."

"You can't have been. You were mine then."

"Oh no, David. We'd been passing that dreary autumn together, amusing ourselves. That weekend was the logical conclusion. I couldn't get out of it, could I? Not after all we'd had of our lives together. It didn't seem fair to you. You were so unhappy and muddled. But I'm afraid I wasn't honest with you."

"James is our son."

"For heaven's sake, stop shouting. He isn't."

"You can't prove it. He was born too soon to have been Andrew's."

"Well, I suppose I could go into a lot of clinical details as to why I know he's Andrew's; I could give you two reasons why I know he isn't yours anyway—you must have thought me a naïve simpleton willing to take risks with you. Be your age. *And* he was born early for a number of reasons I don't propose to go into either. David, don't be a fool. I loved Andrew."

She was in a white and crimson passion by then, spitting her words at me, destroying everything like the wind outside. The dogs, excited by raised voices, woke up and began to howl again in the hall.

"I killed Andrew. Did you know that? I hated him and I killed him. Now I'm glad for the first time."

She was leaning on the mantelpiece after her tirade, now she swung round to me again and her eyes flashed.

"I *know* how Andrew was killed. He was ambushed. You weren't there. Oh, David, for heaven's sake. I can't take any more."

I tried to touch her hand but she withdrew it fiercely.

"I don't mean I shot him, but it was my fault he was ambushed."

"David," she said and she looked hard at me. "David, tell me."

She sat beside me and took my hand in what seemed an odd maternal gesture. I told her everything, the story I had never told anyone properly before and she went on holding my hand, with the tears pouring down her face.

"My poor Andrew. My poor David," she said. "How terrible for you all these years. But it wasn't wilful, just a chain of events."

"That doesn't alter the blame. I've tried to rationalise it all too, believe me. But in the end I know I was wrong."

"My dear David. I don't think anyone can judge you who wasn't involved. The people who were involved, the ones in action beside you, who knew what those days in Normandy were like, *they* didn't blame you. Isn't that what counts? Who are we to judge?"

"I can judge myself."

"Oh no, my dear, none of us can do that, mercifully perhaps."

"No one knew about my hanging round those men I'd killed, except my driver and he probably thought all officers a rum lot anyway. It was *that* which killed Andrew, because I was so het-up eventually I forgot what I should have known, that it *was* an ambush and there would be others to replace them."

"You couldn't have guessed the timing. No one might have relieved them for hours. That was bad luck and that was what killed Andrew, that and a German's bullets. Don't forget those. Do you think there's some good family man

who wonders sometimes as he drives his Volkswagen down
the autobahn about the young man he shot down on some
quiet road in June? Guilt isn't something absolutely personal. It's the sins of the world, David, that we pray are
taken away.''

"Not me. That's an easy way out."

"No, I suppose not you, David; you never thought of
going to a priest, did you?"

"No."

"Poor, arrogant, deluded David."

She mopped her eyes and lit a cigarette and splashed
some whisky blindly into our glasses.

"I've never told anyone, except Aeneas, a little."

"Not Laura?"

"No."

Christina sighed and closed her eyes.

"You have been terrible to Laura, haven't you?"

"I've spared her. She would have agonised over it all."

"You don't know much about loving. You never did. Do
they still haunt you, those Germans?"

"Sometimes; when I'm tired or worried."

She nodded.

"I'm sorry you thought I'd married Andrew for con-
venience. That hurts. I loved him terribly and I've never
stopped missing him. Perhaps it wouldn't have worked. I
was years older than he was for one thing—but while it
lasted it was perfect. That's why I was so angry about James.
David, dear, I can forgive you anything but thinking that."

Even at that moment with both of us tearing truth to the
bone, I did not believe her. If she had been in love with
Andrew, it was natural that she could not bear to think
either that she had deceived him or that he was not his son.

There are some things one cannot even permit oneself to believe. Christina for all her courage and honesty, could not face that. I did not blame her, but I was filled with compassion for her, lonely, vulnerable, deluded as she was.

"Christina, I'm sorry for everything and I love you."

She said, "Yes," almost absent-mindedly.

"You're not listening."

"Yes, I am. Do you know I think the wind's dropping. I think we should go and see Aeneas and I want to go and look at the bridge before it's dark. We'll go in the Land Rover — I want to know how bad that flood is. If it's not too bad some of the men might start repairing it before the tide comes in again, but it depends."

"I said I loved you."

She leaned over me and put her cheek against mine, as she had done two nights ago. (Had it only been two nights ago?)

"Come along, David. The bridge. It's you who isn't listening."

No conversation is ever quite thorough enough, perhaps fortunately. One may rehearse what one says, but then is completely thrown by unexpected answers. Sometimes I had imagined such a conversation with Christina, but it had not proceeded as our recent one had. There was a great deal that hadn't been said. There was a great deal I had wanted to say about James and fatherhood and my feelings, but Christina had left me no room for emotional expansion or manœuvre.

The storm abated, the bridge was repaired, Aeneas recovered (although in a way it was an illness which weakened him and made way for the end) and my leave finished, but the conversation was not re-opened. We had given each other a new and disconcerting view of ourselves and I thought that perhaps we had better get used to it for a while.

There was evidence of the storm everywhere, but when the sun shone and the sea was calm again, one could hardly believe in the force that had battered us so ruthlessly. Our conversation seemed part of that storm.

V

LAURA

SHE WATCHED David settle into his book again, almost
before the train left Limoges station. There was no one else
in the carriage and they had spread themselves and their
possessions as comfortably as possible. It was an old-
fashioned train with upholstery that looked like horsehair,
stiff, black and shiny. She expected the backs of her legs to
be tickled by protruding hairs. There were always horsehair-
stuffed chairs and sofas in the farms she had visited with her
grandfather, where they had drunk strong yellowish tea and
eaten light cakes with bilberry jam and she had listened to
the talk and studied the china or the books on the glass-
fronted shelves. She had been very young then with thin,
tender legs which disliked the prickly chairs; people made
jokes about her legs and the possibilities of her falling down
gratings. On visits to the town she would avoid shops with
bars covering their basement openings, peering down at the
litter of old paper, sweet wrappings and orange peel with
revulsion, and dread that her legs would break or give way,
precipitating her on to the greasy black pavements daubed
with old men's spittle and phlegm and the chalkmarks of
ancient hopscotch games. On country walks she never gave
her legs a thought. What curious things one has feared in
one's life; fumbling one's way along an endless chain of
terrors from the dark to the Bomb and the tomb.

David always said that she was an ostrich because she

would not go and see war films or discuss nuclear warfare at a dinner table. But she was not afraid of illness and death, only of unhappiness and loneliness. John and she had a passion for cemeteries and churchyards, especially in France, where they would spend hours marvelling at the macabre variety of French memorial invention; the railings, photographs, tumble-down shrines, pink and purple plastic flowers, domed immortelles, flowery inscriptions, plaster images, writhing statuary, movable plaques saying 'Regrets'. She had tried to buy one of these for John; it would have had, they thought, many uses, propped against old photographs, failed masterpieces, closed doors. 'Regrets.' There had been one churchyard where she had stayed for hours while John sketched (for an oil later) the old woman who was custodian. It was one of his successful portraits, 'Françoise Leroux'. She could summon up the face and John's representation of it now, the strength of cheek and jaw bone, the knowing yet compassionate eyes and mouth, the fall of iron-grey hair over yellowing skin with its powerful lines of piety and endurance. '*Le Rembrandt de nos jours*' she had heard one cynical woman say in front of it at some gallery, but the Tate had bought it; a plume, as David would say. The old woman had not cared for it, had not perhaps managed to focus properly on it, but John was generous to his models; a few hours' sitting daily in the sun was perhaps the easiest money she had ever earned, with the tombstones in the background and a framework of wrought iron about her as she sat, kerchiefed and implacably good-humoured, the keeper of the dead. Laura had learned every inscription practically by heart and pondered on their significance; she had sat and read her book in various sunny patches, had listened to the sweet chestnuts falling in the adjacent woods and the pattering, scurrying dry leaves with the complacency of one alive, with lunch to look forward to and a lover near by. She had felt smug in that September sunshine, Laura remembered, smug that love lasted and was renewed and that there were three more days before she need return to Germany. John worked quickly and confidently, ignored her while he painted, yet liked to have her about; she watched his stocky, sturdy legs planted before the easel, with sensual pleasure, remembering their strength against hers. This golden oasis of autumn was what she would remember when she was back in Germany, discussing the girls in the Naafi and the shortcomings of batwomen with other wives, when she waited for David to form the next word in 'Scrabble', when she woke, dry-mouthed in the night from some tormenting dream. She thought of herself sometimes as a hoarder, hardly able to roll the present upon her tongue for anticipation of how it would enrich, how seem, in the future. Recollection and anticipation, that had been the stuff of life and now there was to be only recollection, the dwindling of capital, the tarnishing of treasure.

The day after she had gone to London to quiz people about David's new appointment, she had tried to telephone John three or four times, frustratingly. Antonia had been with her; they had been shopping for her trousseau in Farnham. She had left Antonia in fitting-rooms, safely unclothed, while she went to find a call-box and there was never a reply even from Mrs. Malcolm. The feeling of martyrdom had begun already: she was choked with the charred smoke from the kindling.

"Choking white smoke," she had said aloud.

"Tom kitten and Anna-Maria with her rolling pin," said

Antonia. "How gorgeous to read them to one's children. It was always Daddy who read them to us."

"He adores Beatrix Potter."

"Well, don't sound so acid. Why not? Aren't you looking forward to your grandchildren? Don't look so prim. Of course you are. Jack and I hope to trade on your grandmaternal affection and park them with you frequently."

Her immediate reaction had been that John would not care for it and then she remembered that in her martyred future this was immaterial. David would be safely back at Peter Rabbit and Tabitha Twitchit again. He would enjoy them more than *Lolita*. In the afternoon it was impossible to telephone without Antonia hearing; she had finally sent her out with some letters kept from Brownlow while she sent a telegram. There had originally been some doubt about what day she would come to London that week. John rang up in the evening, which he only did in emergency or knowing she was alone.

"Why the drama, honey?"

"What about a fitting on Thursday? I'd like it as soon as possible."

"I get you loud and clear. It's not a good day but lunch would be O.K."

"Why not?"

"Oh, things, things. I'll expect you."

She hated it when he rang off abruptly, unlovingly.

"Mummy, you didn't tell me you were having a dress made. Have you got a new place? You are a meanie not to tell."

"Surprise, surprise," she had said mechanically and suggested a drink.

David was sitting looking exhausted upon the sofa, she

remembered, surrounded by papers, and it had taken a minute or so for him reluctantly to swim up to the surface and find the sherry and the gin. She had a pang of compunction about her manipulation of him. He rarely came home these days without a bulging briefcase; it was worse than the War Office. It was that fearful conscientious honesty that made him work so hard and no doubt that could be blamed for the looming new appointment. He had always cared for the Army, for his men, more than for his family. That was what one faced, in the end, with all men; one would never be first. (Perhaps that was another warning she should give Antonia; priority passes.) But when people had praised him, as they had, yesterday, in her London conversations, she realised again that David was a good man. It did not help.

She had felt completely detached from herself as she made her way on Thursday to John's studio. It was hot and there was a relaxed feeling in London as if everything had been let go; lackadaisical punching of tickets, slow-motion buses, unattended paper-stalls, women in beach dresses in Oxford Street, shop doors stood open and customers swam in and out in long, endless currents. Gushes of old warm air issued from Underground entrances, spent phrases circulated at bus stops, cigarettes dangled, dusty feet shuffled. She waited, exhausted by the day already, for a taxi. There was an old man with a flower basket beside her. "Buy a flower, lady, lovely corsage." She was amused by the word and his pronunciation and turned to look at the white gardenias, then shook her head. It would not be appropriate to be decked for the sacrifice.

"Tell yer what, lady, I'll give you one, for your pretty face. I'll give you one."

He shuffled round in front of her; vanity and manners prevented her from refusing and walking on.

"Have you got a pin, dear? I'll find one."

He took one out of his greasy jacket and then held the flower against her dress.

"Now you've got to have it pinned firmly like, haven't you?" And he thrust his dirty hand inside her dress to secure the pin or with the illusion of doing so. She felt trapped and enraged, with the fear of not making a scene in public uppermost. He leered beerily at her as his fingers scrabbled about in her bosom.

"Don't want to prick you now, do I, lady? Wouldn't do at all."

She stood rigid with loathing and anger.

"There, lady, good luck to you."

"How much is it?"

"Well that depends on what you want to give me, doesn't it, pin and all?"

She threw him half a crown as the taxi drew up and could not rid herself of the feel of his fumbling fingers still pressing her. It was absurd. Anyone else would have got rid of him in a second or two; she was doomed to suffer every nuisance, to listen to every confidence, to be needlessly involved, because she never registered situations in time. Antonia laughed at her over this always.

"Poor old Mum. It's a marvel the white-slavers haven't got you years ago. You're such a sucker."

On John's doorstep she still trembled. Mrs. Malcolm let her in.

"What a pretty flower now that is. What do you call them?"

She unpinned it and gave it to her thankfully.

"Where's Mr. Ledcombe?"

"He's got someone sitting for him, a bus conductress, black, quite black, but he's very excited about the picture, only she will talk and you know he doesn't like that. I mean she goes on and on. Anyway, her sitting's nearly up. Which reminds me, what does the enemy say?"

She looked at Laura's watch.

"I must fly, Mr. Ledcombe didn't tell me you were coming to lunch till this morning and there's not much to eat, but I've washed a lettuce and there's some cheese and eggs, I suppose. Goodbye, dear, be good."

She was gone with a bang of the door. Laura, at the window, could see her sniffing the gardenia as she trotted down the street. There was still a sound of voices from the studio and she felt suddenly shy of disturbing them, so she went into the kitchen and began assembling a lunch tray and finding the sherry. There were odds and ends of china in the cupboard which she and John had bought occasionally for the future house; she touched them lingeringly and affectionately while she hard-boiled some eggs. Then she heard the sounds of leave taking, John's quick, light voice, the deep, throaty voice of the woman.

"You didn't come and meet her. She's gorgeous — bitter chocolate, shiny, rich."

She put her arms round him.

"Do you love me?"

"Yes, yes, yes." He kissed her. "Let's have some sherry, I'm tired. Come and sit down."

She looked at the canvas on the easel; it was going to be good.

"What are you doing as a background? Notting Hill railings and dustbins? Or the cheerful backside of a bus?"

"Come and sit down, Laura. You make me restless standing there being smart. What's bitten you today?"

"The heat, perhaps."

It was hot in the studio where there was never much ventilation. The smell of paint and turpentine, the beloved smell, made her feel sick. She told John about the flower seller.

"So *that's* what's wrong. Some lascivious old man puts his hand down your dress in Oxford Street. *How* old are you, Laura?"

"It's all very well to laugh at me, but I loathed it and he looked as if he were expecting me to like it, as if I'd *pay* him for doing it."

"Now drink up your sherry and don't get so het-up or you'll be hotter still." He paused. "In a way, I'm sorry you came today. I have to see a client this afternoon."

"A client? You mean you're going to do a commissioned portrait? Good heavens, wonders will never cease. A lot of lovely lolly, I hope!"

"Quite a lot; and she's beautiful. It's Anna Reynolds."

"But she keeps on being painted. I wonder she has the time between matinees and evenings and film studios at 5 a.m. What a life! But how nice for you. However did she get round you?"

"I met her at a party."

"Oh, whose? I never thought you ever went to that sort of party."

He smiled faintly.

"I do sometimes. It was a very stagey party. You wouldn't know the people who gave it. I'm going round to her flat to look at dresses and jewels."

"But Thursday's our usual day. I never – I mean – ,"

She felt suddenly confused and looking at John saw her confusion reflected in him.

"Ah well, I suppose one can do nothing about a Royal Command."

"I don't know why we're drinking sherry in this heat, Vermouth would be better or gin and tonic. I suppose it's habit."

"Like Thursdays."

"How did it start being Thursday? Was there a cheap day trip?"

"I suppose so."

Laura wondered whether she had made up her mind; had she come with a problem or a decision? She wanted to talk about it, get it over, but she kept postponing the words.

"John, could we sit somewhere else? It's stifling in here."

"Of course, the sitting-room's cooler. Let's go there, or do you want to eat now? We ought to perhaps."

He looked at his watch.

"All right."

She did not like the idea of signing away love over egg mayonnaise, but there was always some banality to trip one up. They ate in the window, with the trolley between them, as they had done many times, but he was too far away this time to hold her hand as usual. Outside, the roofs and chimneys swam in a hazy pattern and the tops of the trees below them were spiralled in dancing, sun-flecked dust. It had been almost as hot in France in May. John had been lent a house in the south; they had been lazily domestic for ten days, letting the sun thaw their winter bones in the tiny, flagged courtyard by the rustling bamboos. From the bedroom window, where the sun poured thickly in the mornings, was a prospect of red roofs, balconies, tiny terraces, flower-bedecked, a quarter of a palm tree, a third of a stone-pine and a wedge of vineyard. Laura had enjoyed sleepily fitting in the pattern to her waking consciousness, like a jig-saw puzzle. It had been a noisy village, where conversations and imprecations died away at midnight to be renewed at dawn, where cocks crew seemingly all night and carts clattered and bicycles chugged as soon as it was light, not to mention the church bells which punctuated the darkness with a sound of doom.

"It was as hot as this in France," John said. She wondered why she was surprised that he was thinking of France at the same moment. Her mouth was dry; she crumbled her bread and then went on recklessly working it into pellets, knowing that John was watching her.

"What is it, Laura?"

"Oh, nothing. I'm just not hungry."

"I am. Cut me some bread, will you, and I'll have some more salad."

The bread-saw slipped and grazed her thumb, until the unexpected blood soaked the piece of bread she was holding.

"Not that one, even for you, Laura. Can you cut another, or shall I?"

She cut another and absent-mindedly thumb-marked it again with blood.

"Laura, you *are* dreaming."

"You keep calling me, Laura. It makes me feel like someone different."

"Well, I do call you Laura sometimes. Hell, why not, It's a good name for you."

"You didn't like it once."

She sucked her thumb.

"How stupid of me. One changes."

"Have I changed?"

She felt she must squeeze this situation dry before changing it. She could not leave things alone; soon they would be beyond retrieving. The question, inevitably, sounded coquettish; he did not look at her but went on studiously taking the skin from a slice of tomato.

"I have too. Yes, I suppose you have some grey hairs and wrinkles; I've never thought them unbecoming. I like older women's faces, anyway, to paint."

"Except for Anna Reynolds."

"Oh, for God's sake, Laura." He gave the trolley a push so that it rolled away with all the crockery jangling.

"Is that why you're behaving so oddly? I thought you had more sense. Anna Reynolds is just someone I'm hoping to paint. I've only met her twice. She's young and extraordinarily beautiful and I hope I can do a good portrait."

She had never been jealous before of anyone John painted, of his friends, of his life away from her; she had schooled herself into not minding, into drawing a protective veil over her curiosity and possessiveness. But at this last moment, she minded and was prepared to quarrel, be undignified, behave badly.

"How many sittings are you planning to have? Is it true she has a chaperone always, or is it a duenna — I forget what the dividing line is?"

John seemed not to hear.

"I'm going to have an exhibition in New York this autumn."

"You will be able to tell your girl-friends the precise shade of red that hair is and what rinse she uses. New York? John, why New York?"

"Never done it before. My gallery here has a new tie-up with one there and suggested it."

"Another take-over bid? I thought you and Fauntless were sacrosanct."

"It's not a take-over bid. It's a rational leaselend affair."

"Oho!"

"So I shall be in the States for about six weeks – maybe more. I want to go and look up some friends in New England."

"And see the maple and dogwood – and your wife."

"She's in San Francisco and she's not my wife now."

"You didn't tell me. I thought you were both being so civilised about not invoking the law in your arrangements."

"She got a divorce five years ago."

"Why didn't you tell me?"

"It hardly seemed relevant."

"But, darling, I thought everything was relevant."

"Did you?"

Laura lit a cigarette and wheeled out the trolley. It seemed important to pause, to gather strength. When she came back, John was sitting on the sofa and he pulled her down beside him.

"Darling," he said, "why are we quarrelling? We never have. What's upset you so much? I wanted you to be excited about New York – and even about Anna Reynolds. Is it the wedding that's bothering you?"

She let him kiss her. Perhaps it would be easier to go away and not come back. But she pulled herself away from him.

"John, I can't soften the words. I'm afraid I've news about David. He's being given some new job and being promoted. It's a special job and they're fussy about wives and divorce."

224

"And you've always wanted to know what it feels like to be a General's wife? Well, what is worrying you? That's not going to change anything unless you think M.I.5 is going to shadow you on Thursdays."

"John, I always thought — well — with Antonia married . . ." a fearful shyness seized her. All at once she felt she was talking to a stranger, not to John with whom for years there had been endless discussions about plans, houses, decoration schemes, money; the sessions of the Steering Committee he had always called it. Her voice had an imploring note: she recognised it with horror.

"My dear Laura, you have always wanted to have your cake and eat it. Face facts. Why stop having the best of both worlds now?"

"I — I've never wanted that, but it was never possible before."

"Well, it doesn't look as if it's very possible now. Cheer up, Laura darling. We'll have a lovely little trip somewhere when I come back from the States and the wedding's over."

"The wedding is in early October."

"Oh, yes, of course. Well, I hope to be back before Christmas. We might try the delights of Paris again, do our Christmas shopping."

"And what are your plans for next year?"

"None yet, but this portrait commission gives me ideas, if it's any good."

"So the idea of living in France isn't very practicable."

"Holidays, yes; not otherwise, perhaps yet."

"I see."

"You are behaving oddly, today, darling. It must be the heat, what with obsessions about old men assaulting you and now a sort of huffy cross-examination."

She ached to say, "Do you love me?" or to go over in loving close detail every aspect of their relationship and its promise of permanence, but pride prevented her, a diffidence about cornering any human being (let alone the fluid John), a smell of fear. So she smiled instead.

"Dear John, I'd better go and leave you to your appointment. You're right, it's the heat and I'm tired over wedding plans and having to face moving afterwards."

"Where is this college place; Surrey, isn't it? Oh well, not too bad. You'll be very grand. Perhaps David would like his portrait painted."

"He would be so appalled; I can hardly get him to a passport photographer's."

She saw a faint contrition flicker over John's face at her brisk tones and pursued the advantage.

"I'm proposing to do a last crawl round a sale or two. That's why I wanted to come up this week. Darling, I'll let you know. Things are a little hectic. I don't think I'll be able to manage coming for a while."

Before the protestations, she caught the glimmer of relief. John took her in his arms; she could feel herself melting as always, warm, safe, stirred to rapture.

"It's a pity you have to go," he said.

"Yes, don't come down. I'll let myself out. You've never been keen on poker, have you, darling?"

She caught the first train back that she could. Waterloo had a mid-afternoon look that was unfamiliar, no music, a few lost soldiers.

* * * * *

Trains, like this one in France, moving through the rain-soaked umber and burnt sienna of autumn, deadened reality.

The forlornness of cattle huddled under trees, of horses in the lee of a hedge, heads down to the streaming weather, chimed with her mood, but were pictures only. There were patches of sunflowers, absurdly tall and peering, ridiculously gay and golden. Occasionally, there was a farm or the blur of a village, but they whisked past. "There is a book who runs may read" . . . of childish misreadings and misconceptions the most vivid for her; a book mounted on wheels like some speedy sandwich-boards moving with impetus down endless streets pursued breathlessly and unavailingly by a frantic child. Sometimes everything seemed to have been contained as in this speeding book, a leaf half-discernible, half-turned, tantalisingly always the same distance ahead, however hard one pursued it. She closed her eyes, lulled by the rocking train, but seeing still the speeding images of her life.

"There is a book who runs may read": mint imperials sucked through sermons remembered as interminable, whether that was due to childhood or Wales, hymn-singing not as great in depth or emotion as in the chapel up the other end of the village: was it Hermon or Bethesda, sermons not as marked by the 'hwyl' as there, mostly in Welsh, however, with a few explanations thrown in in English for her benefit and one or two other strays. 'Old Marvellous' she had christened the rector because he was given to superlatives, both about Zion and the trout he caught in the local streams. He had married her; his rich voice picking its way through the English service, protracting the vowels, giving an air of exotic mystery to familiar words. His sermon was full of hyperbole and rhetoric since the theme of love was lure to his heady vocabulary. She felt David tremble beside her and had tried to smile at him to reassure him but he never looked at her, only with a fixed face at 'Old Marvellous' about whom he had been warned, but obviously not enough.

"I don't think I heard a word," he had said afterwards when taxed. Laura had heard but it was like background music: the words were beautiful but had no relevance to David and her and what they were doing in church. It was just something going on at the same time. Perhaps if it had not been 'Old Marvellous' and they had not had afterwards a series of disastrous Army padres, David and she might have been more faithful churchgoers. "And that is an excuse like all the others," she said fiercely to herself. She had not thought of Humphrey Griffiths, the Rector, for years. When she had been back with the children at Plas Newydd, *that* time, there was the new man, whom she associated only with her grandfather's funeral; a young man, stiff of neck, wearing his hair *en branche*. She remembered John's mirth at this description of hers; he slapped his knees in a curious old-fashioned way and his head shook when he laughed. Perhaps he had got used to her jokes, perhaps one laughed less anyway when older. They had both been so young then, though she thought of herself as a mature matron; they had been young enough to have scruples, principles, diffidences.

The trouble is that one cannot learn to accept, that is the hard part of being young: the world is manageable, fate flexible. Their childlessness, that had to be fought, there had to be some answer, some out-manœuvring. The kind of person David was, in so far as she ever knew, the measure of love and interest he could mete out to her, that she had not accepted, but had wilfully out-manœuvred. The remedy in both cases had been oblique only.

"I have been marginal always," she said, opening her eyes.

"What did you say?" David did not look up from his book.

"I was thinking aloud. There's a tremendous commotion in the corridor. What do you think it is?"

"Oh, just some French fuss."

If only David had been cruel to her, it would have been some justification, but he had been dispassionately considerate always. That coolness, discerned with pleasure in her mother-in-law, had certainly descended to David. Perhaps even in the beginning she had been mistaken in the ardour of her love for him which crammed the whole world into a fiery ball of passion for him, in the degree of his involvement with her. She had been so afraid that the intensity would fade, that childlessness would wither the marriage. Age had been kinder to David than to John: his mop of hair was grey, John was fair and sparsely stranded: David's face had deepened, lines had become crevasses and fissures, John's had grown fatter. David had the ability to sit motionless, rapt in reading or thought; John was restless with twitching hands; he could only be absorbed at his easel.

She looked at him, wishing he were a stranger and then out of the window.

"David, my God, look!"

The railway line was now skirting a river and a river in flood, not just water brimming over the banks and spreading over the meadows in great pools, but pounding brown water seeking every outlet for itself, bearing all before it. As she looked she saw a dog floating on its back, four stiff paws in the air, then a sheep, two cows, borne downwards, not with the grandeur of their size in death, but as two clumsy carcases buffeted against every obstacle, rushed hither and

229

thither like twigs in a stream. There were ominous planks of wood too and henhouses, great branches of trees. Above the train noise one could hear the muffled roar of the river. The corridor resounded to crescendoes of discussion, ejaculation, apprehension.

"Quite a flood," David said. "I seem to be storm-prone: Achranish and now here."

"You didn't tell me about Achranish."

"Of course I did. There was a gale, like the tail-end of a hurricane. You couldn't have been listening, or you've forgotten."

"You said the weather had been bad, not too good, you possibly said, David, do you think this train's safe? The embankment might crumble."

"If there were any danger they'd stop the train."

"Well, our neighbours seem a little disturbed. They might have told us in Paris or Limoges. Perhaps that's what everyone was murmuring about."

Laura sat back and looked at the river again. There was something unnaturally cosy about being swept past disaster, even though it looked indeed, at the moment, as if disaster was keeping up with them. But here they were in the train, with labelled luggage and comforts for the journey. How long could one remain safe with that outside? At any moment she could see in slow-motion, the embankment subside with a sigh, their train topple over and the water engulfing them, hissing on hot metal, blanketing them in clouds of scalding steam.

"David, do you think we should pull the communication cord?"

"Don't be silly. There are trained personnel sizing up the situation."

230

She started to laugh, immoderately, rather hysterically, while he raised his eyebrows, smiling at her.

"It's just that bloody silly phrase, trained personnel. I see the French as delicious amateurs, all stroking their moustaches now and pondering."

"I have more faith in the S.N.C.F. than that."

His imperturbability enraged her.

"You think we shall just go on in the train as though nothing had happened?"

"Yes." He went back to his book.

"Are you really proposing to read?"

"As far as possible."

She recognised in his dry dismissive tones the iron qualities which had brought him distinction and promotions. She would have preferred almost a sleepy pear of a man whom she could have dented with her thumb and loved with tenderness. There had been tenderness in her love for John and in his for her; they had both cherished and protected each other fiercely in their times together. Each time a holiday was over and, widowed, she had continued her journey back to life with David, it was the rawness of exposure to the world again that hurt. She noted wryly that past tense in her thoughts; one learned quickly, adapted oneself and survived.

Laura looked out of the window again; the river seemed to have gathered momentum still, the torrent of water devoured some small footbridge over a tributary stream as she watched. They were approaching a shed, possibly a house, one of those old wood and stone structures that might house people or cows or both; there was some scarlet creeper up one side of it; she saw it all clearly one minute and the next it was gone, engulfed, invisible and there were

231

great pieces of wood she recognised, still embroidered with the creeper, tossing now in the anonymous flood.

"David. I've just seen a house swept away — well a sort of small house."

"For hens?"

He looked out of the window.

"It's certainly in spate. What a good thing Rocamadour is high up: at least the hotel will be dry."

A ticket collector came in and asked to see their tickets, talking all the time to some people in pursuit of him down the corridor. He shrugged his shoulders and gave a slight tilt of the head from time to time, but otherwise seemed unmoved by the scene outside.

"*Il faut descendre du train à Brive, M'sieur, 'Dame, la ligne est coupée.*"

He squinted at their tickets. "*Rocamadour — hein. Eh bien, il faut descendre à Brive.*"

"*Est-il possible de continuer à Rocamadour par une autre route?*"

Again the shrug. He excused himself rapidly from further discussion and retreated.

"Do you hear that, David?"

"My French just stretches that far."

"I've never understood why your German is better than your French."

"I learned my German by myself when I was grown up and my French at school."

"Why?"

"Some notion of its being useful in the war, I suppose. It was, anyway."

"What on earth do we do at Brive?"

"Find a hotel till the line's clear, I suppose. Fearful bore. At least it's stopped raining."

232

It had, but she did not like the sky which shed a parchment light over the landscape, giving it a flickering stormy radiance. John had painted someone in a light like this, she remembered, a shopkeeper in some little *alimentation* in the village where he had been staying before her arrival once. It was in their bedroom, the smell of new oil paints mixing richly with that of the Caporal cigarettes which a man in the room next to them seemed to smoke all day and all night and which seemed to emanate from the walls and under the door. Where was that hotel? In the south, she thought, remembering picnics in the maquis, rich sausages and warm bread and black grapes that tasted of tea. She could smell the juniper and thyme, the threadbare lavender, now if she tried, the smell that goes with the grasshopper's throbbing that became on familiarity, not a sound but a disturbance of the air. They had lain in the autumn sun, beguiling themselves with that eternal lovers' scrutiny of their early days together; the first time they saw each other.

"You looked at me as if I were selling something, and protecting your young, instantly defensive and eyes like a bird's, fiercely irised."

"Are they like that now?"

"Sometimes, honey, sometimes. And what did you see?"

"A nondescript young man with a block-bustering chin and fair hair and paint stains on his fingers."

"And here we are, how many years later?"

"Let's not count."

"And when did you let me kiss you first?"

"A long time afterwards. A wet day in London with everything shining like black oilskins. I was afraid of you. It seemed absurd, the whole thing, not as if it were happening to me. John, had you wanted to kiss me before?"

"Yes, yes. A hundred times only I was frightened too."

"Do we always remember what we said? We always say the same things. Isn't there anything we've forgotten?"

"Nothing, Laura, ever."

"What sentimental idiots we are."

"No, it's our only capital, the bit of the past that's only ours, so we have to take it out and look at it constantly. Of course, we know it all by heart."

"What was I wearing when you first wanted to make love to me?"

"A creamy dress like porridge with a crimson scarf and you smelt of something delicious, like opening a hot house door at Kew."

"Which hot house had you in mind?"

"The one that has exotic smelling climbing plants. But any hot house will do."

"Oh, pooh! you make me sound like some chic woman with a poodle."

"I always think bits of poodles will break off like biscuits. It's a nightmare of mine."

"Do you *mind* about poodles?"

"No, only about the possibility of finding crumbling bits."

"You're a fool, John. And it's hot and I'm full of lunch and there's an even more beautiful dinner ahead."

But she could remember then, with a cloud passing over the sun, that holidays, adding to their meagre assets, were curiously insubstantial. She wanted to test their happiness on the humdrum and comforted herself that she could never imagine anything being tedious or familiar if experienced with John. And now, there it all was, fixed and embedded and immutable; all past; nothing to add, nothing to change.

The yellow light cast a sheen over the tumbling peat-brown waters, giving it an almost oily look except where it creamed in eddies around obstacles, leaving tide-marks of foam, discoloured, curdled fragments to linger in its wake.

When does one first learn to look at the truth without dark glasses and an oblique approach? Somewhere, perhaps only a moment ago, she had seen her relationship to John brilliantly lit, or is that one of the illusions? Does one learn the truth slowly as one learns other facts, till they become part of one, something one has always known?

John had loved her, but she was not important to him. He had loved his wife and daughter; and made no effort to follow them, to persuade them back. They were not important enough. She had thought herself different, but how readily and comfortingly he had complied with her conditions of what they could have; a day a week with an occasional weekend when she was living in England, ten days' holiday every now and then when abroad. They had never had to be tested by postings to Singapore, Hongkong or Nairobi. It had always seemed to her miraculous that he was grateful for what time she could give him, without continually grasping after more and making her position more difficult. What had been interpreted as concern for her was perhaps only contentment; anything more was an effort and did not matter enough. She had always thought his relations with family and friends cool: naturally, she had had no part in these and had placed herself naturally in another niche of affection. Why should she have ever considered herself any differently regarded?

She had thought of their love for each other as a bulwark,

a fastness, and now it had been swept away as the flooded river swept away bridges and buildings.

What was worse was that it was all the years of her life that had been swept away: the long calms apart from John that she had wished away: Antonia's and Mark's childhood and growing up, David's middle-age, all the peaceful tenure of ordinary life ignored and neglected because all she wanted was the years ahead. What a will-o-the-wisp she had followed over that barren land which seemed, retrospectively, richer and more smiling than one had ever thought.

"*Kennst du das Land wo die Zitrönen bluhmen?*" Lemon blossom, orange blossom: the Nordic dream of the south. How could she have loved John and known him so little? How courted such betrayal? If one is poor or physically wretched, can one be unhappy as well? The tenuousness of Laura's grief seemed stretched to a taut transparency against the disasters of nature outside the carriage windows, the threat of war, the stories of famine, disease, homelessness. Whether one is loved or not must seem irrelevant then, perhaps. If she were to be swept away in the flood she would be decently missed by the children, by David even, but it would not really matter that she had lived or was now suddenly dead.

"I have never been taken seriously," she said.

"What's that? I do frequently."

"Would it matter if we were drowned?"

"Think of my lost pension," David said. "We could have had more champagne at the wedding. I hope no one thought we *had* been a bit stingy."

"Champagne is like Parkinson's Law, but I don't know what I mean by that; supply and demand being equal perhaps. Is that what I mean?"

"Possibly. We must be getting near to Brive."

"In a way I'm glad we are leaving the train. It must be dangerous to go on like this."

"Not only dangerous. Impossible according to the ticket collector."

The train slowed down, they collected their cases from the rack. The station seemed in some confusion, there was no porter. But the ticket collector was there explaining something to a small crowd gathered round him and an enormously tall station master. As he saw Laura and David, he beckoned to them and led them out of the station to a bus.

"*Voici, M'sieur, 'Dame,*" he said with a courtly sweep of the arms.

"*À Rocamadour?*" Laura asked doubtfully.

He said something unintelligible and went back to the station.

"Well, it's obviously going to take us part of the way. Come on, Laura. Let's get seats."

VI

THE BRIVE BUS

IT WAS A country bus, old and dented and inside was a miscellany of passengers. There were two nuns, both young, with shining, pure, fresh faces touched by unusual and barely suppressed excitement, a sailor, home on leave, who kept banging on the window and calling to cronies, a curious, dark-skinned man in a wide-brimmed hat with a guitar who should have been gay but was morose and baffled instead, some men who had the look of having been in their best clothes to consult a lawyer or a tax inspector and were now on their way back to their villages, a sprinkling of black-clad old women clutching shopping-bags; at least one of them had a hen poking its head out with a lively, angry eye. It seemed very much a local bus, humming with conversation and jest.

Laura and David sat in it stiffly at first, aware of their good clothes and luggage and an alien kind of prosperity, but it was a friendly bus. The passengers all seemed to know one another except for the nuns and the dark man with the guitar, whose melancholy eyes stared out blankly and who had the disorientated look of a bartered slave. There were, first of all, friendly, if amused, glances in their direction; then remarks addressed in general seemed to include them too; finally, one or two spoke to them. Laura was relieved. If they were to be marooned in a bus in a flooded country-side or plunged to their death down some ravine, she would prefer the atmosphere to be friendly and unified. David, too, relaxed a little. Laura had looked strained and shadowed for the whole journey; her anxiety over the floods admirably checked but adding to her burden. What burden he did not know; fatigue, Antonia, some depression about the future, even perhaps boredom. She had looked solitary and withdrawn; he had been conscious of her all day in the train, while his life had reeled past his reading gaze, like a drowning man; but it was the past that was drowning him, sucking him under, then as he would try to regain his breath or his balance, knocking him prostrate again, burying him under a mass of deafening water. Aeneas's death, not altogether unexpected, was the seventh wave; one could see it coming rippling over the sea, curving higher and higher, about to bear down on the swimmer, inevitable, inexorable. It was David's old dream which sometimes now seemed not entirely dreamt, where idle helpless limbs struggle feebly to move.

It was ridiculous to be obsessed with sea and drowning when they were apparently surrounded by floods. The drift of the conversation around him, he occasionally understood and he did not care for what it imparted. He wondered whether Laura, engaged now in some chat about food with the old woman with the hen, had also grasped that the Army was being rushed in to help locally, that the devastation was widespread, the hundreds of homeless and missing growing. She gave no sign of perturbation now, except that there was a curious twitch he had noticed lately under her left eye. He wondered whether Laura had had many lovers in the past years; she had been discreet, certainly; no rustling thread of gossip was snipped when he came into the Mess or a drawing-room. But there had been an air of patient content about her, ruffled sometimes by tempests of impatience and irritation or illuminated by a secret smile, which made him wonder. He had found her body disturbing once; now it was just flesh, comforting sometimes, exciting never. Their embraces had been perfunctory and silent. This was perhaps the fate of every marriage: he hoped, for Laura's sake that she believed so. Failing her was one of the enormities that lay behind him. Perhaps it was not compensation enough for Laura to have been left with areas of her life unscrutinised by him.

The bus driver appeared amid loud cries of derisive welcome from the passengers and scanned his load with the assessing eye of a master mariner, before he sat down at the wheel. Laura had watched him in conversation with two railway officials: there had been a great flourish of timetables and scraps of paper.

The bus engine started explosively and noisily; the horn was blown several times to the accompaniment of cheers and shouts, they moved off slowly to skirt the town. Down side roads, Laura could see the Army with D.U.K.Ws. and trucks and occasionally there were vistas of water from which houses rose. She too had been listening to what their fellow-passengers had been saying; the implications of adventure and disaster left her calm. They were moving away from the river, climbing a little; there was something different from hurtling along in an impersonal caterpillar of a train and being in a manœuvrable bus. Presumably they were going to the higher ground above Brive. It was not raining; the early evening light was soft outside.

"Mystery Tour, David. Odd to think there are so many things one has never done and is unlikely to do, like going on a mystery tour in a motor coach."

"I've never been on a roundabout. Mother wouldn't let me go to fairs when I was the right age for them and somehow no one else took me when she wasn't about. And then I was too old."

"I thought subalterns sometimes descended on fairs."

"Yes, I went on the dodgems that way, because one is never too old for them and the ghost train, but roundabout, no."

"Didn't you ever take a girl to a fair?"

"Yes, I took Christina and we did all the side shows, but I was too dignified for roundabouts at seventeen. It was a very remarkable fair, on the Island. There was an old man and an old woman who tied each other up in sacks and then fought their way out. They were dusty and blank and chained, somehow, to fate and each other. I've never forgotten them."

Like us, he thought, seeing the act repeated again for the hundredth time: the sandy dust rising from the bald patch of waste grass where they were performing, their lank hair and lifeless looks, the mechanical nature of their actions, like those of trained animals, the sense they gave of being a pair, bound together not by affection or interest but by casual chance cemented into inescapable habit and bound together for a meagre and unreal life. He could not imagine them comforting each other or sustaining each other, yet they no doubt kept themselves alive by their dependence on each other's ill-humour.

"It's curious that one is haunted forever by people seen only once."

"If they were old then, they'd be dead long since by now."

He saw them dead in a hedgerow ditch, as she spoke, not

grotesque or corrupt, but like dead moles or birds, fading and withering away to be part of grey unfeeling earth. Then he saw the other three, dead in their coppice, stiffening and paling into his ghosts. The age of the dead does not keep pace with ours: he still thought of Willi, Ernst and Christof as young men. But he only saw them now when he summoned them up.

"I can call spirits from the vasty deep" — Glendower arrogant, mystical, the mouthpiece of every Celtic dream and boast.

"Ay, but will they come when you do call them?" Hotspur, wry, cynical, bored, withering, the disbelieving warrior from the North, as scornful of military fanatics as of young staff officers in well-pressed uniform. David always liked Hotspur because he should have been a Hotspur. He had always known he was not, from his school and Sandhurst days, but he had tried. Learning the words was easy enough.

They were out of the town now, it lay behind them waterily beleaguered. The landscape of small hills, veiling the high ground behind, was as gentle as those glimpses of background in Italian paintings, with poplars for cypresses. It had a presence as comforting as the passengers in the bus, some timeless quality, some radiant sense of itself. Laura felt her eyes eased by looking at it, suffused as it was by that light, indefinably peculiar to France, which makes men paint as nowhere else, and which, even now, diminished by the approach of darkness, yet seemed to hold all one could see in its luminous limpidity.

"It's the light that releases the spirit," she had said to John once in France, looking out across a valley as she opened the shutters to the flooding morning sunshine. John had said, "One drinks just enough to relax one, to cradle one. One is rocked and lulled in wine here. At home, where one drinks sherry and spirits, the tensions are dissolved more abruptly and come back like toothache when the drink wears off, unless one is a permanent toper. It's different in France, thank heaven."

"I still think it's the light."

"When I look at you I think perhaps it is. Come back to me."

She closed her eyes; the scene came back too vividly, but she was right about the light. She could almost feel it against her eyelids through the window glass. But when she opened her eyes, it seemed a shade darker outside and the bus, full of cigarette smoke and faint fumes of pastis and garlic, noisier, livelier, more of a world of its own, bowling through obscurity. To all the passengers, except for themselves and possibly the dark stranger and the nuns, of course it was not obscure. They were going home and probably recognised every field and clump of trees as part of the familiar route to the house door where they would eventually be greeted, where the family circle would close round them again, like some ingredient added to the soup saucepan no doubt simmering against their return. They were all going home and the doors would shut behind them; even the nuns would enter again a familiar ritual and pattern, filling empty cells and known places in the chapel. They would all be expected and prepared for, even perhaps, thinking of the returning sailor, longed for. She looked around at the faces emerging from the chiaroscuro of the bus interior, some lit vividly for an instant by a match, or reflected in the glass, some quite in the shadows with a prominent nose or gleaming eyes alone visible. She looked at them all with envy and gentleness, almost with love.

"He prayeth best who loveth best." She had been good at neither; her albatross perhaps was there for life.

Laura put her hand diffidently on David's arm.

"Do you see us like those two old things at the Fair? My poor David, have we nothing to lose but our chains too?"

He had been feeling somnolent and comforted beside her, the bus was thick with animal warmth and he had relaxed into it.

"Chains and burdens."

"And then we could go our own ways. I need not be the commandant's wife."

"I need not be the commandant."

"But you want to be; it's the crown of your career."

"I'm only doing it for you."

"For me, David? Don't be absurd. It can't be true."

He was startled by the terror of her whisper, but merely raised his eyebrows.

"Well, I don't want to make a drama of it, but I thought you were ambitious and I didn't want to deprive you of being a general's wife at the last hurdle."

"But you didn't ever say so before."

"It's not something one says."

"No, David, I suppose not. You wanted to retire?" She had regained her calm.

"Yes, I've wanted to for years so that I could live at Achranish."

"And you stayed in the Army because of me? I simply don't believe it. You're a soldier. You've always done very well—I mean, early promotion and all that, you can't have wanted to have given up what you were so good at. What would you have done?"

"You mean Othello's occupation, etc.? It seems to me that went some time ago, along with the plumed troop and the big wars. That's just the point. Anyway, I wanted to write."

"Yes, you told me that before. I didn't think it was quite your line."

"So you said before, in a harsher voice."

"I can't shout here."

"I can hardly hear you anyway. This bus makes such a noise. Anyway, I would have left the Army years ago if it hadn't been for you."

"So I've even done you out of a golden bowler, have I? Oh come, this is a mood. You're teasing me. I know what everyone thinks of you in the Army."

"Do you, Laura? Have you heard them say – how did old Kingsley avoid Korea and Suez and Cyprus (till the troubles were over). The war, yes, but that was years ago. He's been safely tucked away ever since."

"That's hardly your fault. You've complained about it. I've heard you."

"Yes, but never in the right quarters. I avoided trouble, Laura; excuse – I wasn't quite sure how I would behave."

"David, what are you trying to tell me?"

"That I'm a better administrator than a fighting soldier, to put it nicely. Bluntly, I'm afraid, face to face, I mightn't be able to kill anyone."

"My dear David, you are not unique. In my more cynical moments I always imagine that was why nuclear weapons have been invented. More and more people would find it impossible to kill someone themselves: so they invent a means of killing more and more people with fewer of themselves involved. You need never see your victims, that's very important to us now. We are so civilised that our fingers might waver on the trigger, but never on the button."

"There speaks a typical woman. You've never been sweating, scared, exhausted and fighting for your life. You've never felt the gush of pleasure at having killed and remained alive yourself. Anyway — I was trying to be plain. I'm going to be a general by default. I've no right to be one. Laura, I wanted to give you something. Laura, try to understand."

The bus had slithered to a halt in a village street. A few passengers dismounted, the bus driver too; he was deep in conversation.

"Stories from the front line," Laura said absently. "The bus driver, I mean."

A cat sidled from shadow to shadow, avoiding the pools of light from windows. There was a spill of laughter from a nearby café. A priest in his soutane stopped to talk to the bus driver and Laura looked up a tiny alleyway where the crooked houses leaned towards each other and the scalloped tiles of the roofs rose in angled tiers.

"I am trying to understand. Why didn't you tell me this years ago? And why should you want to give me anything? I've been quite happy."

"Have you? Laura?"

"Yes," she said. "No. But that's irrelevant. You changed. I thought — you were bored with me. And perhaps, really in love with Christina. Was it really only this Army business?"

"In a way."

"Aeneas — he never liked me. That was why I wouldn't have any part in Achranish. He always thought you should have married Christina. He wasn't fair to me, ever. You'll never know how unfair.''

David sighed. The whisky and the stories would be circulating freely at Achranish now and both cottages dark and silent. The owls would be swooping in the twilight and the deer coming down from the hills. James would be listening to the talk, pale, intent, rather dandyish in his dark clothes.

"Aeneas turned you against me in the end. What he wouldn't ever approve you could never wholly accept. Everyone has some odd touchstone; Aeneas was yours. The Old Testament prophet with the Scotch accent and just the same stony prejudices. And don't say '*De Mortuis*' — I haven't that simple sense of honour, being a woman.''

Her bitterness about Aeneas made her mouth feel as dry as if she had bitten into a sloe. She turned away from David, ashamed, but justifying her anger to herself. There was a garden next to the café, full of a tangled profusion of dahlias, great shaggy flowers massed together, their colours muted by the evening light, but still discernible in all their variety. Through the open door of the café she could see some of the ex-passengers leaning against the bar in serious and animated discussion. She wondered what the village was called; there was a curious No-man's-land atmosphere about the terrain they were traversing. Where would their journey end?

David lit a cigarette for her.

"He mattered more to me almost than anyone else, but yes, he had his limitations, of course. You mustn't think I always agreed with him. And I don't really know about his views on Christina — or James.''

"James? How does he come into it?''

"It seems odd that you've never met him."

"Not really, you've been pretty careful that I shouldn't see him, goodness knows why."

"I can tell you why. I was afraid you might see the likeness."

"The likeness. To whom?"

The bus driver climbed in and noisily they were on their way again, with some dog barking at their departing wheels. The last house vanished and there was open country, stony, bushy country interspersed with notices all the way along— 'Chasse gardée', 'Chasse privée'.

David paused but Laura sat so invulnerably beside him, blowing smoke at the old greenish-black felt hat of the man in front, poised so serenely in her own world of judgments, that he decided recklessly to go on.

"To me. James is my son. Now keep calm. The whole affair was over a long time ago."

Laura's voice was cutting.

"Yes, indeed, since he's about eighteen, isn't he? David, have you always— thought this?"

"Oh yes, from the moment he was born."

Laura drew hard on her cigarette. She had spared David for years from knowing the probable truth, at first from love and fear, thinking that the knowledge might so damage or destroy David's feelings about himself that she must protect him at all costs. She could hear the doctor's bland cough-mixture voice now, "Of course, since you won't get your husband to have the necessary tests and examination, we can't be sure that it is indeed he who is the infertile partner. However, there it is, you are a perfectly normal woman, there seems no reason why you should not conceive and bear— any number of children, let us say. But we cannot absolutely find out why your marriage is childless without your husband's co-operation, nor can we definitely blame him, not that blame is the word, you understand, Mrs. Kingsley—there are a number of factors which bring about sterility—as I have explained to you. Are you sure you want the matter to rest there? After all, your husband is a young active man—surely he wouldn't mind coming to see me?"

"He would mind, enormously, and so would I. And there's a war on and he's very much in it. How can I? He'd hate it all and if the trouble did lie with him, and I suppose it looks as if it might—it would make him feel a failure. One can't do that to a soldier now."

"I see your point, Mrs. Kingsley. But aren't you being a little hysterical?"

"I thought I was being particularly reasonable."

"The extremes of both states are very alike. You will regret the sacrifice you are making. After all, we might be able to help your husband—and yourself."

"Does one regret sacrifices?"

"Those made at your age—yes. You're very young, forgive me, you're embarking on a course of conduct—even deceit, one might call it, which is going to alter your whole life, not to mention your marriage. It's going to make you feel frustrated and superior—both dangerous states of mind, Mrs. Kingsley. Come and see me again in a week."

She had left his surgery with a resolute chin. Nothing that she could think of could alter her determination not to involve David. She had so worried about the effect of their childlessness on their happiness, of her failure to produce an heir for the Kingsleys, Aldengrove, the Regiment, that she was no longer sure of anything. Now, having discovered that it was not perhaps she who was sterile, she was determined that she was not going to imperil their marriage by hurting David. That a sense of inadequacy has a far-reaching and disturbing effect on human relations she had found from a survey of her own behaviour over the last year. Since Dunkirk, David had been morose and worried. How could she make everything worse? She returned to the doctor as arranged and listened to his suggestions about adoption. At the back of his advice on the subject, she knew that he was thinking that if David were killed and she married again, adopted children would be an embarrassment. This made her even keener to adopt them.

Mark and Antonia were part of life. Without them she would have been very poor, but of course the doctor had been right. Laura had known this for years. Even silent sacrifices are not a satisfactory basis for any relationship. Better late than never does not apply to telling the truth; there is a time for truth always and the time can pass, and never come again.

"You've hardly seen James until the last year or so."

She felt her way into the conversation again cautiously.

"I used to go and see him a lot, rather ridiculously."

He explained about his visits to the prep school and station, crisply and impersonally.

"I was so excited to have a son. It didn't make me love Mark and Antonia less — you do understand that, don't you?"

She saw David lurking round barriers at Waterloo, reading a paper like a detective, finding excuses for going into shops and cafés in the Surrey village and fought against her rising pity.

"Mark and Antonia don't seem to like James particularly," she said reflectively. "Jealousy – I always thought, apparently rightly."

"It was just a sort of awkwardness with each other and I suppose he and I naturally hit it off."

"That's not necessarily a test of paternity – the reverse, frequently."

"You're mocking me, Laura."

"Did Aeneas know about James?"

"He may have guessed but we've never spoken about it."

If there had been any resemblance, she thought, Aeneas would have divined it. He might have held his peace from one scruple or another, but she did not think it likely.

"And Christina?"

"We've only discussed it once. And I don't want to talk about that."

To tell Laura about the German soldiers and Andrew's death and his love for Christina seemed suddenly impossible: it would be asking for her pity. It would mean that she would start scanning the past and discover how little she knew of him and that the life she had built up so securely and tranquilly for them both, was flimsy and meaningless. If she had amused herself discreetly she had never allowed it to impinge. He owed her the suppression of that aspect of him. He could imagine her pity; Laura was warm-hearted enough to let her compassion turn to tenderness and then imperceptibly to a kind of love. He did not deserve nor need this. He must spare her his rejection.

There was a village built on a hill coming into sight now, studded with lights, like a jewelled castle, against the dark blue sky where the moon rose. Laura watched its golden harvest glow, faintly but stormily rainbow haloed. The beauty of the scene pained her as if she were a young girl again.

What illusions had sustained and nourished David and herself. Her very success at her rôle as his wife had doomed her to be the victim of his sacrifice for her of retirement and Achranish.

"I'm glad about James for you," she said. "Couldn't you resign your commission now? It's not too late. We could manage on your pension, now the children are grown up and Antonia married. I could get a job; you need only make me a tiny allowance until I found something and got settled."

"My dear Laura," he said taking her hand, "I need you." God help me, he thought. The phrase came out awkwardly but pat, like a bad actor's over-rehearsed punch-line. "And anyway, Aeneas always said — anyway, I think I might as well do this job — and I need you for it."

This time he was smoother with it.

David saw the old woman in the sack writhing in the chains the man had tied, struggling to loose herself; only to tie him up, then his frantic efforts to free himself; he saw them as part of each other's act, as each other's burden.

The darkness outside was now almost complete. Periodically, the bus stopped to let someone alight. Sometimes they were met; there were cries of welcome and embraces; the nuns were met by two other nuns whose white coifs emerged ghost-like from the shadows, then the four melted away towards a black mass of buildings. There was hardly anyone left now but the dark-skinned man and themselves.

Laura pondered on whether she should tell David about John. It seemed a fair return, she thought cynically. There was no one but David she could tell about John; it suddenly seemed wonderful to her to be able to talk about it all. But she would not be able to brazen it out briskly; the tears and the humiliation would come. David would think she was asking for his pity, even try to stir other embers of his affection. He might even suggest, oh terrible thought, a fresh start. She did not deserve nor need this kind of love. She could not bear to hurt him with a rejection.

The bus came to its final stop at a station.

"*Terminus, terminus,*" the driver shouted. "*Ici on reprends le train.*"

"*Pour Rocamadour?*" Laura asked.

"*Oui, oui, madam — si vous y allez.*"

There was indeed a little train waiting and they and the man with the guitar got in and it started immediately. He seemed more composed and confident now.

"You are going to Rocamadour?" The dark-skinned man spoke for the first time. "It is a famous shrine; a place of penance and pilgrimage. It was one of the most holy places in the Middle Ages. There is a black Virgin there who can work wonders, who can change hearts." He spoke with fluent conviction.

"Are you going there, monsieur?"

He shook his head, rolled his eyes and twanged a string or two of his guitar.

"Not yet. In time, I too."

Laura and David caught each other's eyes with puzzlement.

It was with difficulty that they read the signboard at the fourth or fifth station the train stopped at.

"Rocamadour indeed; come on, Laura."

They stumbled out on to a dark station, lit only by one or two paraffin lamps. There was a wind blowing with rain

254

on it; the moon was veiled now. It seemed to them both a lost and desolate place. A man was approaching in the distance with a lantern.

"*Monsieur le Général et madame*," he shouted above the wind.

"Oui," David shouted back.

"*On vous attends depuis longtemps, mon Général, madame.*"

Laura and David looked at each other; he took her arm and they walked towards the man with the lantern.